THE DEMOSTHENES CLUB

A Bertrand McAbee Mystery

Joseph A. McCaffrey

authorHOUSE®

AuthorHouse™
1663 Liberty Drive
Bloomington, IN 47403
www.authorhouse.com
Phone: 1 (800) 839-8640

Published by AuthorHouse 06/26/2018

ISBN: 978-1-5462-4749-4 (sc)
ISBN: 978-1-5462-4748-7 (e)

Library of Congress Control Number: 2018907204

Cover design by Sally Paustian

Print information available on the last page.

This book is printed on acid-free paper.

Cover Picture: The Roses Of Sarajevo. A Remembrance Of The Darkness of The Shelling And Deaths Of Bosniaks. Photo By Joseph A. McCaffrey

OTHER MCABEE MYSTERIES

Cassies Ruler
Confessional Matters
The Pony Circus Wagon
Scholarly Executions
Phantom Express
The Troubler
The Marksman's Case
A Byzantine Case
A Case of Silver
A Went Over Case

All of the above titles are available in audio editions. Please refer to Audible.com.

REVIEWS OF EARLIER MCABEE MYSTERIES:

The Pony Circus Wagon
The pre-WWI historical background and international intrigue distinguish this gripping and at times addictive mystery from the standard whodunits.

- Kirkus Reviews

Scholarly Executions
The author hits the ground running with a resolute mystery. An intelligent, intuitive detective who steers clear of guns in favor of a team of talented cohorts.

- Kirkus Reviews

The Marksman's Case
Classy ex-classics professor Bertrand McAbee and his multicultural mystery-solving posse go the distance with a former military sniper turned vigilante. An entertaining mystery, although not for the gun-shy.

- Kirkus Reviews

A Byzantine Case
McCaffrey's mystery thrills with well-drawn characters, solid procedural details and strong storytelling. Historical intrigue and well-narrated suspense make this adventure an absorbing mystery.

- Kirkus Reviews

A Went Over Case
In this thriller, a dying man hires private investigator Bertrand McAbee to find the whereabouts of his brother, missing for nearly 30 years. In his 10th outing, a steadfast gumshoe proves he can handle anything…

- Kirkus Reviews

Dedication

For Monica
The Warrior of Kindness and Civility

CHAPTER 1

Dr. Linda Rhine needed some hefty support in her effort to meet with Phil Pesky, the Davenport, Iowa, Police Chief. At first, through his snippy secretary, Pesky directed her to the principal investigating detective who had closed the case file on the death. On the phone, this detective, Paul Smothers, grudgingly reported that it was an unequivocal, open and shut suicide. Dr. Rhine, Chief Psychiatrist at the Hope Hospital, was adamant that the death was anything but a suicide.

It was only through the intense intercession of the Hope Hospital Board Chair, along with the Mayor of Davenport, that the Chief buckled under pressure and allowed a meeting. Rhine didn't like owing anyone but in this case it was the only way.

And so it was a week since the death that she sat in the waiting room of Chief Pesky's office, an hour beyond the appointed time. Pesky's secretary had a knowing look on her dimpled, overly made-up, millennial face. Rhine was being punished for being a noisome bitch and there was little she could do. She had to pay a price for her impertinence.

A balding man with a considerable paunch came

through the doors to the waiting area. His colossal stomach demonstrated a dubious lifestyle. He stood in front of the cute secretary, uncurled his left hand outwards as if to check on his permission to open the closed door into the Chief's office. She nodded as she snuck a quick, snarly look at Dr. Rhine. Paunch entered and closed the door to the Chief's office.

As a counter to these wounding jabs, Dr. Rhine envisaged the Spanish Steps in Rome, bringing herself into a state of calm as she recalled her visit there last year when she sat on one of those steps in the late afternoon eating a gelato and feeling a marked joy on the occasion. But anger flooded the memory. She was in a state of simmering fury.

About ten minutes later she caught a speck of green light out of the corner of her eye. She wasn't exactly sure of its exact location over by the secretary who now had immediately gotten up, caught her eye, as if to say your moment has come, a meeting with the renowned Chief Pesky. "You may go in now," she said with practiced scorn. Rhine wished she could fling a gelato at her.

Pesky stood as she entered his gargantuan office, in the middle of which stood a matching gargantuan desk. He appeared to be in his late fifties, closely cropped mostly white hair, his black framed glasses revealed crafty eyes. He was the Chief for a good reason. Paunch never got up, mid-forties, there was a sloppiness about him, shirt half out of his pants and with a reddish nose zigzagged by competing red and purple broken lines across a flat nose.

"I'm Chief Pesky, this is detective Paul Smothers. Let's all sit," he stated imperiously. He pointed to a chair for her that completed a triangular arrangement, he at the apex.

Paunch just sat there looking at her with naked scorn.

Pesky flashed a finger toward him. Paunch began, "Well Doctor, here's what I know about this case. Cynthia Power parked her car in her garage, watered down nineteen bath towels which she placed all across the bottom of her double car garage door, the door into her basement, and lastly in front of a storage area that led back into the house through her furnace area. A few extra towels reinforced one area where there was a gap between the garage door and the floor. She then taped a hose to the tailpipe of her Subaru and led the other end of the hose into her car through the driver side window which was snuggly taped to each side of the hose, sealing the window. All of her other windows were also taped tight. Thorough. She then sat in the car, started the ignition, and died of carbon monoxide poisoning. Her next door neighbor smelled an odor and on inspection noticed some escaping smoke that had found its way through the wet towels out into the driveway. Emergency vehicles called and the rest is history. Coroner estimates that the car ran for almost three hours. Conclusion – suicide. There were no signs of violence on her body, the autopsy showed nothing unusual. The best EMT in Scott County investigated about her presence on Facebook and other social media, nothing, not active on them. No known threats and no final notes from her. But she was under psychiatric care," he said with a harsh emphasis. "So why the meeting?" he said now through zippered lips.

Chief Pesky said, "Dr. Rhine, I know she was a patient of yours and that you suspect foul play but really… I don't see how this can be construed otherwise."

"I want to see all of the reports and the post mortem analysis."

"That's not going to happen," Pesky said abruptly. "If you have a question for Detective Smothers please ask it. We're very busy."

Dr. Rhine looked down at her hands which were now pink because of the constant tightening of her fists as she listened to these bureaucratic rhinos. She glared at both of them and said, "I have been a psychiatrist for over 25 years. Cynthia was a patient of mine for almost four years. I know her extremely well. She was not suicidal, pure and simple. I had seen her two days before her body was found. She was ebullient, enthusiastic and full of life, on quests, missions. She simply did not commit suicide."

Paunch reacted, "Then you're saying that she was murdered and that's just pure nonsense. All the evidence is clear. You're placing the study of mental processes over hard and irrefutable physical evidence *Doctor*."

"I am indeed. Did you research her contacts? From what I see her picture and obituary shows up in the newspaper under the phony 'died at home.' Everyone knows what that usually means – suicide. So clear, so quick, so closed. Easy, just put an official stamp on it and the game is over. Case closed so that you can spend 90% of your time trying to figure out why there are so many gunshots in the inner city while a murderer gets away."

Paunch stood up, quickly for the slob he was, pointed his folder at her and yelled, "This is beyond your competency. How dare you…"

Chief Pesky screamed, "Okay, that's enough Paul. Sit!" He glared at Smothers who sat slowly. Then he turned toward Dr. Rhine and loudly, but not at a yell, said sternly, "That's enough Doctor. You have no authority in this matter. You pleaded your case, we've listened and you haven't made your point. Is there anything else you have? Just for your information, I've covered suicides. More often than I want to remember I've heard relatives say 'Oh, he was so happy', 'Impossible, he was so into life', and all sorts of contradictories to the plain fact of suicide. You're a psychiatrist, surely this isn't the first suicide who surprised you?" He finished as he stared laser beams at Rhine.

Rhine responded, half of her energy spent controlling her temper, "You have a point Chief Pesky. But you don't have a point at the same time. This is the first time in my career that I have come down to a police station to challenge a conclusion, an erroneous and ignorant conclusion." She stabbed her forefinger at Smothers and returned the glare toward Chief Pesky.

Pesky stood and said, "Detective Smothers, you can go now. The file is to stay as it is, closed. Dr. Rhine, is there anything further?"

Smothers left as he walked uncomfortably close to Rhine. Rhine stayed seated, Pesky standing. After some tense seconds she said, "Very well Chief Pesky. This meeting was useless. You've dug your heels in. But I'm not done."

He moved from behind his desk and headed toward the door of his office. He opened it and said with mild sarcasm, "Thank you for your attempt at helping us do our job. I have another task at hand and I have nothing further to add to this matter. If you'd please, Doctor." He pointed out to the waiting room.

Rhine left the office, head in full pulse, a migraine beginning to crackle in her head. When she came out onto the street she sensed the fickle May weather was going stormy.

CHAPTER 2

Francine Korbel drove her Cadillac Esplanade over to Oakbrook, Illinois, to attend a fundraiser for Corey Bladel, the six-term Republican Congressman from an ultra-conservative district in the Chicago suburbs. He had little to fear about reelection as he had won eighteen months ago by a 75% plurality. Democrats aimed their fire elsewhere in the State of Illinois. But that election certitude did not hinder his efforts at deepening the campaign war chest Bladel hoggishly filled.

Corey was one of Francine's oldest acquaintances. They had attended the same grammar school in Davenport, Iowa, then on to the same high school, their association with each other irregularly bobbing up and down, mostly down, as they went through those years. At decision time for college, only then, did they truly separate and choose alternate educational paths, he Northwestern University in Evanston, Illinois, Political Science/Government, B.A., and she Columbia University, Economics, Ph.D., at the end of their formal educational journeys.

Corey attached himself to a senior republican senator in Washington, D.C. and with his estimable interpersonal skills had worked himself into a power in Midwestern and particularly Illinois politics. With the timely death of a long-sitting congressman, he pulled every string he controlled to secure enough support from those who count to scare away all opposition to his candidacy for the now open seat. Well, except for a wild-assed Baptist shrew hell-bent on only one issue – abortion pitched as an act of murder, imprisonment for any cooperating doctors, nurses, the affected mothers, and closure of participating hospitals and clinics. What the fervent cow didn't get was that the district was heavily foot-printed by the medical services industry from insurance to direct providers to private abortion clinics and so on. Corey whipped the nutcase badly and sent her back to her Baptist mental prison.

Francine went in a very different direction with her career, she signed on with the agribusiness behemoth Deere and Company in Moline, Illinois. Her ailing mother, father deceased, required the care that only a dutiful daughter could provide, her three siblings psychopathic in their disregard for both her and her mother.

Deere made a generous offer upon her graduation from Columbia and thus she came back to the Quad City area comprised of the cities of Moline and Rock Island in Illinois. The Mississippi River split those two municipalities from Iowa, and its cities of Davenport and Bettendorf.

Her skills and brilliance, she knew, allowed her to shimmy up the corporate ladder headquarters which at the time was a male bastion after one plowed through the female secretarial pool at Deere. Corey once suggested that she get into politics in Washington, D.C. She replied that she was deeply ensconced in politics à la the great America corporate gangland of subtle career destruction and treachery. By the time she retired, a year and a half ago, she was the chief economic prognosticator for overseas corporate sales. Her net worth was at about eight million dollars. She had three homes: one in Moline, one in Naples, Florida, and a small villa in Montenegro overlooking the Adriatic Sea. That last possession was not widely known outside of a few intimates, Corey Bladel very surely not among them.

She stopped at the DeKalb oasis, more or less equidistant from Moline to Oakbrook, a well-heeled Chicago suburb. Interstate 88, sometimes known as the East/West Tollway, rifled, on an almost straight line, across the northern part of Illinois. Only this oasis offered any civilization on the route, a gas station, McDonald's, a Starbucks, and several other quick food outlets. She ordered a skinny grande latte and headed for her next stop – the Marriott off of Route 83 in Oakbrook. If she was put upon she would applaud Corey for his bravery and honesty and pledge $2000 to his phony campaign, unwillingly joining a roomful of sycophants who had their tongues out for some special potion that Corey could deliver, his being the Vice Chair of the Ways and Means Committee in the House of Representatives. But this was all irrelevant to her true purpose on this May night.

She arrived at the Marriott at 6:35 p.m. Drinks were being served between 6:00 and 7:00 p.m. She wore her new jacket/skirt combination, a St. John's knit of midnight blue with thin red piping on the jacket edges. Her one carat diamond earrings, along with her one inch wide diamond bracelet completed the look for which she strove. On bare feet, she stood five feet, eleven inches, her heels got her nicely over six feet. Even at the age of 67, she thought of herself as an attractive package. Yes, there was some surgical sculpting over the past 20 years but her trim athletic body had fought back the attacking forces of aging with pretty good success.

There were about 200 smarmy business whores in the room, males outnumbering the females by about a 2:1 ratio. Four years ago, the ratio would have been 4:1. Liberated women were rocketing their way into the male world of corruption with gathering force. There were two black faces in the crowd and maybe one hispanic. She wasn't sure about the latter. Spaniard? Italian?

Francine had never married. Her tolerance for men and company in general had a use by date of one month. Probably, she thought, people saw her as a candidate for therapy given her decided opinions about things. But she didn't and that was the end of the matter.

She ordered a scotch neat, $12 for J & B piss. One sip caused a slight shudder. A man came over to her and introduced himself, Tom Palmer, a vice president at some local savings and loan. She was tempted to hand over her J & B in order to assist him into his rising drunken trajectory. He was probably in his late 50s. He held out his hand and when she unwillingly extended hers he was a second too slow in the release. His brown eyes had a desperation in them. She was gratified that she could still attract, but my God, not this kind of tuna. She was too smooth to ever act out with rancor in this type of setting. She gave him her 'don't you even think about it' look and with a few quick and long steps sped away from him.

In a far corner she espied Peter Nash, a senior manager at Deere. He was tolerable enough to fasten onto before the tiresome chicken dinner with phony French credentials.

Then there would be the hectoring speech by the shovel-full of manure Corey and only then finally the true purpose of her trip – the very private meeting with the alcoholic congressman.

She knew that she intimidated the introverted Peter Nash, a Harvard nerd with about as much common sense as an Edsel. "So Peter, what does Deere need from the good congressman?" she began with a sour smile.

He stepped back and said haltingly, "Ah, Francine, long time no see. We... just want to show corporate presence. You know how it goes," he said as he gave a furtive look around to see if he was overheard, candid comments anathema for senior Deere personnel.

He was in his mid-forties, about 5'8" and scrawny, all around. Nash was a nervous Nellie, especially when being stared at by an over six foot woman with the practiced intimidation tactics that she had acquired. These very tactics would enable her to intrude on him during the coming agony of the dinner/talk and to avoid wandering scum like Tom Palmer.

By 8:45 Corey was winding down on his stump speech with all the usual platitudes that he had learned to package in a series of oral bullet points. At the end the applause was generous, people stood, milled around. They waited until they could find a clear path to the head table to congratulate him for his brilliant performance along with the requisite promise to be available for help with the campaign at his beck and call, blah, blah, blah.

Francine stayed put at her table as Peter Nash excused himself and left, passing on any kowtowing to Bladel. She wasn't surprised by his behavior but she did think that he was the wrong man for Deere to send to this type of charade.

By 9:40 there were only four people of import in the large room. Waiters, busboys, equipment personnel and the like were scattered across the place doing the teardown. Corey looked back at Francine and his hand shot up, forefinger extended. His two aides, both cute looking blondes, were staring up at him in admiration and probably pouring on the duplicitous praise that fueled poor pompous Corey Bladel. Finally hugs were exchanged and they left. Francine observed the slightest of leers from him, ever so subtle, toward one of the two cuties. She stopped herself from speculating; it added no value to what needed to be done at this meeting.

Corey Bladel was forewarned by Francine that she was coming to the fundraiser. He regretted that he hadn't purged the list of invitees. He sensed the viper from the minute she entered the room. The temperature seemed to drop ten degrees. Fortunately, she came late and attached herself to the little guy from Deere and with him she stayed, more or less, through all of the proceedings. An unlikely pair. She probably used him as a punching bag in preparation for the meeting he did not want to have with her.

As he spoke to his two aides he simultaneously flashed through his mental file. Part of him was tantalized by her, he had to admit. She was brilliant and beautiful, but ruthless and self-centered. Not a woman to cross; she had a memory that was vault-like and as far as he could see it was mostly filled with perceived slights that had an IOU pinned to them by her.

The talk was that she had risen through the ranks of the macho culture at Deere by being meaner than her peers. Female success invariably sparks rumors. The juiciest of them being that she was a dominatrix in a relationship with some vice president or other. The story went that she almost choked him to death and then he sought to end the absurd affair. He was given an IOU by her along with a picture of his being strapped to a bed wearing panties and a bra. Corey didn't believe it but when it came to his rejecting the story as jealous fantasy he found it impossible to do so. In other words, the rumor wasn't beyond the pale given his knowledge of Francine from grammar school and especially into high school. She was one mean cow.

As he was glad-handing the cleanup staff he kept an eye on her, calculating what was in front of him. It would not be beyond her to be wired. Trust between the pair had been in constant erosion in the decades within which their careers developed. Now with her being retired he figured her to be fixated on her money and security. Any potential jeopardy to these was a state of mind that he sensed Francine would not handle well.

Finally, he bit the bullet and went over to her, flashing the most brilliant of his smiles. She stood and he grabbed her and gave her a generous hug. There was no noticeable return. The lioness' body was as firm as a rock. He tried to kiss her on the cheek as her head went back as he went forward. He ended up brushing his lips against her turned in shoulder. She pulled away and said, "I'm not in your district Corey. Save your hugs for your ass-kissing groupies."

"Francine! Always playing hard to get," he said with an empty smile.

"Damn right Corey. This isn't a good place to talk. They have a quiet bar with lots of dark corners. I have questions.

And I know you have some answers. I'll even buy you a drink."

He followed her out of the room and they proceeded down two corridors until they came to the Relaxation Lounge in the Marriott. She was right. It had its darkened corners, customers scarce.

They sat, he ordered a double Manhattan, she a Perrier with a lime twist. She was driving she said. He was feeling anxious, out of his comfort zone. She was his match and, if he was totally honest about it, his better.

CHAPTER 3

Francine sensed Corey's nervousness. She didn't know if its source was she in general or was it more specific to Cynthia Power and her suicide. "I'm here to talk about Cynthia, Corey. Nothing else."

"Okay, okay. I don't know anything. It was a shock to me. I have no knowledge about this Francine. And would you be kind enough to turn down the lasers that you're sending my way," he looked at her, offended.

Of course, she took him for a liar. From what she could make out Corey had started the fire that burned in Cynthia's brain. Cynthia Power had been lit up by something that alcoholic Corey had disclosed. From then on an obsession took her over as she became a plague in her quest to get to a darkened secret. Whatever Corey took for lasers she doubled down on as she watched him squirm pretending to be offended. "You listen to me Corey. When she decided to put that book together it was about success. We all had it. Happy to talk with her, more or less anyway. Her first interview with me lasted almost two hours. She was good at it. Remarkable listener. Patient. I talked about my career at Deere, my experiences at Columbia University. Why I didn't marry. All of it. Nothing to hide, plenty to be proud of. She talks to everyone except you and Peter Waters. Smooth going. No problems. You're doing congressional hearings, then your trip to Poland and Hungary. You're not available."

"But…"

"Shut up Corey. Listen to me! So you get back to your district. She wants to complete all of us. You put her off."

"I was busy. We did talk eventually."

"Stop Corey. You're not listening to me, goddamn you. So finally you put aside some time for her. A nice dinner. You meet her on Rush Street. You're driven there. Limo. She's impressed, then not so impressed when she hears you and you're half-drunk already."

"How do you know any of this? This is typical of you Francine, fire first and then see who's been hit."

"No Corey. You're not getting this or you're pretending not to. Doesn't matter. You fucked up. With her, of all people. What did you say to her?"

"I told her the story of my success. I agree she was a great listener."

"Not only did you bullshit her, you tried to hit on her and lastly you talked about high school. You spoke about the Demosthenes Club. Fine. We all did, that's what her book was largely going to be about. But you stupid, stupid man you talked about Anne Podreski." She stopped, awaiting a reaction from him.

"Well. Yes. Okay. So?"

"You fell into a volcano and brought us with you. Jesus!"

"Listen, if you're going to act this way I'm out of here," he said as he made a feeble effort to push away from the small table.

"You're not going anywhere Corey until I say you can," she caught his wary eyes. "How could you bring up Anne Podreski in the midst of being drunk, hitting on the listener and worst of all say anything to the most creative of us all – Cynthia Power."

"I just mentioned Anne in passing. Can't even think of what I said."

"That's the point Corey. She remembered. Because after that interview with you she was a woman on a mission. She had at me three times after meeting you. The agenda was always Anne. It was all traced back to comments that you made. What exactly did you say to her?"

"Something like, it was too bad that Anne died," he said lamely.

"Sure Corey. And that single comment would cause her to meet with me three times, a fourth surely coming but she inconveniently died. You're full of shit Corey. She wouldn't tell me your exact words, she was too clever for that. She was a bloodhound with a scent in her nostrils. She keeps pestering about Anne. What do I know? Something is lingering in her mind. She's back on the Demosthenes Club and that forbidden place, the lake. You brought her back there with your loose-lipped comments." She stopped for breath.

He gave her a weird look, mouth twisted. "What does it matter? She's dead. Why do you give a damn now?"

"Jesus Corey. You've morphed into a goddamned fool. Do you think that it all ends with death? A rose on the coffin, her encased body and all her secrets?"

"Yes, that's exactly what I think," now alert and pissed off.

Francine looked around the dark lounge. A few seats away a youngish black man was pointing angrily at a petite blonde. What was there was not love. Toward the doorway three men, in their fifties it looked, laughing it up. At the bar a scattering of four patrons looking at a baseball game. The bartender stood to the side of the bar half watching the game. It was a quiet evening. She looked back at Corey.

"Let me remind you of some things since your memory is so impaired. Cynthia was closer to Anne than any of us. They were the odd ones out in the Demosthenes Club. Weak-kneed Liebow wanted gender equality. No trouble finding the males. Never was, was there? I could handle the pressure dealing with the four of you. So could Megan. But these two, Cynthia Power and Anne Podreski? There were always doubts. They both had that vulnerability gene. Because of that they bonded. The pressures were tough on us all. But poor Anne was in the dismal quartile for toughness and Cynthia for suspiciousness. All these years and Cynthia's ignorance maintained its course. To her Anne had just had an accident. Innocence Anne, ignorance Cynthia. And life went on. At age eighteen all of us go our separate ways except for dead Anne, of course. We were all going to do well. White privilege the losers say. It's sheer discipline and perseverance really. But we all succeed. The magnificent seven without Anne. Forget the pushy black jerk. And for all those years, lives led, fortunes made, dreams realized. Suddenly Cynthia sees a light because of you Corey. Cynthia? Of all the people to awaken. She the poet, the artist who had the way about her to make two plus two equal nineteen. The only one among us who was truly creative. Give her a one inch piece of silk and she'd create a dress."

Bladel had enough from her. Her abusiveness was in overdrive. He kept his temper under control as the crazed bull, dressed as a bovine, hammered at him. Two ideas twisted back and forth in his head. Was Francine Korbel wired? Was she otherwise dangerous – even if not wired? He eliminated the first. To say what she said was self-implicating. There was no wire, he concluded. Dangerous was another matter. She was losing her self-control and with that mayhem could occur. Behind the bluster and edginess was a worried woman needful of the reassurance that there was nothing to worry about. But her steely front was a tough barrier.

"Francine, slow down. Look! Please! Cynthia committed suicide. Why? Anne Podreski? No! You? No! Cynthia was a mess for God's sake. Always was. Yeah, she was creative. I'll give you that. But she was also an unsteady woman. I never so much as thought about making a pass at her. Did you see those aides I was talking to? Really – Cynthia? She made that up. And she also made up that I said something incriminating about Anne's death. Her instability was demonstrated by her suicide. Think about the premises to your conclusion." He was watching her closely as he weaved doubt into her position. He saw the waver in her eyes. He pursued the advantage. "She's dead. I'm sorry. But that's it. Let it go Francine."

Fifteen minutes later they separated. She was mollified, not totally, but at least enough for him to buy some time. Francine bitch would be back though. Interestingly, Francine had one very similar personality trait with Cynthia; they were both unrelenting.

CHAPTER 4

Bertrand McAbee didn't have a single 'come to Jesus' moment. He saw his realizations as a 'coming to Jesus' series of events, year after year, until the weight of them all pushed him into making some serious business decisions relative to his ACJ Investigations Agency.

All of those years ago, he had departed from St. Anselm College, a classics professor and occasional administrator. He was encouraged to leave academia by his now deceased brother, Bill, who himself had built an extraordinary career in the investigations business. Bill thought that Bertrand needed a change of scene, thus convincing him to change his career course.

Known only by a few, the agency's initials ACJ stood for three saints from Catholic hagiography, they being: Anthony, Christopher, and Jude. Acerbic brother Bill didn't approve this "cuteness" but in a brotherly fashion Bertrand told him to go to hell. St. Anthony was famed for his finding lost objects. Bertrand figured he earned the reputation from some powerful prelate in advanced stages of senility back in the 13th century – who had the good luck of finding lost objects when he spoke Anthony's name. From there the rest became garbled history. But there were some, Bertrand's deceased mother included, who swore by St. Anthony's power.

As to Christopher, well that was another story altogether. His supposed existence was rooted in pagan myth and the River Styx. The Church itself, abandoned him as a legitimate saint back in the late 20th century. But he continued to exist in the minds and hearts of many as exemplified in the vicinity of the steering wheels of motorized vehicles. St. Christopher's game was to insure safe passage during travel. Bertrand's mother wasn't happy about the "needless" interference by the Church toward this marvelous saint. Bertrand was all in favor of the phantasm as a symbol for his agency's future. Thus Christopher became part of the pantheon.

Lastly, as the third part of the trinity, there was St. Jude, patron saint of lost causes. Jude had a big time following especially for anyone who had to deal with the medical establishment. The Church was not about to be outdone by the damn pagans who already had a like totem in Asclepius, the god of healing. Presumably, Jude was given his standing to face down this pagan impiety. Bertrand's mother was unaware of the covert dialectic surrounding this pair. But she was known to exhort the intercession of St. Jude during tough times. Occasionally, McAbee felt that there *was* some metaphysical hand out there that enabled him to trudge through extraordinarily complex and dangerous cases. Whatever – Jude was enlisted.

So, ACJ was at a crossroads. McAbee was getting old and it became apparent to him that it was wise to consider closing the books on his client-base. The only question that now challenged him was complete closure or partial closure of ACJ. Should he keep his hands in things? The wisdom he had acquired from his living of life suggested that he should keep the heartbeat of the agency going, his tentative solution – cherry picking occasional cases and only those that had the clear ring of the unusual and the challenging.

All of his associates were ahead of him as he found out when he voiced his decision. They had figured it out a long time ago. Pat Trump who was with him from the beginning smiled. Was it with relief? They both knew that her secretarial and administrative abilities had kept ACJ stable as McAbee was constantly battling his instinctive anarchy against order and stability. When she said, involuntarily and rashly he thought, "Amen," everyone in the office became quiet for a few seconds. She was getting up in age, her husband had retired, and she was on solid financial footing, in part, due to McAbee's extraordinary accumulation and sharing of monies from some lucrative cases.

Jack Scholz, the toughest and meanest man McAbee ever met outside of his brother Bill, said, "Good idea." Scholz had been working for the U.S. government for years in the military and then in special ways that were never spoken of. He had helped McAbee in the hardest of times and McAbee grudgingly respected his ability to saw through giant logs, his viciousness and lack of ethics notwithstanding.

Barry Fisk, Yale doctorate and all, was schizophrenic in the sense that he had the emotional intelligence of a four year old and the IQ of a genius. His skill set with artificial intelligence was profound, his hacking abilities without peer, while his personal relationships were of graveyard quality. A bit ago he had been approached by the FBI to help break into Apple software after several terrorist attacks. His hatred for the FBI outweighed his hatred for terrorists. They were told to "fuck off." Because of Barry, McAbee had surged to advantage in many of his cases. His response to Bertrand's announcement was, "You never belonged doing this anyway."

And then finally there was his best friend and confidante Augusta Satin who had been with him through so much. A former Rock Island, Illinois, detective, she was always the 'go-to' when he was gone or when he needed some counsel. She wasn't surprised as she had heard his musings about withdrawing ACJ's reach. She smiled as if to say, finally, he went public. It would be hard to go back on his pronouncement and very especially because of the universal assent of those around the table.

And so McAbee was dismantling the apparatus. Files were being shifted to other agencies, clients thanked. There was exhilaration of a sort but it was mixed with the sadness of the realization that age was beginning its inevitable victory over his life.

He figured that it would take six months to get to where he wanted to be. Pat would come in on a continuing basis. Scholz and Fisk, as long as they stayed in the area, would always be available for a specific job and Augusta and he would remain inseparable, hopefully.

He would keep his offices. Money was not an issue with him and the thought of exiting his suite was just one step too far. There would be a time for that, sometime.

CHAPTER 5

Augusta Satin had been under the periodic care of Dr. Linda Rhine. She sought help after her youngest daughter, a sophomore at the University of Illinois in Champaign-Urbana, got herself romantically entangled with a basketball player at the University. It was untrue love and went against every warning that Augusta had preached as a divorced mother.

The basketball player from the slums of Gary, Indiana, was a sixth man on the team, a 6'3" guard with considerable ability. The pair had met at a rally protesting tuition raises and scholarship declines at this great state institution. Part of the problem with the University of Illinois, Augusta thought, was that it was in Illinois, an incomprehensibly corrupt state. So, no problem with the rally, it was well-placed. The spark that lit the relationship between her daughter, Anastasia, and the guy, Tuwayne, occurred at that rally. Anastasia was a standout student aiming for law school after she finished her undergrad education. All of the road lights leading in this direction were green. Augusta's older daughter, Juliana, now a senior, was heading for med school and there was no doubt that she would get there, part of the reason being that she had kept clear of the Tuwaynes of the world.

It was a feverish call last September that had thrown Augusta under the bus. Juliana was at the emergency ward at University Hospital. Anastasia had been shot along with Tuwayne. Augusta made it to Champaign in two hours and ten minutes under a police escort. Normally it was a three hour drive from her home in Rock Island.

One conclusion was that Anastasia's shoulder wound was so severe that her left arm would forever be a problem for her. Tuwayne had been knee-capped, his career as a basketball player over. The pair had been experimenting with some cheap Mexican heroin when Tuwayne's off-campus apartment had been raided by three druggies who shot semi-alert Tuwayne in his knees and then when Anastasia had made an effort to defend him she took a bullet to her shoulder, a bullet that was only three or four inches from her head.

It came out that Tuwayne was a drug dealer and had encroached into some forbidden zones while selling. He was unceremoniously thrown off the team and, under the threat of expulsion, he left the University heading back for Gary, a broken and embittered 21 year old. Inexplicably he blamed Anastasia for it all, she was careless when she came to his apartment, he said.

To Augusta the only benefit that came from the shooting was that Anastasia was now free of the creep. She withdrew from the Fall semester and got drug rehab for 37 days at a clinic in Minneapolis. When they released her they thought she had a great chance to recover from her budding addiction.

But Augusta also needed rehab. She sought the counsel of her best friend Bertrand McAbee. He recommended some sessions with a counselor ACJ had helped when one of her clients had turned into a stalker. McAbee had been impressed with her coolness under stress. And so it was that Augusta went to Rose Branca. They had only two sessions. Rose sought the intervention of Dr. Linda Rhine, she believed that Augusta needed apothecary intervention.

Linda Rhine M.D. was not a pill pusher – ten minutes in, a prescription, and good luck. Rhine detested the fact that psychiatry had sunk to this level. Augusta and she had connected. Both of them felt a kinship with each other even as Rhine maintained loose professional boundaries. Augusta was prescribed a minimal dosage of an anti-anxiety med in mid-October as Anastasia struggled to recover. By the beginning of the Spring term Anastasia was back at the University of Illinois, chastened, but determined to get back to the discipline that she had developed over the years. By February, Augusta started to relax a bit. Anastasia was again on track. With mixed emotions Augusta had learned that Tuwayne had been murdered in Gary in mid-February.

By early March, Augusta freed herself from the anti-anxiety medication. It had helped but it was no longer necessary. But Linda Rhine and Augusta would occasionally have lunch together.

It was in mid-May that Augusta was called by Linda who asked to meet with her. And here she was sitting at Thai Pagoda on 53rd Street in Davenport. What Augusta most respected in Linda Rhine was her forthrightness. Rhine didn't dawdle in ambiguities. She was a short woman, probably aged in her lower 60s, hinting streaks of what was black hair struggled through her long gray hair. She didn't wear glasses and her stunning blue eyes were alert and riveting. Augusta felt that she didn't miss a trick.

They chatted for a bit about Augusta's two children. Linda shared with Augusta that she had begun dating after a long hiatus. The woman was fifteen years younger. She was concerned about how it would go in the long run. Augusta was happy for her.

"So Augusta! I need your possible intervention and advice. About nine days ago a client of mine was murdered, I believe. I treated her for almost four years. I came to know her very well. A most extraordinary woman, a woman of causes and a woman of honor. You were a detective once, Rock Island as I recall. I know police work is not easy and I suspect that when things are ostensibly clear that there might be a tendency to close cases up."

As Augusta listened she felt that roles had shifted. Linda Rhine was disturbed. As Augusta looked closer she noticed the darkened rings under her eyes, the involuntary squint and the tightening of her lips. She nodded to show her understanding of what Linda was saying.

Linda went on, "To cut to the quick, the Davenport P.D. has ruled her death to be a suicide. They have closed the books. I protested. They tried to put me to shame when I challenged them. Here's the rub," she leaned in closely to Augusta, "I don't believe for one second that she killed herself even though by all appearances it was meant to look so. I believe her death to be a staged event, concealing a murder."

"This is difficult for you. The loss of a client and friend and then a putdown by the police department. I'm so sorry

Linda," Augusta said reflectively. Linda nodded a few times and then looked away, was that a tear in her eye?

"Augusta, you told me during our sessions about your friend McAbee. It was not the first time that I heard that name in my practice. He has come up often enough and not always in the best of ways, even though you seem to love him. Love has its blind spots but it also has a clear-sightedness that I don't underestimate. I have several questions at this point. Would it be an imposition on our friendship to ask you to get me a meeting with him? I know from what you said that he has been contemplating a pullback from the investigations business. Is that a complete withdrawal? I know that you have your hands full with Anastasia and I'm hesitant asking you about this?"

Augusta said, "Linda, of course I will try to help with Bertrand. You are correct in your memory. He is starting the process of pulling back. Let me speak with him and I'll call you. But I will warn you of one thing."

"Yes?"

"I'm not sure how you two will hit it off."

Linda looked back at Augusta and said, "Augusta! I deal with many difficult people."

Augusta smiled as she whispered to herself, 'Well, I warned you.'

CHAPTER 6

Dr. Linda Rhine came into the ACJ offices feeling like what war-torn Syria might feel if it could do so. Her hospital was under severe pressure to expand its psychiatric presence in the community. She was asked by the upper administration to defend the status quo. An impossible assignment as she felt that the hospital's response to psychiatric care was half-hearted if not downright scandalous. She was in a bind as Hope Hospital's chief psychiatrist. Pressure was being exerted against Hope Hospital by an out-of-state for-profit outfit that correctly demonstrated the current inadequacy of beds and psychiatrists in the community. They wanted to open a competing operation.

Furthermore, two of her patients had overdosed last night. One of them was going to live; the other was dead. Both of them should have been hospitalized but there were no beds. They had both stockpiled their dosages and the dead patient had illegally accessed OxyContin.

She had a headache from hell and was now going to have to contend with a Mandarin PI whom she knew about not only from Augusta but other clients over the years. She looked back at his receptionist who had introduced herself as Pat Trump. Nice enough, but a bit edgy and officious. "Bertrand will be with you shortly," she said across her desk, five minutes into Rhine sitting in the office, coiled with *angst.*

Finally, a door opened and she espied two men. Her eyes were drawn toward the short man, barely five feet tall. He was lopsided, the horizontal axis of his shoulders compromised, a clear hump arising from his back and with a scowl from hell. He was so off-putting that if he had been McAbee she would have left the office – the less she had to do with that face the happier she'd be.

The other man was of average height, balding, bespectacled and had his arm around the scowler. It was as though he was guiding him out of the office and clearly away from Pat, the red-haired secretary. There was something going on there, she thought. For what seemed a millisecond McAbee's eyes caught her as he said goodbye to the short man. She had the curious feeling that she'd been hacked by him, that he had fathomed her. She vetoed the fantasy but not with total success.

Only after the short man was escorted through to the hallway did Pat Trump get up and move quickly toward her as McAbee came back into the office. They were introduced by her and Rhine was led into his office. There was an aloof quality to him, her Mandarin-surmise validated.

He brought her to a small table in the corner of his large office. She didn't know if this was a professional courtesy or a practiced statement by him against superior-subordinate relations. But it was a bit coy and she liked it.

Her gaze caught a large number of books that clustered around a massive collection of red and green-covered books.

She had seen this collection somewhere in the past but couldn't remember where.

He said, "Dr. Rhine, I have heard good things about you from Augusta."

His voice was pleasant enough, East coast accent buried somewhere in it. "A good woman. I appreciate your meeting with me."

"Anything to drink? Coffee, Coke?"

"No thanks," she said as she again felt the hack by him. She wondered what he already knew about her and what he was figuring out on the run. She didn't feel judged by him but she felt known.

"I'll tell you what I know Dr. Rhine."

She held up her hand, "Please call me Linda."

"Okay Linda. I'm Bertrand. One of your patients died. Police and coroner say suicide. You say murder. You challenge. They say get lost. This is why you're here? That pretty much is what I was told by Augusta. Generally speaking, am I missing anything?"

"Well no. But as they say, the devil is in the details."

"Of course. I'm listening."

McAbee observed a woman in anguish, her obvious intensity of character doubled by it. He felt exuding from her anger and disquiet, someone fighting too many fires. She appeared to be an insomniac as her blue eyes were rimmed in red with shaded pouches beneath them. There was more going on in this woman than the presenting issue given to him by Augusta.

"It's hard to start this. I've been a psychiatrist for over 25 years. Board certified in case you're wondering. I know what I'm doing."

"Goes without saying," Bertrand said as he observed a defensiveness in her that was surprising to him.

"Well let me start, then. At issue is the death of Cynthia Power. By any chance did you know her?"

"No. I don't think so. But I have to admit that I sometimes know things that I don't know I know. In other words, you begin to describe someone and they begin to come out the fog of memory. But as of now the answer is no."

"I understand that distinction," she gave up a slight smile. "Cynthia was a patient of mine for almost four years. We became friends. There was no erotic relationship between us but I loved her. She was a unique and brilliant soul."

"Why was she a patient?" McAbee asked. He wanted to immediately test her openness as he felt that the doctor-client relationship was no longer in play with the death. But would Rhine open up?

"Initially, she came to me because she was disturbed by her physical deterioration."

"Her age? Physically? Exactly what?"

"She was 63 when she enlisted my help. Her eyes were failing her a bit. She needed serious bifocals. Her knees were hurting her, she needed some physical therapy and some Advil. Several fingers on her right hand were becoming arthritic. She was a right-handed artist. She had some insomnia, she needed to learn to relax at bedtime. She was, in short, a woman coming to grips with age and the ailments that accrue to it." Rhine gazed upwards ever so slightly as if searching for something. She continued, "She was a perfectionist who could not accept that what she did at 52 she could not do at 63, or at least do in the same manner.

This is not an uncommon problem nor is it uncommon for practitioners in my field to treat it with drugs. There's a whole legion of easy fixes. Don't get me wrong; I prescribe them but they are not my first line of defense. With her they wouldn't be. She needed to air herself out. I found her to be an exhilarating presence, a flower that just needed some tending. I hope that by the end of this you will regret not having known her."

There was an occasional soft smile that was leavened with an equal amount of sadness as she went on. Rhine had lost a close friend. McAbee respected physicians who connected with their patients in the way that she did even though it might be professionally unwise. He merely nodded.

"She was a Catholic," Rhine continued, "but was drawn to the wild side of that faith." She looked quizzically at McAbee; he stared back. "Are you familiar with Dorothy Day? The Berrigans?"

"Yes. Dorothy Day was trying to hold together what some would say was an oxymoron – a Catholic Communist. Pretty hated by conservatives in her faith. But social action on issues such as poverty, racism, war, was her forte. You're saying that Cynthia Power was a follower?"

"Oh my yes – believe it," Linda Rhine said with feeling.

"The Berrigans were two Jesuit priests who were obsessed with American militarism. They made a name for themselves during the Vietnam War and then they went anti-war to the extreme. They were arrested with some frequency. That was her brand of Catholicism?" he asked.

"Yes, however she was never arrested. But she had her share of enemies in the community. She was outspoken."

"Was that an issue with her? Upset about rejection?"

"No. I mentioned it to highlight a facet of her. She was into causes. She was a marcher, an activist. Once she got into something she was into it with all of her might. Rejection would not disturb her. Rejection after all has an antidote, integrity."

"How did she make a living?" Bertrand asked.

"She was an accomplished artist. Oils and sculpture. She was exhibited around the country. She was meticulous; her total *oeuvre* was pretty limited. As she grew older there were fewer pieces, arthritis a factor. That upset her terribly."

"Married? Kids? Lovers?"

"No. A few affairs but they didn't add up to anything sustained. She was straight, by the way. There was one relationship that got away from her. The man was murdered. Sarajevo and that whole mess back in the nineties. She was enraged about that murder."

"So presumably you were trying to have her realize that age needed to be accepted. Were you successful?"

"It's never about my success Bertrand. It's about her success. The answer is that she came to grudgingly, but not fully, accept the barriers of age. She wasn't going to run a four minute mile and she needed to say so what? Or, who cares?"

"But your relationship turned into a friendship?"

"Yes. After about six months. I always considered her to be a patient but also a close friend. A bit like Augusta in a way, although I was closer to Cynthia than Augusta."

"Since you led off with a controversial side to her personality, are you suggesting that the radical Catholicism that she engaged with could somehow be involved with her death?"

"No. There was no method to my starting with Dorothy Day and the Berrigans. Just strokes on the portrait that I'm filling in," she stated with a bit of an edge in her voice.

McAbee was slightly suspicious of that statement. There had to be some reason why she went there so early, but it wasn't worth pursuing. "Just to get this in the open Linda. You're here because you are convinced or – you suspect – that she was murdered."

"Convinced is the proper word," she said flatly.

"I'd like to see more strokes on this canvas that you're using."

"Causes! Environmental activist another part to her."

"How out front was she on that issue?"

"Never arrested," she smiled wanly.

McAbee came back at her. "Was she ever arrested period?"

"No, not in America at least. She was very proud of that. Other countries, I don't know."

"She knew when to withdraw and/or she was lucky?" McAbee suggested.

"I concluded that it was both."

"Other groups?"

"Black Lives Matter, another, LGBT. She was a case study for what would be termed ultra-liberal causes. Far to the left of Bernie Sanders, is how I would classify her."

"I'm sure that I don't have to guess how she felt about the NRA," he asked blandly, but with a slight smile. Rhine looked at him to make sure that he was trying to be humorous. She got it as she gave him a smirk. "Where did she live Linda?"

"Davenport. Close to St. Anselm. Modest house but the

neighborhood was… irregular, rough around the edges. She never complained. I believe that she felt safe. The issue never came up in any session or conversation with her. I went to her house twice for a dinner. She was a talented cook. She was thoroughly at ease in her house."

"When was the last time you saw her?"

"Two days before she was found. If she had been on any mind-altering drugs I would have immediately concluded that she was off her meds. She was terribly distraught. The worst I have ever seen her."

"Wouldn't that support suicide?"

"Not at all. She was a woman who would take upsetting news or events and use them to fight against them and herself. Suicide would be the last of her responses to difficult matters. But she was at the stage where she knew battles were in the air. She needed to air out her feelings, her upsets. That's why she came that day. She was focusing the issues, as it were."

McAbee noticed that Linda's hands coiled into a fist, uncoiled and then recoiled constantly. He wondered whether she was dealing with guilt of some sort, as if something bad happened on her watch and she missed an opportunity to set it right. He said, "So the issues? You used the plural. Were they new to you?"

"Yes and no. I'll explain. Months previous Cynthia decided to do a book, interviews, reminiscences and the like on a club that she was in as a high school student. Honor student type of club. Davenport Memorial High School, late 60s. There were only eight students in it. It was called the Demosthenes Club." She stopped and then stared at the green and red volumes. "That's where I ran into those books. I had a class in college on Greek and Roman thought. Those are the Loebs. And of course, you taught the classics. Sometimes I think my mind is out of whack. Excuse me." She brightened a bit, her thoughts wandering away to perhaps better days.

Bertrand said, "Very few people who come here have any idea about those books."

Distractedly she said, "Oh. Yes. I would imagine. To Cynthia again. Members of the club all graduated, except for one who drowned during her senior year. The seven all went on, all with scholarships, and as it turned out extraordinarily successful career-wise. One of them had a heart attack some years ago and died. Cynthia mused that of the six remaining she was the least successful by the alpha dog standards of crazed America. But here are the winds that beset her. She found out, no I should say reaffirmed, something that she knew deep down all along. They were a bad lot. Beneath their supposed success was deep failure. I think that she began to alter her objective, writing an upbeat book about them would be impossible. It took her some months to thoroughly understand this."

"So this was one of her problems?" McAbee asked.

"No," she looked hard at Bertrand. "That realization that they were a dysfunctional group she had already discerned. She just needed a refresher which she got as the book project went along. They all saddened her through the interview processes. They were happy to proclaim how successful they were. But as she probed them she realized that they had become empty, thoughtless. Cynthia was a highly introspective thinker, disciplined and insightful. She perceived them to be dry holes. She became conflicted about the book. She didn't care to be a bitch of some sort outing her former classmates. But that was the trail opening up to her if she went forward."

"Why didn't she just abandon the book? The world is full of dry holes, as you put it," Bertrand inquired.

"I have news for you Bertrand. We haven't hit the issues yet. And for your information she had come to that conclusion. The book project was in her rear window, abandoned." Linda stopped and looked hard at Bertrand.

He interpreted the pause to be a check to see if he was following her narrative but he also perceived a slight piece of theatrics, as if she was about to hit the true target of her visit. He said, "So are you saying that the book project was a disappointment for her but hardly a suicide matter."

"Yes. But now we are getting to worrisome waters." She took from her bag a small writing pad. She placed it on the table. He noticed that there was a printed name on the page top and then a series of bullet points, all hand-printed.

"With Cynthia dead, there are five currently live members of the Demosthenes Club. She would talk about them. I, of course, kept notes. I wrote out a summary of my recollections and of my notes about each one of her former classmates. Allow me to thumbnail them for you."

It took Dr. Rhine about 20 minutes to outline the five club members. McAbee listened attentively and said nothing until she was finished. He commented, "That's an interesting crew. High success. No argument there."

"I regret making this complicated but it is just that the last name that I mentioned, Corey Bladel, the congressman from Illinois, set her off. A heavy drinker and quite handsy with Cynthia's body when they met in Chicago for her interview with him. He said something in his alcohol-drenched meanderings that put Cynthia into a spin. It pertained to the eighth member of the club and the senior year drowning of a girl, Anne Podreski. It was one thing to realize that the club members were still dysfunctional over the decades but did the dysfunction point to a concealment of foul play? This was tearing her apart. Catholic remember? Very, very Catholic. A super-ego on steroids, Cynthia."

"Did you tell this to the Davenport P.D.?"

"No, and I won't. Dry holes, remember?" She said adamantly.

"So you're saying that word might have gotten out about her suspicions and Corey Bladel's mutterings. Enough so that a murder could take place to silence the sentinel?"

"Arguably, yes."

"Lots of ifs in this. Did Cynthia mention Bladel's comments to others in that club?"

"Yes, to one of them in particular, and I'm pretty sure that all of them were alerted about her concerns. But I don't know that for sure."

"You said there were issues. You used the plural. What else?"

"Yes. But this I'm more tentative about. But let me explain. Her lover, I think he was her only real love ever, was murdered while she was in Sarajevo during that horrid siege. Do you recall those times?"

"Absolutely."

"His name was Toma, a reporter of sorts who also worked for the government in Bosnia. She was doing volunteer work for a Catholic group, medical and social care. They fell in love, Cynthia and Toma. Deep, abiding. His murder was a setup, not a random assassination as were most. She never let it go. She thought that the authorities knew more than they were saying. She tried and tried to get information but was blocked. When she came back to the States she still kept trying. No luck. But as I said she'd never quit. A bit ago she caught a break from some contacts over there. Through them she received a police report with a bribe, $5,000. I never saw the report but it rekindled her fire, I'll tell you that," Rhine pounded the table with emphasis, as if to say her disclosures were complete.

"So she was dealing with two brutal hits from the past. But you're still so sure that suicide was not her response?"

"Just the opposite Bertrand. She had everything to live for, don't you see?"

"Does she have family?"

"A brother, Eric, but that's not a positive thing. They're quite estranged. She was going to leave much of her estate, at least this was true the last time it came up, to the animal shelter in Davenport. It's possible she left the house and its contents to him from a comment she made, once."

"That's it? The animal shelter and her brother?"

"As far as I know. Yes."

"What was the issue with her brother?"

"He's politically to the right of Hitler. Her words. She saw him as ethically compromised, dangerous, and from what she said the feelings and reactions were quite similar on his part toward her."

"Was she wealthy?" McAbee asked neutrally.

"I don't know for sure. She gave away a lot of money to her causes. Halfway houses, food banks, environmental organizations. I think that if she had saved her money she'd be classified as pretty well off. She didn't live in want, let's say."

"Who's been to her house since the death?"

"The police. But they were convinced from the outset about their conclusions. Presumably, her attorney got in there."

"Who's that?"

"I hate to say this because I've had my run-ins with him, an ambulance chaser, Matthew Fox."

McAbee knew Fox. He seemed to be pictured on every other billboard in the area. He was a likeable low-life who owed McAbee a favor. The question was – would he remember what McAbee had done for him five or six years ago? Like many people on the far left he portrayed himself as a crusader for justice and fairness. A few weeks ago, McAbee recalled, the local paper *The Quad City Times* had a section called the Parade of Great Homes. There were fifteen listed, his being one; it was an overstated mansion in Pleasant Valley, just to the east of Bettendorf. "That's a hard dot to connect, isn't it? I don't see Fox and Cynthia Power on the same planet."

Rhine sat on that comment for a few seconds before saying, "There are some who would probably say the same thing about me if they heard she was seeing me. I don't know how to explain the connection to Fox. But my assumption is that he's the executor of her will."

"Was she conversant with computers?"

"Oh yes."

"Presumably her personal computer is sitting in her house, untended?"

"Good question. Probably, yes."

"So now Linda, murder? That's quite a leap." McAbee noticed her jaws clench as he asked the question.

"She wasn't the type to wet down towels and place them around her garage and seal up her car door windows. She wasn't suicidal. Her death was too studied, too engineered. She didn't think like that. It wasn't her. It was not the death of an artist. It was *manufactured* and that's a word that doesn't fit her profile. It was a put together murder Bertrand and that's why I'm here. I don't have the time to fight the Davenport P.D. They are set like concrete about this. Can you help me?"

McAbee pondered the request. His relationship with the Davenport P.D. was below sea level, about as low in that regard as the city of Jericho in the Palestinian territories. He knew that this case would involve his pestering of Augusta, the only positive strand connecting ACJ with the police department and its chief, Phil Pesky. If Pesky had his way he would throw the entire ACJ Agency, with the exception of Augusta, into jail. "Linda, no promises. Let me play a few pieces in this chess game and see what I can come up with. How's that?"

"It's a hundred times better than what I got from the police department."

"Some more. You mentioned her brother. Other than his politics, why is he difficult?"

"I asked him about my visiting her house. I wanted to see if there was something there that would give me more hints about what she was mulling over. He was very harsh toward me. He knows that I'm a lesbian. I have been forthright in my convictions – I've been very involved in that community. He made some slurred comments about me and hung up."

"He lives around here?"

"Moline. He's retired. Used to be a real estate agent. Cynthia would talk about him. She felt sorry for him. Referred to him as a lost soul. I never met him and I don't think that will ever happen. How winsome are you Bertrand?" She concluded with a fraught smile.

"If I get involved I'll make some effort to pry him open. Anything else?"

"If, in fact, she bequeathed her house to him. It was an act of compassion on her part. Not love. She thought him sour, sarcastic, and just nasty, at least towards her. I took it as sibling tension gone wild. But an interesting characteristic of Cynthia was her ability to stanch retribution and displace her anger into a positive direction. As I said she was not suicidal, an excellent and fine woman." At that moment her cellphone chirped and she looked at it quickly. "I'm so sorry Bertrand, I have to go. The psychiatric unit at Hope is overfilled and we are short two physicians. My cell number is on my card. Feel free to call me." With that she stood, they shook hands, and she left abruptly.

McAbee noted that she was not a hugger. He saw her as a double of Cynthia Power in so far as their being engaged women.

CHAPTER 7

Barry Fisk received a text from McAbee's snarly secretary, Pat Trump, who had been with McAbee since the inception of the ACJ Agency. Due to that she had weaned her way into McAbee's psyche. He probably couldn't brush his teeth without her approval. But Barry saw her for what she was, a judgmental shrew who used her considerable influence to try to destabilize, if not destroy, his relationship with McAbee. Of course, she would never succeed for one plain reason. Barry was a master hacker and computer guru. There was no one like him in Iowa and only in Chicago might one find a talent such as his.

McAbee knew how critical his skills had been over a variety of his tough and complex cases. Every once in a while he was tempted to tell McAbee that it was either himself or his mean-spirited secretary. But something in the back of his head caused him to back away from an ultimatum. Regardless, though, he was indispensable and they both knew it. And now, because the red-headed vixen was texting him rather than calling she could avoid having to match wits with him, her texting an enhanced piece of passive aggressiveness on her part.

He texted back to her. [I'll be there. Good time for you to smoke in the bathroom and break the Clean Indoors Act of Iowa]. There, let the battles begin.

Pat knocked at Bertrand's open door and said, "Fisk will be here at 2:00 p.m. as you requested."

It seemed to her that the mention of Fisk would bring a subtle smile to Bertrand. It was as if he took some secret pleasure at watching her cope with the little disfigured runt who stood somewhere between four feet nine inches to five feet at best, his shoulders badly uneven, and the hump on his upper back looking like a miniature version of the Gibraltar Rock. And the arrogance of the little freak! Why McAbee put up with him was always a mystery to her. She had been tempted over the years to tell Bertrand that it was either she or Fisk. But she always backed away from this brink.

Bertrand picked up a few of the notes left by Dr. Rhine. It was a dated history of Cynthia Power. He copied down the salient points.

1950:	Born – Davenport
1968:	Graduate – Memorial High School – Davenport
1972:	Graduate – University of Iowa (Art)
1973-1979:	New York City – Metropolitan Museum of Art Assistant to Curator – Impressionist Collection
1980-1985:	San Francisco – Volunteer: Homeless Shelter, later AIDS Clinic, Freelance Artist

1985-1988:	Arizona – Volunteer, Navajo Reservation, Freelance Artist
1988-1992:	Washington, DC – Center for the Humanities Administrator: Art as Mitigation for Terror Collection. Freelance Artist
1992-2000:	Sarajevo, Bosnia – Catholic Action 'Angelus' and Freelance Artist
2001-2009:	Washington, DC – Organizer, Democratic Party, and Freelance Artist
2009-Present:	Davenport – Care of Aunt (deceased 2014), Freelance Artist

It was of note to him that the Berrigans, Dorothy Day and other leftist Catholic movements were not included in the brief profile yet they were the very points of departure that Rhine had used as she spoke about Power.

Other materials, certainly abridged, related to the therapies and discussions between the two women. McAbee observed that Rhine was quite open about her feelings and attitudes and was very clearly not fussy about keeping an emotional and professional distance from her clients, or at the very least, Cynthia Power.

Power came back to Davenport to care for her aunt whose decline in health forced such. At first she rendered care at her house only to eventually place her ailing aunt in assistive care in 2012 to finally her aunt's death in 2014. Cynthia Power's struggles were predictable, the decision to place her aunt in assisted care, her guilt and apprehension, her efforts at focusing on her art career, memories of a horribly failed romantic liaison in Bosnia, her own aging, and within the content of the pages a developing friendship with Linda Rhine. Neither woman was sexually interested in the other but their minds were an interesting match. Dr. Rhine probably knew Cynthia Power better than anyone else did. Her determination that Cynthia was not suicidal was very convincing. On the face of it, there was no outstanding suspect; however, an investigation might uncloak a murderer. He closed the folder and prepared for a meeting with Roberta Wheeler who was being threatened by a former employee who thought he had been fired unjustly.

CHAPTER 8

Francine Korbel attacked the newly built YMCA in Bettendorf: treadmills, yoga, weights, stationary bikes and just about every other device and workout activity into which she could find escape. For days she worked herself into a state of physical exhaustion. This allowed her to sleep each night, though still haunted by the occasional nightmare and the sweats. Her confrontational meeting with Corey Bladel did not sit well with her. The more she thought about it the angrier she became.

Corey Bladel saw Cynthia's death as final, no strings. It was as though he thought that she wasn't a writer? Did Cynthia keep notes about those, just short of being testy, discussions with her about Anne Podreski's death? And where in God's name were those notes? Did the police have them? A friend? Power had shared with Korbel that she was seeing a psychiatrist. Were notes in that office? Yes, she saw that the death was ruled a suicide. And maybe it was. But then again she knew the Demosthenes Club, from eight, well – nine to be precise, to currently five, Cynthia and Anne Podreski dead. Stan Adair died in 2001, well deserved, a renowned and vile class action attorney, gone instantly from a massive heart attack. Arrogant scum bag, didn't die soon enough. And then, of course, the notorious Archie issue, the ninth club member – a brief anomaly.

But the arithmetic left three others, besides herself and Corey Bladel, still out and about. Francine did know that Cynthia interviewed those three for her would-be book concerning the outsized success of the members of the Demosthenes Club. Probably, she tried to reach out to them once again after drunken Corey Bladel alerted her to Anne Podreski. But this was an inference on the part of Francine. The only one of the five that Cynthia Power mentioned to Francine was stupid Corey Bladel, the source of her Podreski obsession.

And if Cynthia had tried to speak with the other three – hah! Fuckers – one and all.

Peter Waters, just recently ambassador to Lebanon. Peter, of the silken-throat. The manicured bass voice of self-importance. He could talk himself out of anything, one of the glibbest characters she had ever run into. She remembered his constantly hitting on Anne Podreski from the moment she was invited into the Demosthenes Club. And all too well she recalled his advocacy for an initiation ritual and then his sheer sophistry within the club at his disavowal of the ritual when the principal objected to it. The 'who me' defense! Was Cynthia even aware of his duplicity? Did she call him and ask for clarifications? Was she as intense with him as she was with her? And what would a bastard like Peter Waters do if his carefully sculpted reputation was imperiled? She looked up his whereabouts. He was in Chicago, Hinsdale, a suburb.

And there was the snake princess, Megan White,

Professor of Sociology at the University of Iowa. She, a wicked manipulator, who had used her looks to captivate the seventeen and eighteen year old males of the club. Francine watched her sow jealousy among them while perfecting the art of studied disingenuousness, a put-on innocence from the depths of guile. She was great at it. Her fame was now far-reaching, a regular contributor at CNN, occasional columnist for *The New York Times*, spouting her psychobabble to the masses. She cultivated victimhood and the denial of personal responsibility. It was all society's fault. She had the marvelous ability of marching idiots to the gates of hell while disappearing from the march. Because she was only an hour away in Iowa City it was likely that Cynthia would have approached her about Anne Podreski's death. And good luck with that Cynthia as Megan the victimizer played the professional victim instinctively. She would try to make Cynthia feel bad about bringing up Anne Podreski and her death.

And then there was finally John Douthit of Silicon Valley fame. He had struck gold, in on the start with Microsoft, Google, Apple and from a newspaper article, Facebook. Estimates of his wealth in the low billions. Douthit the ultimate loner, a calculating son of a bitch, always steps ahead of everyone but pretending to be steps behind everyone. Francine saw through his act the minute she set eyes on him. She recalled Shakespeare's *Julius Caesar* and the comment about Cassius, "Yond Cassius has a lean and hungry look." He was a fucking lone wolf. Francine thought bitterly about him and his supposed shyness and insecurity. He always held back and if she needed support or a friendly ear it would never come from him. But she never confronted him. The club's reputation had restrained her, a rarity for her now, but still an irreplaceable lesson for her in future dealings with subtle aggressors. Attack the bastards. Did Cynthia try to get through to him about Anne Podreski? And if she did, how would he react from his perch in San Francisco?

Good old congressman Corey Bladel, fucking drunk, raising the dead to life.

CHAPTER 9

Barry Fisk drove south to downtown Davenport, thinking about his session yesterday with his court-ordered psychologist. It still rankled him. He was forced by the idiot to fully explain what had caused the judge to require five sessions with a certified counselor. A list of six names had been given to him by the court. Three were females and thus vetoed on principle; one of the males was a Vietnamese, also scornfully rejected. The remaining two underwent intense scrutiny, including Barry's capture of their private patient files. Both of them had become expert in using bureaucratic-speak, neutral to guarded. Ultimately he chose a former varsity football player from the University of Iowa. The son-of-a-bitch had knowledge of aggression, after all. The other guy was too active with the LGBT community and assorted other whiners and was thus into projecting guilt onto good people who did not buy into absurd agendas. There was risk with the jock but he was the best of a bad crew. And it wasn't as if Barry had much of a choice.

So, as commanded, he explained the incident to the dumb-looking pile of muscle. Barry had been at a local haunt, a short-order eatery in central Davenport. Just thinking about the experience infuriated him, as he held the steering wheel tightly. He wished to have a breakfast as he prowled *The New York Times* on his iPad. He was in a pretty good frame of mind given that it was only about 9:00 a.m., the day still too young to set him off. The counselor urged him to continue on about this breakfast that led to the five session mandatory intervention. And so he did. The waitress, incidentally, an overweight, white-haired hag, had come over to him. He was alone reading a story about the controversial makeup of the United States Supreme Court. He didn't expand on that because he assumed that the psychologist-jock didn't even know what the Supreme Court was nor where it was located. So he alerted the jock to listen closely to what was going to occur. And furthermore, what would the jock have done in his place?

So the 60-90 year old hag comes to his table and looks at him scornfully and asks, in a hugely disrespectful way, what does he want to order? He says a glass of orange juice, a cup of coffee, two scrambled eggs, and a *short* stack of pancakes. The filthy bitch starts to laugh hysterically and gurgles out "how *short* do you want it?"

As he recalls his session and the forced recital of the incident he wants to tear the steering wheel from its sockets. The jock-shrink, or whatever the oversized freak is, starts to talk in low and cloying tones about how difficult it can be to deal with insensitive and cruel people who get joy in the plight of "disfigured" people, he says. The fool actually used the word disfigured! By this time Barry has pulled into the downtown garage, close to the ACJ offices. He sits there recalling how he wanted to double down on what he did to the waitress and hurl that full carafe of water in the jock's office at said jock. But he refrains, fearful that the idiot judge will mandate unlimited sessions of therapy for him because the carafe breaks the bastard-jock's nose and ruins his linen suit. So Barry does a monumental psychological swivel and completes the restaurant recital. The bitch is virtually bent in half in maniacal laughter as she breaks Barry's psychological bank by again repeating the word *short*. Barry takes the glass of ice water that she had placed on the table and flings it at her. In golf they would call it a hole-in-one. Her glasses shatter. Her nose goes into full bleed, the pig was probably on a five aspirin-a-day regimen as the blood wouldn't stop. She staggers backward and falls across an adjoining table onto the barely-eaten breakfast of three old biddies who look as though they escaped from some geriatric unit. Hysteria reigns!

The jock pretends to be ignorant of all this but Barry knows otherwise. He has the full police report that details the incident. He again does the undertaker tone of deep sympathy and repeats how hard it is to be disfigured and at the mercy of callous people. He pats Barry on his back at the end of this useless session, a pat by the way that was too, too close to his protruding hump.

So Barry sits in his specially outfitted Toyota for a good five minutes trying to settle his nerves as he contemplates the coming four sessions with the dumb jock-psychologist and hoping that he does not have to deal with McAbee's shrew Pat Trump.

CHAPTER 10

McAbee heard the soft alarm buzz to the entrance of his outer office. He was by himself, Pat Trump had to leave to assist her husband Ed who was in a painful rehab at Hope Hospital. He had fallen down a flight of stairs in their two story house in LeClaire, a small town to the northeast of Bettendorf.

As he came out of his office, one look at Barry foretold a difficult meeting. His eyes were streaked with red lines which were in contrast to the dark pouches under his eyes. He looked as though he hadn't slept for days. He noticed that Barry looked over at Pat's desk, a lingering look. Was he concerned about an ambush from her? McAbee said into this array of observations, "Barry, why don't we go into my office? Pat's gone for the day by the way." Barry said nothing.

Bertrand worried about Barry and how he conducted his life. He lived alone, it appeared that his best friend was his computer. His attitude toward the human race was gravely negative and he was vindictive as hell if slighted. His vindictiveness usually found its sting in some subtle way, his fingerprint on the caused-harm far removed from observation.

He had received a doctorate from Yale University in history but came up as a total disaster in the classroom, his last professorial stint at Western Illinois University in nearby Macomb, Illinois. Years ago, almost by accident McAbee had hired him to do research on a serial killer case. His work was so excellent that from then on he was on a steady retainer basis for ACJ even though his relationship with Pat Trump and Jack Scholz was rife with loads of hostility-baggage. At the end of it all, McAbee was in awe of his skills but he handled him like an unstable bomb.

He was also aware of the incident that had gotten Barry into trouble with the law. He had to testify for Barry's sanity. He knew that this very proud man had been humbled once again as he ventured out of his house into society. Which was worse for him? His failed experience at Western Illinois, a harsh treatment by the FBI, the harassment of him by the Davenport P.D., or this latest event with the waitress? McAbee feared that he was watching the making of an agoraphobic. And God knows, he thought, what other traumas the man had suffered in his life.

"Barry, you look a bit strained. I hope I didn't impose too much on you," he said gently.

"No, you're not the problem. This psychologist that I'm seeing is a moron. And I have four more sessions with him. When I left him I feel ten times worse than before I went to see him. But I don't want to talk about him, it just brings the whole mess up. Why did you need to see me? And by the way, where is *she*?" He looked back toward the outer office.

"Personal business," McAbee said brusquely as he kept speaking so as to avoid the inevitable snarky comments from Barry about Pat. "There was a seeming suicide about a week and a half ago. A psychiatrist friend of Augusta, also a friend of the deceased, is quite sure that it wasn't a suicide. I'd like you to do a workup before I decide to involve with it."

"So, this is what you mean by letting up and backing away from cases?"

Defensively, McAbee responded, "I said I was going to be selective, not done."

"Whatever," Fisk snarled.

At moments like these Bertrand understood how Pat Trump felt. Barry was looking for a verbal fight and if and when McAbee fired back at him his feelings would be hurt and then the practiced pout would take over, Barry the practitioner of aggression and failing in that – the master of passive-aggressiveness. A man with a complex arsenal of psychological traps and counter-traps. McAbee responded gently, "Now that we have clarified my slow disengagement from things let me tell you about the potential case."

Barry sat silent as Bertrand unpacked some of the details given to him by Linda Rhine.

Fisk, after he had spent enough venom, was normally a very careful listener. He never once interrupted Bertrand's recital. When McAbee was done, however, Barry observed, "This whole thing revolves around the psychiatrist and how sure-footed she is. Psychology is a crop of guesswork. For everything they get right, huge errors are made. I'm not saying that she's wrong but from what you say this is an uphill investigation. But it does sound like this Cynthia Power didn't amass enemies the way some of your clients do." He twisted his lips and paused, "It's important to get into her house. If I can access her pc it would make things easier to judge."

"I'm going to speak with her lawyer and see whether I can get into her place. In the meantime, I'd like you to run as deep a check on her as you can."

"Money limits?"

"No."

"Rhine paying for this?"

"Good question. I never got around to talking about it. I will if I get involved."

CHAPTER 11

McAbee pulled up to the Fox and Partners offices, an end unit storefront in a strip mall. In the tracts to the right of Fox's offices, there was a Pizza Hut, a Dollar General, and a large Goodwill store. The mall was located in mid-Davenport, an area that had felt a peaking crime rate. The parking lot had its share of potholes, the entire complex was suffering from architectural dementia.

He had checked the Scott County court calendar. Two trials were on for that day, criminal cases, meth production charges against three West-enders and a Shell Gas Station robbery. Fox would have nothing to do with criminal law, at least of this low-life kind.

Five years ago McAbee had provided assistance to attorney Fox. It was voluntary on the part of ACJ. Fox was very grateful as he swore fealty and promised to pay back ACJ if such was ever required. It went down as follows. One of Jack Scholz's men was keeping tabs on a blackmailing stripper/prostitute. She had been bleeding a prominent heart surgeon of a small fortune, videos and audios of scandalous proportions were in her possession. Her hold on the surgeon was complicated by her having consulted him about an irregular heartbeat. His license to practice medicine was in jeopardy, under her control as it were. The surgeon wept in the offices of ACJ.

During the time of Jack's surveillance a former client of attorney Fox's had been beaten up in an alley outside of a bar in downtown Davenport. This client and Fox had been nastily estranged from each other, the client threatening Fox with a malpractice suit cum appeal to the Judiciary Board of the State of Iowa. He had claimed that one of his two beaters was none other than Matthew Fox himself.

The beating had occurred at 12:55 a.m. Fox, at first, demurred about an alibi, reluctant to supply the name of the stripper/prostitute with whom he was involved. Rightly so. He suspected that his alibi would hit the newspapers because he was on the public enemy list of the City of Davenport, *The Quad City Times*, and assorted other downtown powers. Why? Because he sued them often and won often. Mugging an angry client would be a dream come true in the game of revenge for these powers if he refused to offer his alibi. A dilemma.

That Fox was a lowlife and an unscrupulous lawyer was a known fact to McAbee. Three clients of ACJ that had been mauled by him. In two of three cases Fox had been particularly unethical in Bertrand's judgment. But McAbee was in a moral dilemma. Fox and his car had been video-recorded from the time of 11:55 p.m. – 2:34 a.m. at the stripper's apartment on the night of the beating.

Fox would probably have given her up as an alibi except for her potential hold on him. A kind of 'out me and your troubles are just beginning counselor.' Who knew?

Augusta had gotten wind of the beating and Fox being

a suspect at a breakfast meeting with a Davenport P.D. detective. When she mentioned Fox to McAbee he had been reading Scholz's surveillance report and its explicit mention of Fox, the man of the omnipresent billboards. Just about everyone in the Quad Cities knew Fox. Conscience overrode *schadenfreude* as McAbee arranged a hasty meeting with a frantic Fox who upon hearing of the surveillance and the video was overjoyed. McAbee said that he would get the word back to the Davenport P.D. and the detective on the case of the downtown beating. And so it went that Fox slipped the publicity. When Fox later asked McAbee how much he wanted for this favor, McAbee declined. Fox, in genuine shock, almost walked away clicking his heels. McAbee wondered about an afterlife and whether his good deed would erase some of his dubious behaviors. His conjectures vanished in an eye-blink.

Matthew Fox was in his mid-forties. He had been a fine quarterback at Bettendorf High School until in his senior year he suddenly quit the team in mid-season. There was a local uproar that had a shelf-life of two weeks. He never played again as best McAbee could discern from his Google search. He graduated from Luther College in Decorah, Iowa, and from the Drake School of Law in Des Moines, Iowa.

Fox came back to the Quad Cities where he churned away for two years with a litigation firm of dubious repute and then went into his outsized game of personal injury litigation. McAbee figured that 25% of his revenue was returned to marketing. Somewhere along the line he had become fluent in Spanish, he became a known and generous contributor to African- American causes and put himself out as an avenger against the persecution of the little guy, minorities in particular.

He came into his offices unannounced. The suite was elegant, garish almost, positioned in the wanting strip mall. It was outfitted by practiced hands. He hadn't seen a César Chavez picture in some time. The deceased Mexican civil rights leader had been resurrected in the office as a prominently squared picture of him was hung alongside of Martin Luther King and Pope Francis I. This trinity took up one side wall, each picture about three feet square. McAbee wondered who had been there before Pope Francis, Mother Theresa?

Across from the wall of heroes there was a receptionist. She had the requisite good looks, blonde, sculpted frame, and a generous outgoing face at first glance. But at second look, behind the sun, McAbee sensed the potential for storms.

"May I help you sir?" as she looked at her watch. It was 4:45 p.m.

"Yes. I'd like to see Mr. Fox."

"Oh, I'm afraid that's not possible. If you have a case for him you will have to go through his paralegal staff first. Unfortunately, all three of them are in Mason City at a workshop," she smiled.

"No. I want to see Mr. Fox. I would like to see him now," he said as non-threateningly as he could.

"Not possible, sorry," she stood up.

She was a good six feet. He couldn't tell if she wore heels. But he did know that a joust with her was possible. He caught her name on the side of her desk, "Look Savannah, I know he's here. His Mercedes is behind back. The vanity license is ATTYFOX. He knows me. If you'd be so kind. Just give him my name and occupation, Bertrand McAbee – ACJ Investigations. Here's my card. I'm quite sure he'll see me. If he won't then we'll talk about Plan B." Plan B had yet to develop in his mind.

She looked hesitant. After a few seconds she said, "Please sit. I'll see." She left and went to a door to her right where she punched in a code. She wasn't wearing heels.

McAbee sat. He scanned the magazines on a long glass table. Some of them were in Spanish, some were African American in orientation, and then there were the usual – *Reader's Digest*, *Time*, and *Sports Illustrated* among them. They were neatly exhibited and they were all of recent origin. One of the consequences of Fox's marketing skills was the care that he took to maintain an image. McAbee thought of the many offices that he had visited in the past where the magazines were six months old, badly dog-eared, stained, and over-touched to the point of being mangled, and bacterially challenged.

Savannah came out from behind the locked door and held it open, "Attorney Fox will be happy to meet with you. This way." She took him back through a corridor with eight doorways to separate offices. At the end of this hallway McAbee was shown into a central office, a semi-circle. This was the Fox den, for sure, the place of exhibitions.

Matthew Fox was not ignorant of the presence of ACJ in the community. The agency had a reasonably good reputation given that most P.I. firms were engaged in shady works. He recalled all too well his meeting with the man who stood in front of him, McAbee. His ass had been saved back then when he was screwing that blackmailing bitch who had headed back up to Canada after her apartment had been riddled with a multi-round blast from a semi-automatic. Fox figured that the scheming cunt would need a calculator to add up all the suspects. Whoever was behind it merited an Emmy or an Oscar for righteous conduct.

But the man in front of him was someone who confused him. He figured that anything was possible from this geezer whose gaze felt like stripping lye. It was not time to put on his gregarious and highly extroverted act.

He left from behind his file-full desk and walked across his carpet and extended his hand, "Dr. McAbee, what a joy to see you again. This time under such different circumstances." He winked in a way that could be called loud, part of the act, as his mind was racing about why McAbee was here. He noticed that McAbee's hand had surprising strength. "Come, come, let's sit." He led the still silent McAbee to a work table, he sitting at the end of the rectangle so as to keep McAbee to his side. At this point he observed that the son-of-a-bitch hadn't said anything yet. He was uncomfortable with him. McAbee wasn't helping. They sat. Fox said, "Just for the record, I cannot help but reiterate my gratitude to you for your coming forth on my behalf."

"I'm sure that you would have done the same," McAbee said.

Fox had his antennae up for irony. He couldn't tell but he was sure that caginess was a feature in this P.I. He advanced the meeting by saying, "I take it that this isn't a social call, good sir." He gave his shallow smile, no teeth showing.

McAbee said, "You're right, it's not. I need a favor. It

concerns a former client of yours, deceased. I would really appreciate your help."

"Of course, of course. I'll do whatever I can do without jeopardizing my license!" A big hearty laugh and a private sigh of relief that the blackmailing bitch from that night was not on the agenda of this somber bastard who sat looking at him as though he had just risen from a casket.

"Cynthia Power," he said.

"Ah yes. Yes. Cynthia, a sad story. Nicest woman you'd ever want to meet. Couldn't believe it when I heard about her suicide. Just terrible. I don't know how I can help though – just a really nice woman." As he spoke he was buying time trying to determine why McAbee was interested in this. No answer was coming to him.

"If I may. She has become a matter of interest to ACJ."

"Well, I'll be damned. I'm surprised. Everything is in place in her estate. Very clean. She avoided the probate process. My paralegal has begun to inventory her possessions. The distribution of her wealth and property is unremarkable. She avoided any public record. A very private woman."

"Out of curiosity. How did you two connect? You're such an extroverted guy and she was so, let's say different, it seems. I'm trying to get a fix on her. An answer to that question might be helpful."

Fox didn't know the answer to that question. Her choice of him as her attorney always baffled him. When he told this to McAbee he sensed that he wasn't believed. But actually his answer was a rare episode in truth-telling.

"I know you're a busy man Mr. Fox so let me tell you where I need the favor. My firm needs access to her house, especially her personal computer, and her private papers. The matter of this case is the potential that Cynthia Power was murdered despite the findings of the Davenport P.D. I am in need of a foothold in case she didn't suicide."

"Hold on." He went back to his desk and buzzed Savannah. He asked her to get the Power file and very especially any results of the inventory. When it was retrieved, he spread it out and scanned the pages. In surprise, he said to McAbee, "There was a turned off personal computer in her house. Maybe she just wasn't the geeky sort. She was an artist, after all." Again he was pretty sure that McAbee wasn't buying but he was being honest.

"For the record, she was conversant with computers."

"Well, that's why you're a P.I. I can't say much more without violating what I see as a sacred trust. I've already crossed the line in a way."

McAbee leaned forward and caught Fox's eyes dead center. "Here's the deal Fox. I want you to answer some questions. I expect you to. I don't need to hear about sacred trusts. Let's start this way, what are the main conditions around her will? Who gets what?"

There was a certain menace to McAbee. He wasn't violent. Fox didn't feel that his safety was threatened. But the room had become pressurized. "Between you and me. The house and its contents when they are adjudicated go to her brother. A jerk of the first order. Her car and all of her monies – investments, bank accounts – go to the Humane Society. Anything else is incidental, lawyer fees and whatever."

"When does the brother get control of the house?"

"It's no longer an investigation scene for the cops. Never was taken to be anything other than a suicide really. Look, the place is locked with a realtor's lock. No one can get in there, brother included, until this all gets settled at the courthouse. Next week probably. If you're trying to get in there, you can't. Neither can her brother." There was a silence in the room. Fox became uneasy.

McAbee said, "I want access to the place, now. You present, you not. The people who will go over that place will leave it cleaner than it is now. No one will know."

"I can't do that."

McAbee said, "Yes you can – you will."

CHAPTER 12

Professor Megan White cleared her calendar, not an easy deed given her extraordinary rise to academic and journalistic fame. By her secretary's count she averaged eight calls a day from various media for comments about stories that had made it out of the clouds and into the bloodstream of the nation. Megan had become a public intellectual. To accommodate her fame the work done on her physical appearance had been performed over a five year period. Only a close watcher, and there were plenty of those maggots around, would have seen the nose job, the eye lids, the throat, the teeth, the jawline, her thighs, stomach, arms, and the ultimate remake, the full facial lift, made her 68 years slide down to a cool 40. She was a cougar and proud of it.

Her training in Marxist sociological principles of analysis was downplayed in her bio. She worked hard at being the voice of reason and non-prejudice. She became so good at it that even Fox News had called her. Yes, it was O'Reilly and yes, he blew up at her by constant interruptions. Someone had done the spadework on her training and the semi-crazed host was lying in wait for her. But for her crowd what had happened was a badge of honor, her being still another victim of this right-wing male-chauvinist zealot. Invited back again six months later, she told the Fox producer to go fuck himself. O'Reilly was in terrible need for someone to defend the terrorists from ISIS. Fox was right, she was a sympathizer for the 'misguided' men. She understood them well. It all went back to Western imperialism.

Her principal argument was that if we were being bombed, our maps redrawn and so on we would celebrate those who fought against the oppressors. But she knew that she had to be careful with such views. Iowa, a relatively peaceful and vanilla state, had its share of vets and yahoos. The University had rejected her righteous appeal for a bodyguard. Her legal team had been notified of this. They would sue the goddamn place out of existence if something happened to her. Her elation knew no bounds when O'Reilly was fired by the fascist Fox network.

She hated the idea of the coming meeting with Francine Korbel who should have had a gender transformation back in high school. The big-boned heifer with the low voice driven by some erratic testosterone storms was one babe you would not want to meet on a dark and stormy night. Actually, not even a bright and calm day.

And this all went back to Cynthia Power, supergirl, whose superego would leak guilt and *angst* over the death of a goddamn ant. But Francine Korbel? She probably celebrated with a bottle of champagne when she stomped on an actual ant. But Korbel was scared and because of that attention had to be paid to her.

Every one of the eight members of the Demosthenes Club had talent pouring from them. Success was inevitable. Both their ACT and SAT scores registered from the 95th to the 99th percentile. Good old insecure teacher Sam Liebow had to have parity among the genders, so, of course, Megan was chosen. So also Korbel, but then he chose badly and picked Cynthia Power, tolerable but not a driver. But then he dove deep into neurosis and instability – Anne Podreski. Jesus! Anne, a loose weathervane in a tornado. Liebow was hell bent on spotting talent, advancing a select group of high school seniors, and forming a club around them. Liebow, the high school wonder from the gods was similar to the gods, the embodiment of good and evil, smart and stupid.

Megan liked the look of her wardrobe. She felt classy but with a slight Bohemian touch. Expensive enough to separate herself from the purse-conscious comers in the department, sleek enough to bury the fatties but modest enough not to appear to be some dumb, rich housewife. She was a Marxist with a dacha she thought ruefully. She knew Korbel would be decked out in corporate overkill, not the kind of look that would succeed at this Big Ten University in Iowa City, Iowa.

Brendan McBirney, a professor in the University of Iowa writer's program, was sitting with an editor from Holt, who preferred to be called Kidd. They were at the Bistro in downtown Iowa City. Kidd, an old friend, was regaling McBirney with the latest gossip from New York publishing houses. Their lunch called for a second bottle of wine as they relaxed in familiarity and trust. This was a rare feeling for McBirney as he found the Writer's Workshop a sphincter tightening prison of sorts.

As they talked and laughed, even an occasional guffaw, his eye caught at the entrance to the establishment, a woman of more than six feet, dressed to the nines. He nudged Kidd, their both sitting in a booth with a view of the entrance.

He said softly, "Now there's a regal woman. She just needs a crown, a staff and a few fan bearers."

"Maybe she's from Michelin, a star-giver," Kidd said. "Or maybe a star taker. Tough looking lady."

The pricey restaurant was almost full. McBirney watched with curiosity as the woman and the hostess seemed to tussle a bit. Finally she was shown to a far corner where she sat. She looked at her watch. "She has a great pissed-off look about her. I'm doing a short story. She'll be my inspiration," McBirney uttered.

Kidd said, "I wonder who she's meeting? If it's an unfaithful lover he, or she, is a goner."

McBirney now saw the batty left-wing Megan White enter the place. "Kidd. Sit back. One of our primo contessas has just come out of her casket and I'm almost positive she's headed for the behemoth. This might be great theater."

The tall one didn't get up as Megan White stood in front of her. There was no handshake or smile. White sat. "That's what a lunch would be between two domesticated lynxes who disliked the hell out of each other. I hope they keep their paws holstered. I have to stop looking at them. My stomach is freezing up," McBirney said.

Francine Korbel had purposefully come fifteen minutes early only to be finessed into Megan's preferred seating area. Megan appeared before her in phony academic elegance, an Eileen Fisher outfit that bespoke faux Bohemian. They ordered from the limited menu, neither interested in any alcohol. Informal chatter about the weather and the drive across I-80 lasted for about two minutes.

Korbel led. "How many times did Cynthia speak to you other than about the book she had been contemplating?"

Megan worked up her phony CNN smile. "Once. In this very spot. Look, I feel terrible about her suicide. Surprised, but when I think about her, not shocked. You sounded very upset on the phone Francine. Is there something I should know?"

Francine wasn't caught off guard by Megan. Denial. Only hard evidence would shake her, she knew this. She decided to call her bluff. "You should know that she had at me three times. A fourth surely on the way but her inconvenient death was a stopper." Megan just sat in silence. Francine pressed, "Her book about our success is not why I'm here. As you know," she paused for a bit as White's eyes did a premonitional flitter, "she became fixated on the death of Anne Podreski."

"But…"

"No. Let me finish. I already spoke with stupid Corey. He threw her enough bait. What did you say to her when she raised questions about Anne Podreski?"

"Hey, wait a minute Francine. Did someone make you the prosecutor in chief? I don't like your attitude. Back off," she parked her professional smile, replacing it with a belligerent stare. "Anne Podreski is long dead. That's what I told Cynthia. She came up here a few weeks ago. She sat right where you're sitting. My favorite table by the way. Cynthia was spooked. She mentioned Corey but she didn't disclose what he said in any exact way. Just that his comments had thrown her into some psychological hell. I told her that I couldn't help her and that Corey was probably drunk and was trying to get under her skin, or into her pants. Who knows with that scum?"

"And?"

"And what? By the fourth or fifth time she tried to reenter into the matter, lunch was thankfully over. I told her in very precise terms that I did not want to talk about this again. Anne Podreski's death was a sad accident. Period. And just so you know I don't appreciate your pawing around this stuff. Cynthia is dead. Anne Podreski is dead. Stan Adair is dead. There's only five of us left. Let the dead stay dead for Christ's sake Francine."

The waiter brought the food and left rather hurriedly in Francine's estimation. Because this was Megan White's preferred table he probably knew that she was a nasty shrew and wanted nothing to do with her and/or he sensed the tension between them.

"Did she take any notes?"

"No, of course not. I thought she wanted to back check for the book she was going to write. The alleged book about our club's success was dead and buried I found out immediately from her. I had no idea that Anne Podreski was the main feature. I thought she sandbagged me. Why are you trying so hard on this?"

"Why? Why?" Francine was incredulous. "We're all five of us at a great place in our lives. We succeeded just like Sam Liebow predicted. That's what inspired Cynthia to think about cobbling together a book about us. Anne Podreski is an 800 pound gorilla in this whole saga because of Corey's big mouth. *Why?* Are you serious?"

Megan White glared at her. Then she looked around the now near empty restaurant and her eyes lit on two men who sat gazing at the two of them. She pursed her lips. She said, "That guy over there, the one with the white beard, he's a wacky right-wing sonofabitch. Writer's Workshop.

I've crossed swords with him a few times. He's a smart ass. But back to you and your hysteria – there's nothing to talk about. I don't know anything and that's my advice for you. You don't know a goddamn thing! And you know what," she raised her hand and did an imaginary scribble in the air, the waiter came, she pointed to him to stay and she removed a credit card and gave him back the leather folder, "I don't want you to bother me anymore. Lunch is on me Francine and as far as I'm concerned, this is the end of things with us. You've become a pain in my ass!"

The waiter came back, she wrote in a tip, signed the bill statement and threw down her napkin. As Megan was getting up, Francine said ominously, "In your dreams Megan – this is over. Stupid arrogant woman."

Megan White sped out of the restaurant and was that a middle finger she directed at that white haired guy?

CHAPTER 13

Bertrand downloaded the article from *The Quad City Times*. It was titled "The Magnificent Eight." It was written by a long-time reporter at the paper, Jane Murphy, and published three years and one month to the current date. There were three pictures. One of them of a social science teacher at the high school, named Sam Liebow. He appeared to be in his early thirties. He had bushy eyebrows, long unkempt hair, and a gaping smile. Further on, there was a picture of the eight students who comprised the Demosthenes Club. They were in two rows, one seated and the other behind, standing. They went 'L-R seated': Anne Podreski, John Douthit, Stan Adair, and Cynthia Power. 'L-R standing': Megan White, Peter Waters, Corey Bladel, and Francine Korbel. McAbee studied the eight closely. Three were dead: Anne Podreski, Stan Adair, and Cynthia Power. An unlucky front row, he thought. He noted that only Anne Podreski had a warm smile. The others were on a continuum from somber to at best a half smile, Cynthia Power and Corey Bladel managing the latter. The last picture in the article was a stock photo of John Douthit of Silicon

Valley fame, the reporter playing to his wealth and success. The article read as follows:

> Back in the late 1960s a highly awarded educator, Sam Liebow, at Memorial High School, was tasked by Principal Andrew Holder to be a talent scout for gifted students. Once identified in their junior classes, he was to gather them together and form a club of sorts for the purpose of having them develop lifelong friendships and a support network for each other.
>
> Liebow hit a leadership homerun with the 1968 graduating class which has found extraordinary success even though marred by two untimely deaths. Eight students peopled the Demosthenes Club, named after the famed Athenian orator of yore.
>
> Of the six living students, probably the most well-known is John Douthit, the investment guru living out his days in San Francisco. He has been written about in leading financial publications, such as *Barrons*, *Fortune*, and *The Wall Street Journal*. His wealth has been calculated to be in the low billions. When asked about his memories he said, "It was an interesting group of kids. Lots of memories about Memorial High School."
>
> Then there is U.S. congressman Corey Bladel representing Chicago's ring suburbs. Known as one of the key insider politicians of the Republican Party, Representative Bladel said, "I'm enthusiastic about this article. In every respect there was

> marvelous competition around us. I miss Anne and Stan immensely, of course, and I regret that the rest of us have scattered around the world in a way. Regards to Memorial High School."

Bertrand was so far unimpressed as he wondered whether or not this band of students was really all that close, noting the word 'competition' in Bladel's comments. He continued reading.

> Dr. Megan White is a constant presence on several cable news outlets, a sometimes guest columnist for *The New York Times* and a leading expert in the field of victimology. She is a Professor of Sociology at the University of Iowa. She recalls fondly the mostly friendly debates within this gifted group. "We, all of us knew, either consciously or sub-consciously, that we were on a fast-moving train of destiny. Each of us with unique gifts."

McAbee recalled watching Megan White, was it CNN? He thought her to be haughty and a bit pontifical. He couldn't recall what issue she was speaking to or exactly when he saw her. The article continued.

> Francine Korbel, Vice President at Deere & Company, has traveled to 89 countries around the world. She has put in millions of miles and has met thousands of people. She feels that the intensity of her experiences in the Demosthenes Club was instrumental in forming her confidence to succeed. "The Club was a great idea. I will always remember

> matching wits with the other members of this select group. Great idea." Cynthia Power is a known free-lance artist and has been a volunteer in a variety of efforts to "create a better world... The Demosthenes Club helped me form a good idea of where I wanted my future to point to. It was a notable experience while in high school."
>
> Peter Waters, currently United States Ambassador to Lebanon, was unavailable for a chat but the following was texted to this reporter, "Great leadership experience, great place, Memorial High School. Best to the remaining members of the Demosthenes Club!"
>
> Annie Podreski died while a senior at Davenport High School and Stan Adair, a successful attorney, died in 2001.
>
> This reporter was unable to locate Sam Liebow who, if alive, would be in his mid-eighties.
>
> The current principal of Memorial High School remarked that he thought the Demosthenes Club a fine idea and was considering the possibility of bringing back some semblance of it.

McAbee wondered what had inspired the reporter to attempt the piece. He sensed a bit of frustration. The former students weren't exactly forthcoming with interesting stories about the club. Notable also, was any mention by them of gratitude toward Sam Liebow. They seemed to be pleased to have been a part of the club because it helped them mature but love, or even affection, was not part of the mix.

For some reason Cynthia Power became curious as to

why the six of them ended up where they were and how they got there. That would be compelling especially for a woman like her, a person of imagination and intelligence. Maybe an interesting book might have come from her efforts, but it seemed to dissolve with her disgust toward them.

But there was something else in the story. It was what was missing.

He called Eric Dawson, the associate editor of *The Quad City Times*. After two minutes of telephone hopping, Eric answered.

"Bertrand? Hey! What's up?"

Eric owed ACJ. It performed a stealth review of his private office and home phone line seven years ago. Both had been tapped illegally confirming Eric's suspicions. Not only had ACJ discovered the tap but also sourced it back to an associate of Eric's at the paper. The legal department of *The Quad City Times* had forced a dismissal of the guy. The anonymous disclosure of the tap by ACJ had kept Eric clear of the matter. Newspapers were very adept at keeping secrets, McAbee noted.

"I need a favor," McAbee declared.

"Shoot."

"Your paper printed a story, three years and a month ago. The reporter was Jane Murphy and it involved a club from years ago at Memorial High School. The Demosthenes Club was the name. You remember?"

"Yeah, faintly. Douthit. Anything about him and his experiences in Davenport and Iowa is a big deal. What do you need?"

"I'd like to speak with Jane Murphy. I need your introduction. Complications?"

"Jane retired about a year ago. She lives in town. I can call her. As I recall, this was more or less a puff piece. Is there something I should know?"

"No. Just working out a detail for a client. Crazy business as you know. You doing okay?"

"Yes, I am Bertrand. Thanks for asking. There's a chance at an editorship but I'll have to move. I do remember what you did for me. I'll speak with Jane and be back in touch. I have to read the article to make sure that there are no problems with sources or confidentiality. Please understand that in case she's hesitant. Oh, and fyi, Jane is a bit troubled."

"Got it. Thanks Eric."

CHAPTER 14

Jack Scholz was annoyed that rabid Matthew Fox insisted that he be present when Cynthia's house was being searched. He knew Fox from the countless ads on television and the omnipresent billboards around the Quad Cities. Someone, somewhere, had mentioned that in one of Shakespeare's plays there was a line about killing off all of the lawyers. For whatever reason it was written, Shakespeare had gone up in his opinion.

Jack pulled up outside of Cynthia Power's modest house. Parked by the curb was a high end black Mercedes. It was out of place in the neighborhood. It told Jack that Fox was already there. He had three people with him, two men and a woman. The two men were retired Navy Seals who had worked for Jack on some of his clandestine missions. The woman was none other than Augusta Satin. On the last major case that McAbee had entangled himself with, as usual over-matched, she had demonstrated to him that she was damn competent. Yes, she was a bit too ethical, too lawful, but even that as a given she was solid. He couldn't use her, or even speak with her, about some of his wet work, but for this search of Power's house she was fine. It was a big compliment to her but she was probably blind to it.

The four of them went up to the door, Jack rang the bell. He heard the chime echo through the house. The door was opened. For reasons he could never ascertain, not that he was given to much reflection, there passed between him and attorney Fox instant hate. It was like a downed electrical line skidding and sparking across a road. He wondered if his team picked it up.

"Limited time here. Did you really need four people?" Fox looked dismissively through his disgust and it was all aimed at Jack Scholz.

"Why do you care about the numbers?" Jack asked acidly.

"Because this estate is in a trust, not going through probate. I am accountable by law for everything in this house. That's why," he said this as he stepped forward to within a foot of Jack's face.

Augusta watched this encounter with alarm. She knew that Fox was a blowhard and a bluffer. Fine, she thought. But he was in danger of having serious damage done to him. She knew enough about Scholz and his hair-trigger temper which if it did not explode now would be used later to exact retribution on the unsuspecting Fox.

She came forward, patted Jack's shoulder and said to Fox, "Mr. Fox, we are aware of all this. We will be most careful. Our search is very exacting and if we need to remove anything we will have you tag it for later retrieval." She knew that she was speaking in her most professional and official police voice. If Jack would hold back, this operation would not take long. She also knew that Fox would probably fade in the presence of a black woman as he was known for his cultivation of that community.

"Very well. Just trying to stay on the right side of the law." He stepped away from Jack and out of the doorway allowing entry to the four of them. Fox went into the living room, sat down and started to use his cellphone.

Augusta took Jack aside and said, "I'm not trying to interfere with you Jack, but I think that the scene needed some relaxation," she smiled.

He nodded slightly as he brought the group together and issued his instructions for the search of Cynthia's house. Augusta appreciated that Jack had asked her to participate in the search. It was a subtle compliment. Just so long as he didn't think she was prepared to become a follower of him and his ways.

At the end of it all, three hours, the search was of import for what it didn't turn up. The hard drive from Cynthia's computer was gone. It had been removed carefully. No sledgehammer. One of the guys did some fingerprint takes in that vicinity.

Augusta found a partial yellow notepad, barely half of it filled with writing. Oddly, it was under Cynthia's couch. She scanned it quickly. The writing was erratic, scrawled in some places. She could explore it later. In good faith, but only with Jack's approval, she showed it to Fox. He quickly looked it over, noted it on his phone and said, "Immaterial," then taking an iPhone picture of the notepad.

In a closet in a room Cynthia had used as a semi-studio, Augusta discovered two medium sized plastic bins. One of them had an assortment of what looked to be diaries and correspondence and the other was filled with small picture albums and framed photos. When these were brought down to the first floor Fox took a quick look and also approved their removal after taking a picture of each bin from his iPhone.

CHAPTER 15

Jane Murphy was on the sauce once again, not quite drunk but definitely not sober. She had been forcibly retired by the newspaper brass. Forty goddamn years and then she was treated like sewer water by the bastards. Now the call from Eric, one of the nicer of the phonies down there. Would she be kind enough to speak with some P.I. named Mackafucker or something? A puff piece she did a few years ago. The Demosthenes Club. Did she remember the piece? "Yes, of course I remember," she said slowly trying the keep the slur from her voice, always hopeful that they'd add her back to the staff, part-time would do. Deep down, not that she liked to go there often, she agonized over not working there anymore.

Her profoundly stupid daughter had imprisoned her in her small apartment. Two DWI's in two months had done the trick. They took her car away from her, a condition set by the sorry-assed judge who owed Jane many favors, conveniently forgotten by the black-robed fraud whose scandalous conduct she had personally hushed up.

Her daughter got control of her money, most of it anyway, all in a concerted effort to keep her from the liquor store a mile away, a mile too far. So she became a frequent user of Uber for stealthy trips to the liquor store. Daughter bitch knew that she was using but was unable to find her hiding places. Once in a while, Jane would sacrifice a half-bottle of watered down Beam just to make her and her overbearing boob of a husband think that they had busted her. Good luck with that.

This Mackafucker was coming in another hour. She straightened out the place as well as she could, took a badly needed shower and sprayed the place down with a lavender concoction.

She closeted boxes of notes from all the interviews that she had done over the years. Once upon a time she thought that she could put an interesting book together on Quad City personalities. Well, she could put it together easily enough by selecting her pieces from over the years. But who would buy a book about various cuts of pork? Anyway, she didn't have the energy. It was she against the fucking world.

She looked down at State Street from her third floor window in downtown Bettendorf. A maroon Camry pulled up to the curb outside of the apartment building. Out of the car came an older man, glasses, balding, average height and weight. He looked up toward the third floor, she backed away. It had to be Mackafucker. She quickly went to her piece of paper which had the man's name on it. 'McAbee, Bertrand. Demosthenes Club.' Hurriedly, she scanned the apartment again. She was ready.

The building, yellow-orange brick, had been around since the late 1920s. It had held up pretty well for its age and its location a few blocks north of the Mississippi River. A bicycle path paralleled the river as well as railroad tracks that skittered along the river somewhere north to Minnesota or southward to Missouri. The freight trains went by pretty often and when they did they sounded horns that could be heard miles away. While it had to be a joy to see the great Mississippi River through its seasons the train blare had to take a toll.

Jane Murphy was widely known in the area. She had written pieces on Quad City personalities over many years. On occasion she would snare big names who would find themselves in Davenport or one of the adjoining cities. Her biggest score, Cary Grant, died in Davenport the very night she interviewed him. McAbee had heard that the piece was not allowed to be printed, the rumor had the Grant family responsible. It was said that Murphy was never the same. McAbee couldn't remember the source of this information. But the fact that it hung around in his head led him to give it some probability.

He knocked at C-4. The woman who opened the door was apparitional in the way that ghosts would appear in black and white films from the 1940s and 50s. Her white hair was long, falling well below her slim shoulders. She was barely five feet tall and she weighed as a feather. The whiteness of her hair was matched by the whiteness of her face but with a touch of added pigment. Her face was extraordinarily narrow, enclosed.

The color in this picture of snow was in her brown eyes, eyelids and brows already snow white. The emptiness of her eyes caught McAbee, was it beyond sorrow? He was psychologically punched as it were by this unexpected vision.

"Come in," she said in a voice shadowing her visage.

McAbee thought séance as he said, "Thanks for seeing me." He felt that he would have to follow her pacing.

The place smelled of some odorizer recently sprayed. The apartment seemed to have been created out of a square, zoned irregularly into three parts – a bathroom and kitchen which he observed to his left, a bedroom, whose door was almost closed and the living room into which he was led. She walked in a glide, her ethereal qualities still maintained. She pointed to a rocking chair as she sat across from him on a loveseat.

"Can I get you something to drink?"

"No, no thanks." Her voice seemed to come out of her sunken chest. It was as though her words climbed up to her lips, was there a time delay of some sort? "My name is Bertrand. I appreciate your seeing me."

She nodded, looking up and down at him. She said, "I'm Jane, as you know. I'm going to have some tea. I need a minute." She walked to her kitchen area.

McAbee knew that there was some disconnect here but was not able to pin it down. She came back so quietly from behind him that he was slightly startled. She sat. Her tea was in a drinking glass with a few ice cubes. Well, iced tea, perhaps. But probably not.

"What is it that you want from me?"

"I don't know what Eric said to you. So I'll repeat what…"

She held up her right hand. "The Demosthenes Club, he told me. I retrieved my notes and reviewed them. What is it that you want to know," she drew off a healthy gulp of tea.

"When I read your piece I sensed that the interview did not come easy, that the club members were reticent?" McAbee felt that he had to be very careful with this woman, that lurking beneath the studied appearance was a roadside bomb.

"You're correct. It was a very difficult assignment. Sometimes I would approach a story assuming that it would come easy. Lots of material after I finish interviewing. Too much. Editing massive. Just the opposite actually with this one. There was some sort of wall there. I couldn't penetrate it. It was clever of you to fathom the silence from them. Stoney withdrawals. There was no affection in that group. It was as though the club was an evil that had to be passed through for future success. There was estrangement and what I printed from them was pap. They had to give me something. You figured it out, my subtlety. I don't think that anyone caught it."

"A little bit ago one of them committed suicide, Cynthia Power."

"I'm surprised that she was the only one. Beneath all of their success I sensed many of them were personal failures. Perhaps too ignorant to realize that they were. Cynthia Power seemed to be the most aware of life. Reflective. The bottom line about them was they didn't seem to like each other. There was a visceral-like undercurrent of distaste among them."

As she spoke McAbee was hearing a very insightful woman broken by life. The tea wasn't tea, but her sadness was sadness. Maybe that sadness gave her the gift of insight.

She got up suddenly and said, "That's all I wish to say today. Here's my phone number," she hurriedly wrote it and almost forced it into Bertrand's hand. The door to her apartment slammed hard behind him.

As he went to his car he wondered whether there would ever be a good time to visit this hurting woman.

CHAPTER 16

McAbee phoned into Memorial High School. When he asked for the librarian he felt pushback winds from the receptionist. Schools across America were on high alert for would-be terrorists, murderers, and gun-toting psychopaths. After he cleared the obstacle-logs put down by her inquisition she put him through to Helen Krill. He explained the purpose of his call. She listened and told him she'd assist in his quest. The library at Memorial kept extraordinary files about the school, she said. Helen Krill sounded like an optimistic person, an antidote to Jane Murphy.

He parked in the visitor's space to the right of the main doorway to the school, an aged edifice that fought earnestly against rehab attempts. The handicap ramp chewed up tons of concrete. He chose the steps, fifteen later he was at the doorway. A sign informed him to ring the bell to the right of the door. He did so as he noticed two cameras fixed on him. A buzz unlatched the door and he entered the building. A plaque showed the place was built back in 1934. There was a smell to the building, a mix of vinegar, Clorox and some kind of deodorizer, a mammoth struggle between them with no clear victor.

There were two turnstiles diagonal to a small aisle that ended at an X-ray machine that looked as though it was absconded from an airport surplus store. A guard came forward. He was in his sixties. His severe limp and almost grotesque squint caused McAbee to wonder if there was a new agency in Davenport – Rent the Unsuited. Everyone in the building must have felt safe with this guy around, he thought ruefully.

"Take everything out of your pockets and put them on the tray," he said indifferently.

McAbee did so. The X-ray machine groaned or was that the moving belt that slid McAbee's materials through to the other side of the machine? Permission to proceed beyond the guard-post came in a mutter, "The library is straight ahead to the right." The squinting guard hobbled back to what appeared to be a small walk-in closet. McAbee's eye caught about twelve school-vicinity screens that provided the man with entertainment.

Helen Krill was in the fifties zone. Her dress was casual, black slacks, beige turtle neck. She had a pleasant face, smile lines around her lips. McAbee, for some reason he couldn't locate, saw her as saucy and mildly cynical.

He introduced himself and reminded her of his visit.

Pertly she said, "Thanks for the reminder. It's so busy around here that one tends to forget." She waved her hand around the large empty cavern of a room.

McAbee laughed. He had a weakness for kind women who knew how to send a taunting arrow into him. The question was could she take one back that was aimed at her? Before he left he'd probably send one her way.

"I brought out the binders for the student newspapers

for the 1966-67 and 1967-68 school years. They were pretty wild times in Davenport. Interesting, watching the students have a go at the administration. Battles galore. Now the students just ignore them. Self-absorbed. Do you want some coffee or anything?"

"Anything? You passing out whiskey in this place?"

She laughed. "I'm sure it's around somewhere but I don't know where, and look at me I'm a research librarian!"

"Definite inadequacy," he said smilingly.

"I'll put you over there by the window while I look for the whiskey. The light should help your vision."

"I need all the light I can get. I'm as blind as a bat."

She nodded in agreement and walked over to the table area where the over-sized ledger books were located. She said, now with humor and earnestness, "I'm here if you need me. Don't shout, just flap your bat wings."

McAbee sat and started his research into 18 copies of the *Memorial Informant* for 1966-67 and to the 20 copies for 1967-68 school years. Helen was correct, they were interesting times. Vietnam, the Beetles, and the 60s revolution had made their way onto the consciousness of Davenport teenagers. McAbee leafed through the pages with relative alacrity as his eyes were alert to the names of the Demosthenes Club and the teacher-founder Sam Liebow. While he was doing so he wondered if Jane Murphy had troubled herself with these newspapers when she did the piece three years ago. He was inclined to think not.

His first hit occurred on January 27, 1967. The story featured an interview with Sam Liebow. He was forming a club called after the great Athenian orator, politician, and leader named Demosthenes who lived in the fourth century before Christ. Sam would be collecting names from the teachers and staff of the school and also applications from interested students. Minimum entry requirements were a 3.5 GPA and junior standing. Rigorous vetting and interviews were to be used. Membership was limited to eight to ten students.

In April of that year, eight juniors were chosen. The picture of the eight accompanying the short article was the same one used in *The Quad City Times* piece. So Sam Liebow had his club and great things were expected in the following school year. That was the entirety of mentions for 1966-67. He looked up and saw Helen Krill about 30 feet away examining a book binding. She became aware of his glance and said, "Need something?"

"Yes actually. I'm finished with this first tome. There are two articles that I'd like copied. How do I go about that?"

She came over. "This can be arranged for a price."

McAbee reached for his wallet. "Sure, what do you need?"

"Well, 25 cents a page is the usual price. Looks like you're dealing with two pages? I'm not good at math. But does 50 cents sound right?" Her smile was delightfully coy.

His scan of the 1967-1968 tome found six articles about the club, more than he expected. He asked Helen for copies and volunteered a $20 bill which she refused on the grounds that an employee in the registrar's office had taken money to change a grade, was discovered, and fired. And then a reign of terror was initiated under the rubric of bribes. No one at the high school was to ever again receive any gift, no matter how trifling, from anyone that would even remotely be construed as compromising. Even apples were on the list.

"So you see sir, I'm of an age where my career choices have been whittled down, where craziness is ubiquitous because of one misstep by an errant employee, and lastly, so that you don't think me an obsessive-compulsive witch, I do thank you and appreciate your offer."

Her smile was electric. McAbee said, "I understand. There are an amazing number of rules imposed on us because of one faulty person or group. Extraordinary tension going on. I think of this often when I fly and I have to put up with the agony of our airports and all of the protocols. Airplane crews are now more into law enforcement than service courtesy. And by the way, I don't see you as easily compromised." He smiled, so did she, as she took the tome over to the copier.

Bertrand was of mixed emotion when he left the high school, at once glad to be gone from the building but down a bit from leaving Helen Krill, a sparkling presence.

He drove back to his office anxious to study the six articles from the 1967-68 school year. Two of them had been lengthy and a quick read had alerted him that he needed to study them closely.

Pat was at her desk and looked up at him in surprise. "Well, the elusive Dr. Bertrand McAbee. Good afternoon."

"Pat, I definitely heard your signals through the day. What have I missed?"

"Well, to be truthful, nothing. I listened to three potential clients, one of them for about a half hour. All three I referred to other agencies. I keep hearing the sounds of bales of money dropping into shredders. Some of these cases you would have taken a few years ago. But I will continue my role of gatekeeper for you. Having any luck with Cynthia Power?"

"Still up in the air on it. Something is there that's troubling. A bad pulse. I'll be in the office for a bit."

He removed from a folder the two sets of copies, reviewing again the articles from 1966-1967. He was most interested, however, in the 1967-68 pieces which after a brief perusal at the high school library perhaps foretold the present inquiry.

The six articles dated to the following months: September, October, November, January, March, and April.

The September piece spoke of a complaint filed against Sam Liebow. He had allegedly discriminated against a black student who had sought membership into the Demosthenes Club back in the Spring of 1967 when Liebow was soliciting for students. The teenager was named Archie Sanders. His complaint indicated that he felt that Liebow was particularly hostile towards him at an interview, that the hostility had been passed on to the chosen eight who when later questioned by Archie had been equally hostile towards him. School authorities would investigate the charges even though Liebow was vehement in his denial of any untoward conduct directed at Sanders. End of article one.

The October article made the front page of the student newspaper. The then principal, Andrew Holder, announced that Sam Liebow was innocent of the charges but because Archie was so persistent and forceful, thus demonstrating leadership, he was granted membership in the club. Everyone was overwhelmingly pleased, including some school board members who had received calls about the issue. So, at one point there had been nine members in the club. Jane

Murphy's profile had nothing on these events, a big deal to McAbee on all counts.

A small piece in November told of Archie finding peace and love in the club along with some details of club achievements. Peter Waters placed first in a statewide debate tournament. Corey Bladel was elected president of the senior class. John Douthit was a finalist for the Davenport Rotary Scholarship and a champion swimmer in the state competition in Des Moines. Megan White led an outstanding effort to collect monies to assist the poor in anticipation for payment of gas and electric bills for the coming winter. Cynthia Power had received two blue ribbons for her oils at an art fair in Des Moines. Anne Prodreski had entered the Miss Scott County contest which would eventually see the winner compete for Miss Iowa and potentially Miss America. McAbee noted the absence of Francine Korbel, Stan Adair, and Archie Sanders relative to notable achievements.

Front page again in late January of 1968, article four. Archie Sanders had petitioned the elected seven member school board to make a five minute presentation. It was allowed because the superintendent suggested that granting it would serve as a commendation for his principal's decision to have Archie become a member of the celebrated Demosthenes Club, or so the student reporter, Sean O'Malley, speculated.

The five minute accommodation morphed into a 20 minute harangue by Archie who pretty much tied the whole educational community to the Ku Klux Klan. The Davenport P.D. had to forcibly remove Archie from the meeting which led to further charges by Archie of a racist system of justice and violent cops.

In his loud recital in front of the school board he resigned from the Demosthenes Club claiming once again vile treatment by Sam Liebow and that all of the white student members, save one, were also aggressors against him. It was not mentioned in the article which of the eight was the 'good' student.

Reporter O'Malley concluded his article with a quote from an unnamed teacher, "Misunderstandings of this nature are a drain on school spirit. Let's hope that everything settles down or this will be a spoiler for the rest of the school year."

The headline on page three of a March issue of *The Informant* read as follows: "Demosthenes Club Triumphs." All eight of the students in the club had scholarships to universities across the country. Sam Liebow was complimented by the principal for his fine efforts even though, sadly, because of budget problems the club was being dropped. The finance committee of the school board had refused to reconsider a request made by Sam Liebow who unsuccessfully pointed out the merit of the club. Reporter O'Malley quoted another unnamed source to this effect, "The school board is vindictive. When Archie spoke out as he did the Demosthenes Club was in the gun sight of a retaliatory school board." McAbee wondered about the use of unnamed sources in this kid's reporting.

An April issue of the paper was shrouded in sadness. Anne Podreski was found dead in a small man-made lake in Scott County Park, an extraordinarily large park north of Davenport. The Demosthenes Club was having an overnight camp out to celebrate the success of its members as the school year was approaching its terminus. Somehow Anne had slipped away from the group's romp in the lake and inexplicably she had drowned. The lake's deepest parts were no more than six feet. Within the article, again written by Sean O'Malley, there was a series of groanings about Anne. How smart, how beautiful, how gracious and so on. As was O'Malley's wont, he went to an unnamed administrative source toward the conclusion of his piece, "Unfortunately it is the Scott County Sheriff's Department that is conducting a review of the incident. But no foul play is suspected." It was noted by this same administrator that the drowning took place in an unincorporated section of land and thus the investigation was to be managed by the Sheriff's Department rather than the City of Davenport Police Department.

There were no further references to the Demosthenes Club for the remainder of the school year.

McAbee went back to the comment about the Scott County Sheriff's Department and the Davenport Police Department. The administrator had used the word 'unfortunately.' It was not the first time that the investigative competency of the Sheriff's Department had been referred to over the years.

CHAPTER 17

Augusta sat in Bertrand's office looking over at him with a slight regret. She had more or less tossed the Cynthia Power case into ACJ and she was beginning to see that there were too many complications. She respected Dr. Rhine but she also thought that the Davenport P.D. probably had their conclusions well-based. Linda had a propensity to mix therapy with friendship and this might have colored her thinking about Cynthia Power. After all, if Cynthia did commit suicide Dr. Rhine had failed to see it coming. Linda was, above all, quite sure of herself thus doubling her *angst* over Power's death.

Bertrand, after quickly fingering the different material in the bins that she had brought from Cynthia's house, said to her, "Lots of stuff here. Any analysis?"

"No. I thought it best to bring it all here. She was 67 years old. A lot of years. I thought we'd find more, actually."

"The hard drive?"

"I don't know what to say about that Bertrand. One of Jack's men examined the PC very closely. The removal had been done professionally. He got a match off of prints from her house that were clearly hers, and that's all he got around her PC. The conclusion – gloves were worn. *If* it was a murder gloves would most likely be used, of course, the removal of the hard drive points to foul play," Augusta concluded.

"Why weren't these bins taken?"

"Jack thought there would be too much potential neighborhood presence. Carrying bins out in a close-knit neighborhood area would be too risky. Hard drives are one thing, bins another. Also nothing says these boxes weren't gone through. But Jack thought that time was a premium, because of that a murderer wasn't going to stick around. They would want to be far removed by the time she was dead, he thought and I agree. The big thing, though, the notepad under her couch. Almost positive it wasn't seen, no less examined. It was clearly small enough to pocket if it had been seen. All of this on the assumption that she didn't take her own life."

Bertrand told her of his experiences with Jane Murphy and the Memorial High School library. And he concluded with an unaccustomed darkness, "The more I look the bleaker this gets. It sounds as if Sam Liebow found a lot of talent but also a lot of dysfunction. There was a ninth kid also. He elbowed his way into this esoteric crowd only to either select himself out, or he was shunned out by the other students, or some combination of these. Ever run across the name Sanders? Black family?"

Augusta responded, "You trying to age me mistah? I will remind you that this all went down in 1967 or so." She smiled at Bertrand who looked glum.

Lightly, he said, "No, I'm not trying to age you. I know that you were a baby. But I also know that you grew up to be a tough cop-babe," he was in full smirk, "and that you ran into a lot of people."

"Lots of Sanders around. Black, white, and everything in between."

"I know. Just throwing darts."

"You seem to be holding back on involvement. I see why. It's a case that's sprouting in a lot of directions. And for God's sake, please don't get into this on my behalf. I know that I was the intermediary between Linda and you. And fine. You looked at it and you can just hand it back and tell her to engage with another agency if she wants to press on it. You can always tell her that there is potential foul play. Just don't involve because of a concern about my feelings. I'm serious."

He gave her that weighing look of his that meant he was still wavering. He would tip soon and then he'd either go at Cynthia Power's death full-bore or he'd pull away and not look back. The fact that he had already spaded this much ground indicated to her that it would be difficult for him to walk away. But every once in a while she had seen him do it. And there was that one time about five years ago that he remarked that his decision not to take on a case was one of the best decisions he had ever made in his life.

"Augusta, I'd like to prowl through these materials. I'll stick around the office and I'll make the decision tomorrow."

"Need me to hang around?"

"No. I'd rather have you be my fresh eyes."

"Understood."

They exchanged hugs and Augusta left knowing the part of McAbee that was impenetrable and remote as hell was now in full operation.

CHAPTER 18

Cynthia had a large, curled type of writing. It took McAbee a bit to accustom himself to it. He scanned the half-filled yellow pad. It began with a conversation that she had with a man named Corey. After reading two pages he decided to lay the pad aside, knowing already that the jottings were critical to Cynthia. If there was a case here it would probably be found in this yellow pad.

He went to his small office refrigerator and took out a can of Diet Coke and six McVitie's digestive cookies. He knew that he was in for a late afternoon and a long night. When McAbee was dealing with issues such as what Cynthia's materials suggested, he would first delve into all of the other materials that were probably not or less relevant. Only then would he go back onto what seemed pertinent. He understood it to be a personality tic. He simply accepted it as a given. In bin number one he found 21 small diary books. They began in 1977, each given to a specific year, many years missing. The last one ended in 2009. Clearly, she was not a dutiful diarest. The entries were sporadic; sometimes two consecutive days, and then nothing for months. He focused on the Demosthenes Club and its members. In only three of all of the diaries was there a mention of club members.

In 1984 she had lunch in Chicago with Corey Bladel, who proved to be the same Corey mentioned in the yellow pad that he had laid aside. The diary entry read:

> In Chicago for a conference. Met Corey for lunch at an Italian place on Rush Street. Giannis or something like that. He picked me up at the hotel lobby. We walked there. Same old Corey. Hands too loose on my body. Still a braggart. An unrepentant political animal. So far to the right. But he'd probably flip left for a large donation. Clearly wanted to come back to the hotel for a tryst. Not my type. Glad to see the end. Asked about other Club members. All doing well. Admires particularly Stan Adair. Not too thrilled with Francine Korbel (probably gave him a whack on the head if he came onto her), a rising star at Deere apparently. Have to go.

A 1996 entry, is an otherwise very sparse entry year she wrote at length. It would actually comprise about a third of the verbiage in this entire year's diary.

> Took time out from Cardinal Krasner's confab. I had dinner in Vienna with Peter Waters. Waters has the ambiguous title of Roving Ambassador to the Balkan Territories. That could involve up to eight distinct countries depending on past, present, and future sovereignty definitions.

At last I cornered Peter. We had a tense dinner at the Vienna Hilton. He was staying at the American Embassy. Peter has become quite the stuff-shirt. I'm quite sure that he'd rather have not met with scruffy me with all of my Sarajevo and Srebrenica rage.

He claimed vast ignorance about some of the slaughter in Sarajevo – events that I saw with my own eyes. He seems to believe that he can lie at will. When I challenged him he simply shrugged. I see him as a coward who has given up independent analysis. He manifested indifference to the slaughters. In those cases where he had to agree because there are tapes of sniper-killings in Sarajevo, he just shrugged. He sat there staring at me as though I was a fool for being concerned. I asked him about Srebrenica, the slaughter of the Moslems by the Serbs. He flinched. Said he knew nothing. Why does he need to lie? He was in Belgrade for God's sake. I tried to bring up Toma with him. He waved his hand at me, dismissively. He said 'I don't know anything about this stuff. Please stop, I'm not your counselor.' I don't believe a word he says.

I know that he is a careerist at the State Department and he yearns for probably some major ambassadorship or a powerful post in Washington. So he sat there, an obnoxious walrus of a man as innocents die.

Am I surprised? No. He was a debater in high school. Very competent. Won awards in Des Moines. But debate? Really! Basically teaching kids the art of sophistry. Give them a position and

> they'll win the argument. But with me there was no debate, he simply sat there, imperious, impervious, unreachable and ultimately a cruel advocate for the sin of omission. He would have done well representing the Papacy during World War II!
>
> Our dinner ended in less than an hour. He didn't like being pushed by me. He had important obligations to address, he proclaimed. He walked away from me with a studied and pronounced finality. Wanted to scream at the bastard. But to what effect? Truth be told! I hope I never see this man again. The Demosthenes Club was, as I see it now, an incubator for raw ambition. I wonder if Sam Liebow understood the depravity that was nurtured. We were all smart beyond our years but I think also selfish too beyond our years. Was I this bad? Or was I never in the real core of the group?
>
> I think of poor Anne who was always trying to find favor and acceptance from them (and from me also) but they shunned her once she entered the Miss Scott County contest. She became an unworthy. And then Archie Sanders! A nasty business. I close now. Discouraged. Peter Waters!

Cynthia had used the exact same diary books year in and year out. He noted that they were published by a company called Memorables Diaries out of Green Bay, Wisconsin. The missing years? She either didn't order them or perhaps she disposed of them.

The last entry relative to the Demosthenes Club was in 2001.

The luncheon had been arranged for us by Corey Bladel. Stan Adair died from a massive heart attack that he suffered during a trial in downtown Chicago. He could not be revived. Adair had acquired a national reputation as a litigator especially in class action lawsuits. All of the members of the club had come for the funeral except for Peter Waters

By 2:00 p.m. we had gathered at the Palmer House. Francine Korbel was in one of her designer suits, her four inch heels got her to well over six feet. She has mastered the corporate posture of importance, steely eyes and a readiness for combat. I know that she had detested Stan Adair as a senior at Memorial High. Why she came is a mystery to me. In fact, as I think of it, Francine didn't really like anyone in the club, not that that was hard to do when I think about it.

Megan White, always a bit over-dramatic, was in from Iowa City. She wasn't inconsolable although she went through the motions as she tried to cast a positive light on Stan's life. John Douthit (more of him later) just stared through her and then quickly walked away from her. That action stranded Megan with Francine Korbel and Corey Bladel. Francine, hand on chin, was presumably paying attention to her ramblings but constantly sneaking glances away from her and Bladel.

I stayed seated to the side as my ankle was still in a state of recovery from my fall. I was apprehensive about the forthcoming luncheon for the five of us, so relieved that Peter Waters was 6000 miles away – ever since our meeting in Vienna the thought of him repulses me.

And now to our wealthy John Douthit. When he fled from Megan White he saw me and then hesitated. Our eyes caught, he looked down, saw the ankle cast and probably felt obligated to come over. Of all the characters in the club he was the most inscrutable. He never reached out to anyone. He was a good match for the ancient philosophy of Stoicism, in other words, he was a studied piece of ice. I said 'hi,' he said 'hi.' I waited. He wasn't used to that I'm sure. He was a master of waiting out people – using silence as a weapon to get people to divulge things. He was gifted at that in high school. In fact, I always remembered him that way. Some kind of serpent, staying his movement until he found a way to strike. I believe that he saw everyone as an opponent. Did he get this trait from his family business? They were funeral directors. According to the papers he now has untold wealth. Finally he says, "Your foot?" I say with equal brevity, "broken ankle." "Sad about Stan." "Yes" I say. He started to look at his watch. His scintillating presence had an expiration date. "In the U.S. now?" "Yes back," I say. At this point Corey Bladel speaks aloud. "The buffet is ready," as he points to a smallish room to the right of where we are. The buffet lasted no more than 30 minutes. The stress of being together was too much – further being accented by the death of Stan. I likened it to the last supper for deaf-mutes. Douthit was the first to leave, followed by

> Megan White who had an interview on WGN, she informed us in Megan-style humility. The whole affair was empty and I regretted coming to it. The fact is that we have little in common and truly there was no friendship among us. Never really was.

That was it. Other diary entries were of no significance to him. Her correspondence was surprisingly light. Cynthia was not a compiler or its extreme a hoarder. She kept two groups of letters and cards. Both were tied with a lace ribbon. McAbee was hesitant. He knew this to be a huge flaw in his adopted role as a P.I. He had an abhorrence about invading the space of innocent people, doubled, if not trebled, by their being possible victims of murder. He was pretty sure the materials spoke of love and intimacy. He got up and walked to his office window and looked at a darkening sky and the flow of the Mississippi River. He felt a sadness for Cynthia.

In the first pile he chose a letter from the middle of what appeared to be a grouping of about 25-30 letters and cards. He removed the letter from a slightly discolored envelope. It was dated April 3, 1982. She would have been about 32 years old. He read it for what it was – a promise of enduring love for eternity from a man who signed off as David. McAbee pursed his lips as he read 'promise,' 'enduring love' and 'eternity'. He understood the sentiment but not the underlying logic that experience had proven to be wanting. He took out the last piece, a greeting card. It was dated February 14, 1983. The card was blood red with a pink heart on its face. Inside, he read, 'Cyn, sorry about all this. You will always be a dear. Maybe in another life.' David. The return address on the envelope to this card had it in Virginia Beach, Virginia. He reflected on the sadness that probably poured through this relationship but he saw no good reason to probe further into this affair from 35 years ago. He carefully re-bowed this grouping and proceeded to the second cache.

There were no cards here, all letters, ten in number. The four stamped letters were posted from Bosnia Herzegovina. The writing was by a right-handed person whose lettering tilted left. Each word had crimped lettering and at first glance was difficult to decipher. The others were probably handed to her in some way; that was beyond discovery. But all of them were by the same hand.

Because of the diary mention of a testy Vienna dinner with Peter Waters and his position as a U.S. diplomat associated with the Balkans, McAbee felt compelled to probe these more thoroughly than the first batch from Virginia Beach. He spread them out observing that they appeared to have been handled often, smudges, small rips, and smearing. On two of the letters he noticed a clear bleed in the ink caused, probably, by water. Or was it tears?

All of the letters were dated in the custom of Europe, day-month-year. All of the letters were signed with one name, written large and with a flourish, Toma.

Cynthia had a lover, a Christian Bosnian, who lived in Sarajevo. The letters spoke of love and the highest regard for the humanitarian work of Cynthia that was supported by the Roman Catholic Church. The Church was historically rooted in parts of Bosnia/Herzegovina. Pope John Paul II had shown a keen interest in the civil wars that had erupted in the shattered Yugoslavia. It became apparent that Toma was a government official but also a news correspondent.

Cynthia, sponsored by the Church, an organization called Angelus, was a social worker, educator, nurse, and perhaps a fixer of sorts – an important go-to person relative to the European Union, the United States, the Vatican and probably otherwise unknown entities. There were a number of comments in the letters that drew McAbee to that conclusion.

The course of the correspondence extended from 1992 when Bosnia/Herzegovina declared independence through to May, 1995. Their trysts were written about lovingly by him, remorse was expressed about the brutal sniper killings and shellings in Sarajevo perpetuated by Bosnian Serbs from outlying hills and apartment buildings surrounding the city. There was a noticeable slide into depression by Toma. He referred to the letters written by Cynthia and how they gouged his spirit. The last letter ended in a short paragraph. Toma was attaching himself in a few days to a small NATO mission bound for Srebrenica which was north and east of Sarajevo. The eastern part of the city of Srebrenica had been overrun by the Bosnian Serb military and there was considerable fear that the Moslem population there was endangered.

McAbee knew in fact that at a minimum 7,000 Moslem Bosnians were systematically slaughtered by the Bosnian Serbs. Nothing like this had happened in Europe since the reign of Nazism.

On the last page of this last letter, in the florid handwriting of Cynthia, there was a short note. It read, 'Monsignor Forte informed me this morning that Toma had been found dead this morning by the Latin Bridge. My heart is broken.' Bertrand sat back and groaned within himself, both for the couple and for his intrusion into this sacred and hidden space. He felt sullied and ill at ease with himself and the business that brought him into this cave of secrecy and hurt.

The second bin was only half full. At the very top was an 8 by 10 portrait photo of Anne Podreski. He thought that it had recently been retrieved by Cynthia. On the back, in neat penmanship, there was this: 'Cynthia, please accept this and root for me. Anne.' There were two 5 by 7 framed photos, presumably of her mother in the one and father in the other. There was a small album that held only 20 or so photos. He was brought back to Cynthia and Toma who were in various poses and both in obvious joy with each other. McAbee guessed that this was probably Cynthia's one great love. The photos seemed to have all been shot in and around Sarajevo.

At the very bottom of the bin were some loose photos and a scattering of Memorial High student newspapers that covered the Demosthenes Club. The loose photos were of members of the Demosthenes Club and in addition of Sam Liebow. There was a black kid in one of them. McAbee assumed, given that it was in the stack, that this was probably Archie Sanders.

One thing was clear to him as he closed this second bin. Cynthia was not a sentimentalist who clung to each and every moment of her life.

He got up, stretched, and looked back at the yellow pad. If there had been foul play perhaps evidence would be found in it.

CHAPTER 19

He went back to the yellow pad glancing over the first two pages again. There was enough there to surface the incident that troubled Cynthia. A note attached to the top of page three indicated that Corey Bladel was the last of the five she had interviewed for her soon to be aborted book. Peter Waters had merely sent a 26 page vita to her.

At first her writing was tame, Corey hadn't changed. Extroverted, bragging, full of himself, too handsy, moderately intoxicated. He was more than willing to share his success with her and how important the Demosthenes Club had been for his 'wonderful' career as a politician. Some notes were taken by way of bullet points by Cynthia. Material one could get on Google. Then the writing changed, she was quite disturbed by Corey's leg under the table touching hers. The 'buffoon' was still a 'buffoon' she wrote.

> I kept at him about the Demosthenes Club and why it was so important to him. He was finally focusing. Mentioned us all. I said 'but no one really liked each other. It was a pool of sharks'. He's such a bullshitter. I wanted to see how he'd handle that.

> He finally relented and distinguished between "like" and "respect." 'I respected everyone, but like is another matter. I liked you,' the phony grin and the leg again pushing against mine.

The writing now became aberrant, odd. The Corey interview:

> Corey says every one of us had talent. Even Sanders, remember that black kid, but he was a pushy ass. Every time you looked at him you were a racist. And poor Sam Liebow leaning over backwards to win Sanders' approval and each time being fingered as a racist by the bastard. Or words to that effect. All the time Corey's drinking. Hides it well but it had to be affecting his inner machinery. He starts to make a comment about the others now. Douthit, one lucky play on Microsoft, then a streak and suddenly the sullen swindler is a billionaire. Then he tells me how much Douthit respects him even though he wouldn't contribute a nickel to Corey's campaign. Everyone in the club gets scolded. Megan White 'has a stick up her ass.' Francine Korbel 'pumps testosterone up her ass nightly.' Peter Waters is a 'fraud,' a 'phony.' Not me of course. He's a politician but God knows what he would say about me to others, my not being present.
>
> Anne Podreski. I mention Anne. He looks at me as though I'm stupid. Puzzlement all over his face. I say things were never the same after her drowning. We were all warned about the booze. I don't think

she ever had a drink in her life, but as I say this he looks at me in disbelief.

Then he says, 'don't pretend Cynthia. You know as well as I do. Accident my ass. She was punished, left, ignored. Peter!' He skidded off to another topic. I tried to get him back on but he wouldn't say anymore. I think he knew that he had stepped falsely. Then he quickly pulls out his cell. I think he pretends that he has to go. Sorry and all that. Limo waiting, back to hotel, no longer handsy. We'll do it again Cynthia, good luck with the book, call if you need more, goodbye. Cold as ice all of a sudden. I think he forgot about my not being at the lake when Anne drowned.

Cynthia continues as McAbee opens to the fourth page.

I can't sleep. Anne is present in me. She's taking possession of me. Anne, simple, innocent, raised strictly, bright but not street-wise. Family poor, I think. Tells me that she is going to enter the Miss Scott County contest. If she wins that, Miss Iowa, and if she wins that, Miss America. I'm impressed. Supportive even though I don't care for the whole enterprise. We're not overly close but I felt sorry for her. As I look back who was I to feel sorry for her? She had good looks and was a talented violinist. But I knew the others in the club. They tried to destroy her. Mean characters, everyone in their own way. And she was always trying to win their favor, impress them. They preyed on her insecurity. And

I was not at my best, too many personal issues at the tough age of 17. They found out when Sam Liebow informed us at a club meeting. Megan White snipped, Anne was turning herself into a sex toy. Stan Adair (RIP) told her it was a good career option for a Vegas showgirl as he laughed at her. Corey Bladel offered to take some nude photos of her with his new Nikon. Peter Waters told her he lost whatever little respect he had for her, even though he ogled her constantly. Lastly Francine Korbel told her to withdraw immediately as it made all of the club members look like fools. To this day I remember the hatred and the comments, except for Douthit, I can't remember his reaction. He was there but quiet. I spoke in support of her but I wasn't heard as Sam Liebow chided us all. Liebow never had control of us. Poor Anne was blood in the water. She was a gift for the sharks who now loved to feast on her. The perfect victim, needy and beautiful.

So much is coming back to me. I am ashamed of my past. I should have been kinder to Anne. I think back to that night. It was a weekend, Saturday, middle April. There were packs of Coca Cola, beer and a few bottles of rum. A big bag of ice. Hot dogs and hamburgers at Scott County Park. Someone smuggled the rum and beer. I don't recall who. It was a beautiful Spring night. We all came. Picnic grounds. A campfire was lit. My memory fails with details. Liebow was present with his wife. They left early, maybe 7:00 p.m. The booze just appeared as soon as they left. We were all in rebellion of course. We were full of ourselves. Protest music, Simon and Garfunkel, Joan Baez, whatever. We wanted to show our adulthood. We drank. I had beer. Hated the taste, still do. I was not a drinker. Anne trying to impress, of course, drank. I remember seeing her secretly grimacing at the rum and Coke taste. I doubted Anne had ever had a drink in her life. But she had to impress these vile characters. She was egged on by a few of them especially when they saw her touching the edge of drunkenness. I got sick. I ate too fast. Vomited. They just ignored me, I smelled bad, got some puke on my pants. There was a small lake there, close to where we were. They wanted to swim – clothes off. Besides being sick, needing to puke again, I was having my period. I wouldn't go. I must have napped, I felt so rotten. They came back. Anne was dead! I shrieked, I cried. I went to the lake. Where? What? Someone got the cops. Anne was on the ground, face down. She was dead. They all said that they were playing and Anne just disappeared. Douthit found her too late. They didn't notice. That was the story. I couldn't add anything. I wasn't there. But they all agreed, she just disappeared. It was the end of the Demosthenes Club. I think that it was the end of all of us in a way. I felt we were cursed. But I never thought anything other than what was said about her death. And now Corey! Anne was punked? This will have to be pursued. I will not let it go. Something else happened out there that night and some, if not all of them, know. Ingenuous fool that I am.

McAbee felt her pain. She was an introspective woman who was capable of looking into herself and searching out her faults, even as when she was a 17 year old girl. A harsh gaze back into her then self-absorption, that teenage malady, pretty inescapable.

He continued on into the pad. He read on about Francine Korbel. Cynthia meets with her specifically about Anne Podreski. McAbee thinks that the hard disc that is missing was perhaps devoted to the formal history of the Demosthenes Club, to her interviews about what had happened to each member. But this yellow pad? This might involve her inquiry into Anne Podreski and just maybe she never entered any of her investigation into Anne's death into her PC. If there was foul play in Cynthia Power's death it could easily be argued that it was this investigation that was the cause. Cynthia may have foreseen how dangerous her inquiry was. Why else would she conceal the pad under her couch? Augusta had been clear. Cynthia was very neat with the exception of her studio and even then, for a working artist's studio, it was pretty ordered in her estimate.

McAbee read over the pages devoted to Korbel, the retired Vice President from Deere & Company. He couldn't get a feel for the relationship. There was no 'like' there but then again there was no 'dislike.' Cynthia seemed to accept Francine Korbel's edginess, frankness, and even her sarcasm. It was as if the relationship was picked up where it had left off all those years ago.

He read:

> I called Francine again. She had been very receptive about my book and had cooperated very

> openly about the Demosthenes Club and its effect on her future success at Deere. I'm sure she just assumed that I was doing follow up. Of all the club members, I still see her as the toughest of us. Francine could freeze a boiling Satan with her stare.
>
> We met at the Ramada in downtown Davenport. She asked about my progress on the book. She seemed interested. I used great caution with her before bringing up Anne. Francine could tell me to go to hell and just walk away. I had one asset working for me. I am almost sure that she abhorred Corey Bladel. In fact, I think that Francine probably had issues with the human race in general. When I would mention any club name, such as Megan White, her lips would curl noticeably.
>
> I went to Corey very indirectly, spoke of his 'wonderful' career and then I worked into Anne. Francine's head flew back about two inches as I watched her closely hear me do a roundabout report on Corey's revelation about Anne's death. I say that he had unsettled me about her death, as if he assumed I knew what everyone else knew. I left it there and went on. She didn't bite and I left in on the table.

McAbee appreciated Cynthia's tactic. She would let Francine stew about it. Korbel was seen by her as a goal-oriented women who would be incapable of letting a standing nail stay standing. Thus he read about a second meeting between the pair.

> We met again, a week later at Starbucks on 53rd Street. Francine was edgy, not mean, but a bit wired. She said that she only had fifteen minutes. I brought up Anne again, almost instantly. I told her that I was upset. She emptied a truckload of sarcasm at Corey Bladel saying he's a stupid ass, inflated ego. The mind of a roach. Why would I pay any attention to the moron? She patted my hand condescendingly. Don't lose sleep, her final message before leaving, her coffee concoction barely touched. One thing is now clear to me. There's smoke around Anne and that means there was a fire that was there.

Cynthia Power was not above sarcasm. There was an innocence to her, yes, perhaps it was her idealism – this inferred through her vita, but her analysis of Demosthenes members had indignation about them.

> My third meeting with Francine was not pleasant. She began with her corporate laser that was meant to stop me in my tracks. I came back at her hard, pressing her about Anne. She told me that I was an obsessive with Roman Catholic cancerous guilt. Anne is dead. She drowned. She was drunk. I came back to her with Corey. She dismissed him as an alcoholic. Finally she strutted away angrily telling me over her shoulder not to be in touch with her again about this matter.

A new page was devoted to Megan White, the University of Iowa professor.

> Drove to Iowa City for lunch with Megan. Poor Megan is in love with herself. She looks great until I look closely at her and observe the mini-scars all over her face and neck. The caked makeup almost succeeds. Her arrogance has only gotten worse over the years. She thought that I was there to draw out more data about her greatness. If she knew that I wasn't doing the book I don't think she would have met with me. I tried to ease into the Anne Podreski issue. I believe there is no easy way to go into it. She was quicker off the mark than Francine. Instant defensiveness. How could you? Stupid Catholic! Crazy Corey. And it went on and on. Our relationship, flawed when we were 17 years old, broken at 18, slightly recovered when I was doing the book, and now irretrievable with the mention of Anne. She stormed off. She barely ate anything.

McAbee was impressed with Cynthia's perseverance but he was beginning to understand her frustration and also her suspicions.

The last written-on page had little.

> Corey refuses to respond to my requests for another meeting. Peter Waters is unreachable and, of course, John Douthit was as still and deep as a Norwegian fjord. When I informed him that I wasn't doing the book he shut down once and for all, I think.

There was nothing else in the pad. She either gave up, perhaps committing suicide, or did she scare someone in this club to cause her murder. McAbee left his office at 11:55 p.m. Several concepts swung around in his head. Cynthia Power had a high sense of ethics. The Demosthenes Club had been peopled by difficult teenagers. The drowned Anne Podreski was a doomed beauty in the midst of these same teenagers. Lastly, though, he could not shake the conclusion that there was something disturbing around the Davenport Police Department's all too quick dismissal of Linda Rhine's complaints.

He recalled Dr. Linda Rhine's comments about Cynthia's gaining some new information about her lover's death in Sarajevo. She was a woman beset. Maybe she did commit suicide.

CHAPTER 20

McAbee arrived late the next morning. During the drive to downtown Davenport he continued to mull over whether to take on the case of Cynthia Power. There certainly were oddities. But, then again, suicides were frequently loaded with unknowns and missed signals.

As he was about to enter the up-bound elevator he heard a voice to his back, from the building entrance. He turned and saw Helen Krill, the librarian at Memorial High School. He was delighted to see her again but as she rushed toward him she seemed unhappy, maybe angry.

Slightly out of breath, she said curtly, "I need to speak with you. I'm very upset. You have an office here, right?"

"Yeah, of course Helen. Come up with me." Her hands grabbed the rail that circumscribed the elevator. She was looking down and biting her lower lip. This was not a social visit. He told Pat that Helen and he were going to have a talk in his office. Helen shook her head at the offer of anything to drink.

McAbee sat at the table off to the side of his desk. He invited Helen to sit as he ran through several scenarios that would cause this affable woman to be so upset. After they sat he said, "Helen, what's up?" while observing a leery woman.

"I'm really puzzled. I don't understand your motivation. I was about to call the police when my principal told me to come down here and confront you. Just to make sure, he says."

McAbee still had no idea where this was heading. "Helen, excuse me. What are you talking about? Motivation? About what?"

"Please! You came to the library yesterday. I copied what you wanted! Remember?" her voice rising to a near scream. "I came in this morning and both of those newspaper binders are gone. The very ones that you were interested in. We have no backup for them. They're gone and we have no film on them. If you give them back to me now, no questions will be asked. I'll say it was a misunderstanding even though you had to have broken in last night. This is against my principles but I'll go along. Hand them over McAbee." She held her right palm outwards.

It was at this precise point, a silence across the table, when McAbee knew that he would have to take up the case of Cynthia Power. Whatever doubts he had, and they were there, evaporated.

Helen Krill left his office about 45 minutes later. He was almost certain that she believed him. However, McAbee now concluded that there was some force out there trying to eradicate evidence. That doesn't happen unless something had to be covered up. Dr. Linda Rhine's suspicions had climbed into a near certainty.

CHAPTER 21

Augusta, stunning as ever, came to the booth where McAbee sat at the downtown Ramada in Davenport. As he watched her cross the restaurant floor he noticed the glances and some of the double-takes from the diners. She wore a black flare skirt, a deep red blouse and a tan sport coat. A gold chain and large hooped earrings caught the glint of sun that splintered across the room. She had aged a bit, more ribs of silver in her medium length Afro and she now wore glasses, black-rimmed, that gave her a look of wise elegance. She commanded the room. Their love for each other was unquestioned by either of them. He stood, they hugged. He said, "Hey."

She whispered, "Mistah."

They talked about her girls, Augusta now relaxed that the missteps of her one daughter had been righted. They ordered, both light salads. Finally she looked at Bertrand and said, "So Dr. McAbee does not as a matter of custom ask people to lunch without having an agenda. And why would I doubt this conclusion as Pat, rather insistently, urged me to come here? Simple. You need me to do something. So, Mistah, let's hear it," she said in full smile.

McAbee felt bad as he was about to turn the smile into a frown. He began, "So Augusta, I went through the materials that you and Jack had taken from Cynthia Power's house. Almost all of it interesting but maybe not of consequence to her death I think. But the yellow pad was curious. Cynthia was doing an investigation." He recounted the details of the Demosthenes Club and Cynthia's separate meetings with a few of them, his visit with Jane Murphy the reporter, his trip to Memorial High School, his ambivalence about the case. And then the turning point – Helen Krill this morning and the theft of the two years of student newspapers. "So Augusta, I have decided to go after this matter. I need your help of course."

Augusta looked at him pensively as she placed her right hand under her jaw. "I'll do whatever I can. Let's hope this one doesn't expand like what the universe is doing as we speak."

McAbee smiled. He was aware of his tendency to have cases explode on him. "I don't think this will happen on this one; however, I have learned to be cautious." He noticed that her right hand maintained under her jaw. He was hesitant about asking her to do what he felt to be necessary. Relenting, he said, "Augusta, I need some things that I can only get through you." Her hand went down to the table top as if she expected a request too far. "I need investigatory files about two cases that are seen as closed. The one refers back to Anne Podreski's death in April of 1968. The other, the details around Cynthia Power's supposed suicide."

"Bertrand, I anticipated Cynthia Power. You know that I'm on thin ice with Chief Pesky. Your last few case resolutions have alienated him. The last time I ran into him over at the Blackhawk Hotel, totally by accident, he barely said hello to me."

"I know this is going to be tough, Augusta. Is there any way around him?"

"I'll try him first. If that doesn't work, I'll have to go to your infamous Plan B."

"Plan B?" McAbee asked.

"That means there has to be another way. Sneaky. Dangerous."

"Dangerous?"

"Yes. Because if it fails and he gets wind of my involvement we would forever be banned within a square mile of police headquarters. As you know, he thinks we're involved romantically and he shudders at the horror of the idea." She threw McAbee her million dollar smile.

McAbee found himself becoming a bit defensive before catching himself. He said, "Yes, I suppose he thinks he'd make for a great replacement?" He noticed that she looked down momentarily, caught off guard by his comment. He assumed that he had hit a target.

Recovering herself she said, "Oh Bertrand. Fear not. You're my guy unless you keep making crazy requests. Let me work my way through this. But the Anne Podreski thing? Fifty years ago? I understand why you're asking about it, but that's ancient history."

"Cynthia Power was shaken about Anne's death. A slipped comment was made by Corey Bladel. Maybe it's just remorse because she wasn't swimming with the others when Anne Podreski died. But I'm thinking that there is more to it. She seems to have been really ethically centered whereas the other club members are an odd lot."

"So what are you going to be doing while I'm climbing the Chief Phil Pesky cliffs?"

"I have an appointment with Cynthia's brother, Eric, in an hour."

Eric Power lived in downtown Moline, Illinois. The twelve story building was once a hotel, converted years back into apartments. McAbee had never been above the ground floor of the building and that was years ago. He was struck by how many years had passed in the interlude between now and then. Shabbiness was the now operant word.

He pressed the button to Eric's apartment number on the panel at the first floor entrance.

There was a quick and sharp "Yeah?"

"Hi. Bertrand McAbee. We're still on?"

"I'll buzz you. 9C. Go left to the end of the hallway. Doors open."

Eric's door was ajar. Bertrand knocked gently as he said, "Hi."

"Yeah. Come on in. Be careful of the stuff. I know, I know, I don't need your advice."

Bertrand was overwhelmed as he entered into the main living room. He stopped as he gazed out through a picture window at the I-74 bridge that spanned the Mississippi River between Moline, Illinois, and Bettendorf in Iowa. As his eyes took in the room, however, he realized that he was in the lair of a *bona fide* hoarder. The room was like a crime scene created by some violent horde of voracious Vikings. Eric was nowhere to be seen.

"Over here," he growled. McAbee looked over to where he heard the sound come from, he saw an archway and a few feet behind it a lime-green refrigerator. "Be careful where you step."

McAbee could not see any floor area where he could move, without stepping on a piece of paper, or some questionable object, or boxes to make an unfettered step toward Power.

He did the best he could hoping that he wouldn't disturb any mice that might be munching on all the junk that this man had accumulated.

Eric Power was sitting on a short stool. He was sorting marbles from an oversized plastic five gallon container into five different half-gallon topless milk containers. The methodology behind the sorting was not apparent to McAbee who observed a thin man with thick glasses licking his small mustache. His thinning hair seemed to have been free of barbering for years, matching his apartment in disorder. "Pull up a seat!" he said in a way that sounded abrupt, words shortened with consonants stressed at the cost of vowels. McAbee thought that if bulldogs could speak they might sound like Eric. He noticed a steel beige folding chair a few feet to the right of Eric. McAbee went to it removing two shoeboxes that impeded him. As he looked around to see where to place them Eric barked, "Just put them anywhere." McAbee placed them on a three carton-high set of boxes. As he was sitting, he noticed that the chair seat was smeared as it were with uneven sectors of rust.

Bertrand began, "Eric, let me say at the start I'm sorry about your sister's death." Power continued to toss marbles into the containers giving no eye contact to him. McAbee let the silence sit.

Finally, Eric said, "Yeah. Sad story. What exactly do you want?" The clicking of each marble was methodical.

"There's some evidence around this that suggests that she didn't commit suicide."

The clicking stopped. He looked at McAbee for a few seconds as he rubbed his chin and slid his index finger across his mustache. Finally, he said, "You know mister you gotta be careful with those comments. The cops were certain that she suicided. How well did you know her?"

"I didn't. I've been asked to investigate her death by a close friend, a psychiatrist in fact. Her judgment runs counter to the police. I've done some spade work on the matter. I'm beginning to think that the psychiatrist is right."

"Does any of this crap affect the will? Oh, and that psychiatrist? A goddamn dyke."

"No, I don't think so. The will is fine as far as I know." He did not remark to the comment about Dr. Rhine.

"Well good, because I get the house and the contents of her place. I need more room as you can see," he said in a semi-snarl.

McAbee fell silent as he heard the marbles clicking once again in the sorting process. So Eric was not all there, also there was a good chance that this might be McAbee's last run with him. So he counseled himself into patience. "Yeah, that's not an issue. I imagine that you'll have possession shortly. Do you know her attorney?" He was trying to gain some time and understanding with the man.

"Yes. Fox. He called me. Sounds like a weirdo to me."

"Oh yeah. He's pretty controversial with all of those billboards around here." McAbee smiled ever so slightly as he was creating a path into this character.

"They're all a bunch of crooks." The crackling sound of marbles grew louder. Extra hard throws in angry dismissal of lawyers.

"I'm trying to figure out your sister Eric. Could you help me a bit?"

The marble-sort now came sporadically and a bit softer as Eric spoke. "She was thirteen years older than me. My father was ten years older than my mother. My father was a mean bastard who died when I was eight. I have no good memories of him. My mother was a good-hearted flake. Cynthia took after her. That's what she was. She regularly got herself into radical Catholic crap. The Berrigans! Can you believe those fools? Dorothy Day another one. She lived in a fairy world. We were night and day with each other. The best I can say about Cynthia was that she was smart and a good artist, she made some money at it. So, at least, I get her house and stuff. But in reality I really didn't want anything to do with her." The sorting picked up again. He had said his piece, click, click, click.

Bertrand queried, "Did you guys ever communicate?"

"Rarely. We had to speak on burying our mother. We disagreed about it. I just wanted her cremated – cheap as possible. Don't believe in all that casket and burial crap. But she wanted the casket and a funeral mass and tombstone and on and on and on. I gave her a thousand dollars and told her she was on her own."

"When was that?"

"89," he barked quickly, impatiently.

"She seems to have been out of the country for most of the 90s," McAbee said tentatively.

"Yep. She came back once for a month or two in, I

don't know, 96 or 97. She wanted to make up with me. She whined, 'We're all alone now Eric. We should be friends.' I brushed her off. If she wasn't a communist she was one of their dupes. I felt sorry for her. She was like my mother. Impractical, irresponsible. She was downtrodden, though, I'll tell you. She had a boyfriend, whatever, over in Sarajevo. He was killed. It crushed her. Crazy bastards over there in the Balkans and she in full foolhardiness volunteering to help them in their misery. You see that was the problem with her, she had no common sense." The marble sorting had stopped momentarily as he gazed at McAbee for a few seconds.

McAbee said consolingly, "It's too bad that the two of you couldn't connect. That probably upset you?"

"Nah. Listen to me. She was my sister but that's where it all ended. Don't you see? I didn't want anything to do with her."

"Sounds like you don't miss her?"

"I don't. I don't give a damn. She should have left me everything. Fox tells me that she gave her money to some goddamn animal shelter. Can you believe that?"

"She left you her house," Bertrand said noncommittally.

"I know. I know."

"I really appreciate your candor with me Eric. But allow me to get back to her death. Were you surprised when they told you that she committed suicide?"

There was a lengthy pause. "Yeah, at first. She was religious, at least she was to the best of my knowledge. You have to understand that I probably last saw her around 2009. We had lunch. Her insistence. She had decided to move back here. Our meal didn't end well. For all of her left-ness I am way to the right. She really disgusted me. She'd send me birthday cards. Every year. I never sent one to her but she just wouldn't accept my wanting nothing to do with her."

"I can see that," Bertrand said sympathetically. "But now I'm telling you that she might have been murdered. Given her kindness and concern for others, why would anyone want to kill her?"

"Your guess is as good as mine. She was trusting. That's a weakness in my book. She went around with jaw out setting herself up for a punch. Maybe it caught up with her. But look, the cops were certain it was suicide. My advice to you is let it go. At the end of it all her life was a failure. Anything else?" The marbles started up again, click, click, click, click.

McAbee determined that he had to keep channels open for a return visit. Thus, he maintained a very sympathetic approach to this man mangled by contradictions, hatreds, and anger. But he found it increasingly difficult to listen to Eric Power. There was one item that he needed to pursue. "One other thing if I may?"

"Yeah?" he looked at his watch.

"You mentioned the Balkans. Crazy people. That entire history is very interesting. Long memories. Some people say that they're still fighting the Turks, six centuries later." He smiled at Eric. "This boyfriend that she had. You said he was killed that it crushed her. I realize that that was over 20 years ago, but do you think there is any connection there?"

"Nah. But how would I know? She just mentioned it, there was a sob story there but I didn't want to hear it. She did have one close friend around here. She might know more about that Balkan crap, who knows?"

"Name?"

"Boy, don't remember. But I know there were close once. Cynthia leaned on her to help with all my mother's funeral stuff. That's all I can tell you." He stood up.

McAbee thanked him and left, careful not to disturb the trash and any living thing underneath it all.

As he drove across I-74 toward Iowa, McAbee opened all of the windows and the sunroof of his relatively new Toyota Camry hybrid. He needed lots of air.

CHAPTER 22

Francine Korbel had been put off by Peter Waters' secretary five times. She was told that the former ambassador was engaged with world affairs, but that he would return her call as soon as possible. Emails were attempted and met with the same scornful neglect. That game extended through ten days. She finally got through to Peter's wife. After some studious work on Google, she ascertained that she was Peter's fourth one, the other three divorced, one of those now dead. This latest fixer-upper was a graduate of Wellesley with bloodlines into a Boston banking family. Peter was Francine's age, 67. The new model, Courtney, was 37. Peter was her third husband. The cow was keeping up with him actuarially, in fact, she would probably be hitting her sixth husband when she hobbled to his age. These thoughts filtered through her mind as she had to listen to the phony New England voice coyly telling her to go to hell. As cutie Courtney droned on about how busy Peter was Francine was deciding just how she was going to eviscerate the bitch and her fucking stuck-up avoiding husband.

"So I hope that you understand, most gracious of you," Courtney concluded probably just about to disconnect.

Francine interjected. "Courtney, you have been most kind. I totally understand your predicament. I know Peter so well," she said as mildly as she could staunching the acid that was leaking from her orifices. "But let me leave this message with you for him. You might want to write it down. It's a bit complicated. If I don't hear from him by tonight, his secretary has had my number for ten days, I'm going to come over to Chicago and inform your two bullshit papers there about his drug usage while in high school and his knowledge of the drowning of Anne Podreski."

"How dare you! Drug usage? High school? Anne Podreski?"

"Just do what I told you, you dumb bitch!" She disconnected. She knew enough about Peter Waters to know how jealously he would protect his reputation. Even though he was supposedly retired, his tongue was probably out for a new posting hoping by this time to ditch Courtney-skank even if it meant he had to go to the Congo.

Courtney flew into Peter's study, her lips were taut and pale, almost white. Her intense brown eyes looked like armed missiles. Of course, during his courtship of her, or was it her courtship of him, he had never seen these qualities. For the past three years, since their marriage, she would roll onto a firing range about every other week and hang there until her guns were totally spent. To his relief they hadn't had sex for over a year. He had already consulted his attorney on how he could disentangle from this Boston Medusa. He was told that her history during divorce procedures was very injurious toward the escaping husband.

"And who the fuck is this crazy bitch Francine Korbel? Why am I being exposed to some trash from your high school who is busily contemplating outing you about drug usage and some drowning? And the way she spoke to me! I still cannot believe it! The goddamn nerve! You better straighten that crazy bitch out and have it that I never see or hear from her again!"

Waters saw that she actually stamped her right foot hard on the oak floor. He identified with Odysseus sailing through Scylla and Charybdis. His horrid wife and Francine! Although Courtney was one tough shrew she was a lightweight against the likes of Francine Korbel. He should have called Francine ten days ago when Marilyn, his secretary, first brought her call to his attention. Emails, of course, would almost never be answered. Waters kept telling her to put off Francine even though Marilyn had reported to him that Korbel was becoming quite agitated. Sometimes delaying tactics worked in diplomacy among civilized countries. But with Francine Korbel? His thought flew to North Korea. He would have to speak with her. Megan White, the cobra, had texted him a bit ago informing him that Francine was on the warpath. But he already figured that behind it all was Cynthia Power. Drunken Corey Bladel had set up a chain of dominoes with this big mouth. And this was all breaking around him as he was edging his credentials forward through some allies at State for an ambassadorship to Iceland. Perfect. Anorexic Courtney who didn't weigh more than 90 pounds would shiver to death in that godforsaken country.

He tried to explain to his still shaking wife what the issue was all about. That Francine Korbel had missed her true calling by not becoming a professional wrestler. A pain in the ass, "I'm so sorry dear that you had to deal with her.

She's probably off her meds again," he said while being secretly pleased that Courtney had gotten a good kick up her scrawny, disappearing ass. He concluded by saying, "I will call her and calm her down. These are issues that go back to problems she had in high school. We were in a club together and she didn't fit in. I think that she was a good candidate for transgender surgery but she was before her time. I will also tell her in no uncertain terms never to speak with you again. The nerve of her," he said with this practiced and phony candor.

She didn't say anything, merely wagging her finger as she left his study. Many missiles had not yet been fired. He dreaded the next few days as he hoped for a call about Iceland and Thor's intervention on his behalf.

The last time he had seen Francine was at Stan Adair's funeral in 2001. They had sat as far apart from each other as good manners allowed. All through that time with her in the Demosthenes Club he had been secretly scared of her, not that anyone knew. Well, maybe he told Megan White once when they were high on grass. He couldn't remember but he was sure that if he had shared his fears with Megan she'd never forget it. Another wacky harridan whom he had gingerly stayed in touch with her over the years, after all they were both obsessive careerists.

His hand went to his iPhone. Then he decided to use his landline. He didn't want her to have his cell number. If he concealed it from her as being a 'private caller' it would create the conditions of war.

"Francine," he said in phony cheer. "I know you don't believe this but I have been tied up terribly. No need to tease my wife." He cringed awaiting her response. There was a long pause. She was probably injecting testosterone up her ass when his call came through.

"Cut the bullshit Peter. I'm not comfortable talking on the phone with you. Did you get my message clearly from your wife? Secretary?"

"Oh yes. Been meaning to call. You have no idea how pressed I am. But I'm okay with the phone. This is a landline after all."

"And landlines are so protected," she said in irony. "Very well. Hear me out. As you know, Cynthia is dead. I saw your wreath at her funeral. You've always been so generous."

He couldn't ever tell whether her graciousness was in the grip of constant irony. "Couldn't get there of course. So sad. A good woman."

"Yeah. Well this former good woman met Corey who was on one of his constant groping and drinking runs. He brought up Anne Podreski and her drowning. I know that what was said was explicit enough for Cynthia to start digging. Perhaps a new book with us as the creeps given Corey's stupidity. And now as I try to gather us together I am being met with hostility. I met your sweet friend Megan in Iowa City and the stupid woman storms out of a restaurant that we were eating at. Fucking denial. And then you holed up in retirement with your fourth fucking wife, avoiding me."

Coming back at her carefully he commented, "Francine, Cynthia is dead. Death stops things, inquiries. Anne Podreski drowned. She was drunk. We all were. It was pitch dark. She blacked out and died. Corey Bladel is a drunk. Maybe he's having some guilt pangs and shares his feelings with Cynthia. You knew Cynthia – all heart, all ears. Her super-sized conscience kicks in and then she goes off track. It's the off track part of her that committed suicide. My analysis – drunken and guilty Corey meets sensitive and moral Cynthia."

"That's a real smooth take Peter. Very creative. Your interview for her book about the Demosthenes Club? She told me that you brushed her off and faxed her your *vita*, all 20,000 pages of it. She felt that's all she'd get from you. But when she tried to reach you about Podreski and Corey's comment you stonewalled her, no *vita* – just stone silence."

"Francine, you're in a warp. This is enough now. I have nothing else to say."

"You're not getting this. So I'm going to have to lay it on you. I don't think that Cynthia would have committed suicide! I spoke with her three times post Corey. She was as far from suicide as you are. And one more thing before I hang up. Next time you'll come to me you bastard. You were all over Anne Podreski. You never let up on her. After she rejected you, I heard it, we all did. We were surprised at how firm this very weak girl was. Then you started, unrelentingly, to harass her about the Miss Scott County contest. That she was loose, too ugly, and so on. Your horniness for her turned into a hatred. Don't think for a second that observant Cynthia didn't see all of this you fool. And then, of course, there's the lake."

Peter had had enough. "I've tried to be diplomatic with you Francine. You haven't changed. Get back on your fucking tractor and plow some fields. Don't bother me again." He disconnected. But he knew it. He had been stung by this wasp.

He looked up. Courtney just appearing, was at the door

tapping her foot. This was wacky nut day. Was there a full moon? He growled at her, "Well you heard me. I put her in her place. She won't bother us again," as he sat up straight and spoke in full bluster.

Courtney stared at him in disgust for a few seconds before turning and walking away. Peter wavered about the next steps. Corey Bladel was best left stewing in his own juices. And then there was John Douthit. He'd have to think about that but for now he'd let truculent Francine try to invade Douthit's castle. Francine was in a howl but she was far, far, away from doing any career-harm and that's what counted.

CHAPTER 23

The minute McAbee came into his office he knew. He had made it a priority to get there on time, but because of an accident on River Road (Iowa 67) he had been held up for fifteen minutes. This allowed Barry Fisk and Pat Trump to engage unfettered in their campaign of mutually insured destruction. There was an instantaneous sullen silence in the outer office. Pat was staring daggers and tapping her hand on her desk while Barry, sitting in his specially fitted chair, had his small legs vibrating like the blades of a helicopter. He disliked this war between these two. He had tried on numerous occasions to conciliate the pair but if anything, he worsened their relationship. If they had been married and both armed he would have sought a court order to forcibly separate them. Their relationship was the worst dysfunction at ACJ.

Lightly, he said, "Well, I see the two of you have met on the field of battle."

Neither of them responded. In fact, neither of them looked at him, their glares fixed. McAbee was offended, the peacemaker as he saw himself. He said to Pat, an employee and not just a contractor, "Pat, I'm here now. I'll see Barry in my office."

"Please do," she retorted in agitation. This was unlike her. Barry must have hit her hard with one of his verbal onslaughts. He stood in front of Barry and said, "Let's go to my office."

When they sat down Barry came at him. "You see. You see how insolent she is? I can't believe you keep..."

"Barry! That's enough. If and when she leaves me I'll leave also. That's it. She's essential to me. When I'm not here and you come in I just want you to sit and be quiet. Do not engage with her. She will be under similar orders in regards to you. I just cannot accept this. You are both dear to me. Make me your reference point not her. When you leave she will hear the same words."

"Okay, okay. But..."

"No buts. I need you to do some digging for me. Is your calendar clear?

"Yes," he said in despondence.

"The Cynthia Power case. I'm into it. Something bad has happened. It's not what it seems to the police. I'm pretty positive that she was murdered. A professional hit job if there ever was one. Murder is now my working hypothesis. I have some records here that I'm going to give to you. The Demosthenes Club. I was at Memorial High. I had copies of the student paper run for me whenever it was mentioned. That very night after I left, the two volumes disappeared from the school library. It was the trigger that has caused me to get into this."

"There's no microfilm of these student papers?"

"No. That's not to say that someone, somewhere, doesn't

have copies in their attic but in answer to your question no. No copies anywhere at that school. Everything is coming back full circle. There's something awry about the Demosthenes Club. Cynthia Power got a whiff of it and then I'm pretty sure she was murdered."

"I see. This mission precisely?"

"Go full bore into all of these names on this sheet." McAbee handed across a paper that had the eight names, a ninth – Archie Sanders in brackets – and the teacher Sam Liebow. He included other names, the student reporter who seemed to have an ear for gossip, Sean O'Malley, the principal, Andrew Holder, during that period, and an old school board member, Dale Pauley, who had been on the board for ages.

Fisk left with McAbee by his side. Pat wasn't at her desk. As Barry entered the elevator he placed his two fingers near his lips and pretended to smoke. The doors closed. It was his petty way of telling McAbee that Pat was a smoker and was probably in the women's bathroom doing just that. He breathed deeply and went back to his reception area and awaited Pat.

When she came back he asked her to come into his office. She hesitated before doing so. They sat. He noticed that her eyes were puffy, her face distorted by a quiet rage.

"So Pat, talk to me."

"Ah Bertrand. I know that you respect Fisk. I know that he's in the 99th percentile as a researcher and a computer whiz. I know that he has been an enormous help to you on many cases, especially your really hard ones. I know all that. But I can't allow his abuse any longer. For some reason, I remind him of the Wicked Witch of the West. I return fire on him but he goes below the belt using the very skills that you so admire. He dug into some things about my husband Ed. Some things that Ed and I had to deal with a few years ago. Very private. Absolutely none of his business. This morning he unloads it on me. I felt naked. Mentally raped by him. My vulnerability is only Ed and that's where he hit. As soon as he saw you weren't here he just burst out that Ed had a gambling addiction. Lost us a lot of money. Fisk found out. He kept going at me. Unrelenting. I can't work here Bertrand. You won't or can't do anything about this. He's just too valuable to you. But I can't take him anymore." She started to cry.

Bertrand was stunned. He knew that she and Fisk exchanged barbs but Barry had taken it to a new level. Pat Trump was not a crier. "Pat, I'm so sorry about this. I've always seen you as someone who could give as well as take. But that's when the field is pretty even, no land mines. He changed the nature of your relationship. This is what I just told him before he left. He is to come in and sit. Not a word with you unless there is some overwhelmingly professional reason for doing so. Obviously, I'd like you to reciprocate. Will you give it a try?"

She stared hard at McAbee. He was unsettled by this. He wasn't prepared to drop Barry Fisk. Unbeknownst to Pat was that Fisk was in therapy precisely because of his inability to relate to others in a positive way. He felt that he could not disclose this to her without, ironically, replicating his behavior towards Ed's privacy. If Pat made her continuance at ACJ a drop-dead proposition, he would be in a swamp while engaging with the Demosthenes Club and his further continuance in the investigation game.

After a considerable delay, Pat said, "Okay Bertrand, I know that you do care for me. I'll give it one more try. I'd like you to put a camera with voice activation in the office. When he is here for a meeting I will put it on. If he violates your conditions you will see for yourself. You always talk about the transparency principle. But if he violates your command and you see it and refuse to do anything about it I'm gone from that moment on."

McAbee had never experienced Pat's wrath as he did now. He felt that he had looked the other way for too long and this had caused Pat to proceed in a way that left him obligated to accept her demands. Ultimately, she was right. He responded, "You're right Pat. Get it installed."

CHAPTER 24

Within two days of their meeting, Barry Fisk sent fourteen encrypted files to McAbee. Each file was loaded with information. Bertrand had only asked for thirteen probes but Barry couldn't resist sending Plutarch's *Life of Demosthenes*. It was meant to tick off McAbee as Barry had insinuated himself into the classics, specifically Plutarch, the second century C.E. pagan priest and scholar who wrote the *Essays* that Barry, after a rapid read, put down as being trite. Plutarch's *Lives*, on the other hand, he found to be interesting. Barry knew well that McAbee was familiar with the Plutarch piece and would be angered by what they both knew was an insult. McAbee had it coming for his protection of his chain-smoking secretary.

For years Pat had taunted him, looking down her nose at him and smirking at his physical appearance. She kept encroaching on him as they parried back and forth. Finally, in exasperation, he nuked her by launching into a hack of her stupid husband Ed's medical files. He was hospitalized for a gambling addiction. Then it was onto some casinos. Good old Ed was shoveling their retirement monies into casino furnaces to the tune of $2500 a week for about two years. The hospital intervention was pretty rough on the two of them. He enjoyed reading about Pat's near breakdown all the while hearing in his mind McAbee's plea that he reach out, show compassion and engage with the outer world.

Fortunately, McAbee never asked him how he came to know about Ed's problems. Well, he probably knew given all of the rotten tricks he had performed for that corrupt agency that pretended to be ethical. Hah! If truth be told, he didn't like McAbee either. He with his soul-searching questioning and hidden judgmental gazes. To hell with them all.

Bertrand appreciated that Barry had sent files and had not come into his office. Pat was still raw and even Barry's abiding by the terms of McAbee's decree, the sight of him might be enough to start a forest fire in Pat's mind. The full print job took him to 633 pages of material. The materials were prefaced with the following cover piece.

Bertrand,

> Literally, there are thousands of pages that I could have sent to you. Five of the club members are fairly to very famous. John Douthit, wealth beyond count, a mystery man in many ways, has been in numerous publications, the subject of many lawsuits, etc. Corey Bladel is an oft-quoted congressman and is in the news with frequency. Megan White has published over 50 articles and has written three books just to name a few things of what this assignment could have led to. Francine Korbel was a Vice President at Deere and showed up in a number of trade journals, etc. Peter Waters was a highly placed diplomat and is a co-founder of

a foreign studies think tank. Lots of stuff there. The dead attorney (fortunately back in his grave from where he came) Stan Adair, also many lawsuits; a plane crash got him a lot of fame, money, and press. Cynthia Power was in relative obscurity compared to the above and Anne Podreski, of course, scant. The ninth, Archie Sanders, has pretty much fallen off the map, but there is a bit. I did not have to edit much relative to Sam Liebow, the principal, Andrew Holder, the school board member, Dale Pauley, and the student reporter, Sean O'Malley. Before you run into the last enclosure I took the liberty to send only the material that I thought could help. As per our custom I have given a one page analysis of each of the thirteen you asked about. As to the last enclosure I send this just in case your copy is too far up in your library casing, this being the slick Athenian Sophist Demosthenes.

Bill enclosed, please have your secretary remit ASAP.

Barry

The thirteen summary pages, Barry didn't dare send an analysis of Demosthenes, came right after his cover letter. Pat had already removed the bill and was surely cutting a check. It was a *pro forma* procedure with Barry whose distrust of everyone was accepted.

Each of the eight members, Archie Sanders excluded in McAbee's mind as a graft that never took, told the story of life. As he read each summary he was impressed by them.

Anne Podreski never had her chance at success. Cynthia Power seemed to be a good soul who found her way into a canyon of Type A characters. She wasn't a good fit for this group as was true of Anne Podreski. Archie Sanders had the sense to get out of it. Maybe it was naked racism, maybe some other factors, but whatever the true reason for his departure he ran for the hills.

In typical fashion McAbee went after the peripherals first. He withdrew the summary pages for: Sam Liebow (Club Founder), Andrew Holder (Principal, Memorial High School), Dale Pauley (School Board), and Sean O'Malley (Student Reporter).

He would work out from there, hopeful that they were still alive. As to Plutarch's piece on Demosthenes he smiled to himself. Barry would forever be what he was, a prize fighter with fragile fists.

CHAPTER 25

Dale Pauley had been elected to the Davenport School Board at the age of 25. He was from rural Scott County but his local grammar school was within the Davenport school system boundaries. His family was in the auto, truck, and tractor repair business. In 1965, he ran as a conservative just as the issue of busing and segregation was blowing up school politics in Davenport and other larger cities across Iowa. He had been considered fair-minded by the tiny number of eligible electorate who voted for him every three years hence until he retired from the School Board in 2012. Even his enemies, and he had his share, had respect for him.

Bertrand knew Dale Pauley from a case that he had worked back in 2010. Dale was being muscled by an agricultural group out of Des Moines to sell a 50 acre farm lot which would be turned into a gigantic hog confinement complex. Dale knew the devastating impact that this plan would have on his town and the area in general, stench and ground water devastation, to name a few. The Scott County Sheriff's Department was unwilling or unable to quell the strong arm tactics that were used against Dale because of his refusal to sell. These involved a barn burning, damage to tractors and numerous hang-up and threatening phone calls, to name a few. On one of the rare occasions where McAbee would personally insert himself into a Jack Scholz counter-assault campaign, the hostile offer was withdrawn and the issue died. The pig confinement operation was moved to nearby Cedar County. The firm's corporate headquarters, after it had been demonstrated to be fully involved in the campaign against Dale, had experienced an arson attack that had destroyed the prize-winning architectural three story building in Des Moines. Dale knew nothing of the particulars, of course. Interestingly, the Des Moines firm had cancelled its building insurance policy with State Farm two weeks previous to the fire. Thus the fire inspectors did not see complicity on their part. The firm's president, however, was beside himself as no one had cancelled the policy. But someone had, apparently. Barry and Jack, each in his own distinct way, were surprised at Bertrand's vehemence about the whole issue, but they did as asked.

He arrived at Dale's business unannounced. The polite secretary asked him to sit as she took his card into Pauley's office. Within seconds, he came out and sped over to McAbee for the requisite handshake. Dale was short, wide, and in shape. He looked younger than his age by a good fifteen years. 'Country-living' he would say if asked. His most notable physical feature was his light blue eyes that gave the impression of being set in constant inquiry.

Courtesies done, McAbee came to his point. "So Dale, nice as you are and your convenient location 20 miles away from me, I have not come here to have a chat about your well-being." Dale gave him a broad, knowing smile as he flicked his right fingers up so as to give McAbee the floor.

"I need you to recall something from way in the past. 1967, 1968."

In his high tenor, Dale said smilingly, "Bertrand, I have a hard time remembering my name, but let's give it a try."

"Do you recall anything about the Demosthenes Club? Sam Liebow, the teacher, the principal of Memorial High was Andrew Holder?"

"Ah! I do remember. Tough situation. Our president of the school board took a hard hit on that one. I remember the black kid came in and railed against all of us. He put on a good show. Can't remember his name…"

"Archie Sanders."

"Yeah, sounds right. So he has to be escorted out of this place by the cops. The superintendent of schools asks for a recess and an executive session. Personnel, he says. After a break, the room is cleared. Only the seven school board members, the superintendent and the board secretary present. Before the superintendent could open his mouth the president tears the man's head off for allowing this kid's tirade. Why didn't he know this kid was off his rocker and so on? We all looked bad and by the way what the hell kind of club is this? His rant almost as bad as the kids. You mentioned Liebow. I think that poor guy was scapegoated in turn for the whole mess. Should have known and all that."

McAbee commented, "Pretty predictable I guess."

"Well there was more. You have to understand I was still new compared to the others on the board. It was a buddy system, of course. The long and short of it was this – payback. When the principal forwarded a request to fund another round of this club it was DOA. I remember Liebow making a personal appearance to ask us to reconsider. It was a chance for the president to humiliate him. He did and not to my credit I just sat there and watched. I do recall an article a few years ago in the paper, very successful people. Right?"

"Yes. Most of them. Eight really. Three of them are dead. The living five have done very well. But it seems that there were some underlying problems. Anything like that?"

"No. I can't remember. Oh… Wait. There was a drowning right? One of the eight. A girl. The superintendent and the principal appeared before us on it. Another executive session, meaning nothing gets public. There was a picnic and it seems that there was drinking. That the girl's blood alcohol was high. They wanted to protect her reputation. In those days you could. Strings were pulled. It went out as a very sad accident. Bertrand, you're really pulling me back into the past. You know the principal? Andrew Holder. A good man. He died a few years ago. He would have known more. Long time ago. Superintendent, board president, they're all gone. I'm afraid that I haven't been of much help."

"No. You have Dale. You gave me two more names, the superintendent and the board president, and then you killed them off," Bertrand said with a smirk.

"That's happening to a lot of people in my age group no less those two. They'd be a 100 by now. Before you leave Bertrand, I have a question for you. You don't have to answer, of course. Those characters from Des Moines trying to damage my property and threatening my family? The arson out there? No one was ever caught, right?"

"Yes, to the best of my knowledge."

"Did you know anything about it?" His questioning eyes taking in McAbee fully.

"No. But if you believe in a just God that's where I'd place my bet."

"I believe in a just God Bertrand. But I don't know about an arsonist God."

"Maybe you should expand your theological considerations," Bertrand said lightly.

When McAbee drove away he saw Dale at his front door. He was waving. McAbee noted his inquiring eyes.

CHAPTER 26

McAbee was feeling lucky. He decided to drive to Muscatine, Iowa, a river town southwest of Davenport. It had once been a button capital in America. As small cities went in Iowa it was prosperous: successful factories, some mid-sized farms and an outlying agricultural base. The general area had about 25,000 people.

Sean O'Malley was President of Muscatine Bank & Trust, another successful student from the 1968 graduating class. The bank was off of Highway 67 which roughly paralleled the Mississippi River now once again flowing on its north/south axis. The place still had the feel of an old fashioned bank. Three tellers sat behind marble counters; it was a one floor building with a vaulted ceiling. It had a studied look that the bank made obvious efforts to maintain, a substantial feeling to it projecting old Midwestern values whatever they were.

McAbee's luck did maintain. Sean O'Malley was available after McAbee had informed his secretary that he had questions about the Demosthenes Club from Sean's days at Memorial High School. He was gracious as he took McAbee into his office, with its full view of the Mississippi

River and the shoreline of Illinois. He was of medium height and weight. He had a practiced set of graces as he steered McAbee to a plush chair across from his desk. He asked McAbee if he wanted a cup of coffee. He declined. McAbee noticed that O'Malley's hand trembled as he raised his cup. McAbee, pretending not to see this, remarked that the view of the river was superb. He told O'Malley about reading his articles from 1967 and 1968, complimenting him on his work. That he was a P.I. and was engaging in an investigation about the causes of a suicide a bit ago of a Demosthenes Club member. He knew that he had O'Malley's full attention as he concluded his framing of this interview, "The sense is that Cynthia Power's death is somehow related to this club. And to be honest with you there seem to be some mysteries surrounding it."

O'Malley nodded. "I'll talk with you off the record." McAbee consented. "They were one screwed up lot of kids, first off, all smart, most of them weird, and most of them arrogant as hell. Sam Liebow, have you run into that name yet?" McAbee nodded. "Well, he was one of those goofy teachers in high school who run around trying to gain favor with the students. Generally, he was laughed at. So I think as a defense against that he came up with this idea, the club. He got a list of all of the high scorers on the standardized tests, high GPAs, and sought their applications."

"Did you apply?" McAbee asked.

"I was going to but decided against it. Just didn't want anything to do with Liebow, too much for my tastes. If you're asking whether I would have been chosen if I had applied, I don't know. But I know this. I would never associate with the ones who were chosen. I saw that Cynthia Power died.

I sensed suicide all over the piece but I don't know for sure. Know that some of them are pretty successful. John Douthit is big-time, for instance. Strange bastard."

"Do you remember Cynthia at all?"

"Oh yeah. Probably the nicest of them all, arty, spacey. I think she had a good heart. Are you asking whether being in that club in high school could be causative of a suicide in later life? That's too speculative for me. I don't believe that any of them were enhanced by their experiences with each other. They were dysfunctional like their teacher, Liebow. What I saw is most of them sending death stares at each other."

"Do you remember Archie Sanders?"

O'Malley laughed. "I do indeed. Let me tell you. Archie should have been chosen on the first draw. Very talented. He was right. I think Liebow went against him on racial grounds. But kids were going crazy in America. Easy to catch the flu of radicalism and causes. Archie was besotted with the Black Panthers. From then on everyone was an enemy and if you weren't really an enemy he'd make you one pretty quickly. I'll tell you this too. When their hands were forced and Archie was allowed into the club those eight others were probably nasty as hell. Like being allowed into a snake pit." He laughed again.

"I noticed an approach that was used by you in your articles. You seemed to have some sources high up in the administration. Anonymous was close to you," McAbee said lightly.

O'Malley nodded for about five seconds as he drank off the remainder of his coffee, hand shaking as he leaned into the cup to shorten the distance to his lips. "I had two deep throats. I used them in a number of my articles. None of them had anything to do with Cynthia Power as I recall. More for Archie and then of course, Anne Podreski. Boy did they put a heavy blanket over that situation. There was something about that drowning that was being covered up. I just couldn't get at it. My sources were very reluctant or ignorant, perhaps."

"What about Anne?"

"Look, she was an only daughter of a divorced mother. She was so innocent and insecure. If she was told to be mean by one of those scoundrels in that club, she'd be mean. Nice, nice. So suggestible. Some of those characters didn't like me and suddenly she turns on me. Mean. But it wasn't her. She was a puppet. They saw her vulnerability and used it against her. But I had no secret source about her death, nonetheless I believe that she being in that club was causative of her death. I really do believe that. So going back to Cynthia, adding another 40 years, looking for causation? Who knows? Not as clear, certainly, as with Anne."

"Just out of curiosity, do you have copies of your articles from your stint in high school?"

"Oh God no. I'm sure they're all packed away at the library there."

McAbee didn't say anything about Sean's expectation. He left Muscatine to head back to Davenport. There was one more peripheral – Sam Liebow.

CHAPTER 27

Congressman Corey Bladel had just finished a hearing at the Capitol building. It was a boring session about an issue that was long decided by leadership. The fix was already in. Corey was in the know about outcomes on most of these special hearings – only on occasion crossed up by the Speaker or one of his stooges, this being one of those times.

Upon returning to his offices his long-time secretary Bernadette signaled to him that she needed to speak urgently with him. Her mid-fifties eyes had that special stare. He had learned the hard way to be observant to her flagging. He flipped his hand over which was his way of telling her to come into his private office. They both knew that after one of those phony hearings that he needed privacy. Usually this meant some large gulps of bourbon. When he turned she was upon him, stopping a foot away.

She said in a half-whisper, after all there was a roomful of aides and secretaries many feet away on the other side of the door she had silently closed. "There was a call," she looked at her red Fitbit, "45 minutes ago. Lots of somber tones in the voice. He was *the* assistant, note – not *a*, to an old classmate of yours from Davenport Memorial High

School. He said you'd know the name, John Douthit. Hell, everyone knows that name. He gave me the number. Before he hung up he said to tell you it was *imperative* that you call back. I knew you'd want to know."

"Thanks Bernadette. I'll take care of it."

He watched her leave noting that she was still a damn good-looking cougar. From the bottom drawer of his oversized desk he took out a decanter and poured himself a half glass of Jim Beam, more or less four ounces, from a liter decanter that was regularly kept full by good old Bernadette.

John Douthit never was a contributor to his campaign chest. They hadn't spoken since Stan Adair's funeral in 2001. This son-of-a-bitch was no friend, all the way back to the Demosthenes Club. The call was surely about Cynthia Power. Someone had reached him. He was feeling that he was being tagged with the blame, the cause of Cynthia re-igniting the Podreski drowning. But Douthit? The man who pretended to have been chosen by God and given special wisdom enabling him to make a fortune. How had he been lured out of his cave? He drank off two ounces of the Beam before picking up his private landline to call his classmate from high school days.

He encountered the somber tone of *the* assistant. He sounded like a horribly morose funeral director in just his simple, "Hello."

"This is Congressman Corey Bladel returning a call to John," he said forcefully.

"Hold on," he replied flatly.

Not one sign of courtesy from the bastard, Corey noted.

After about 30 seconds the great John Douthit came to the phone. "Corey, thanks for returning my call. I'll get right to the point. I'm concerned about Francine. She's been trying to get through to me. But I will not take her calls. I know, though, why she's calling." Corey speculating once again about his source. "From what I can make out you said something to Cynthia Power about Podreski's death, suggesting that it was not an accidental drowning. Is this true?"

Corey was being spoken to, once again – remembering crazy Francine at the Marriott – as some kind of lesser being. "Yeah? Is that right?" Defensive now. "Cynthia was a poet. She was prone to hearing voices. I said something like it shouldn't have happened and then suddenly she hears foul play. As we both know she was unstable. That's why she committed suicide. So relax out there John and keep ignoring Francine. She retired and now has nothing to do," he was trying to relax the tension in his voice so as to relax Douthit whom he knew would not have made this call unless he was unnerved.

There was a long pause before Douthit in his measured and deliberate way said, "What you're saying and I'm hearing does not sync. I understand that you're a bit of a drunkard. I had some research done on you Corey. You think you're in a safe seat in your congressional district. You're not really. I have many resources. Believe me on this, I will use them to crush you politically. This whole thing must die quickly. The next time you call me it better be about how this whole issue is as dead as Cynthia Power and Anne Podreski," he disconnected.

Corey Bladel took the decanter and topped the glass, eight ounces full now, and went to an armchair and sat. He had a pretty good view of the Capitol areas. As he gulped down the Beam his hand was shaking. He felt dizzy. He had just spoken with the equivalent of an assassin. In a whispering voice he said to the office furniture, "And how the fuck am I going to do that Douthit, you sonofabitch."

CHAPTER 28

Sam Liebow resided in an extended care facility named Caring Manor. It was located in the lower west end of Davenport, about a mile north of the Mississippi River. Long ago in a past iteration it had been a hospital. As history moved it became a long-term psychiatric facility, more popularly known as an asylum. It was shut down in the late 1970s, an affront to human dignity declared a local newspaper. It stood idle until 1991 when a grifting entrepreneur bought the premises and surrounding land for a pittance. The place was refurbished and turned into a long-term care facility.

McAbee had been there once. It involved a tightly contested will concerning the intellectual competency of a male patient who had been recently diagnosed as having the onset of dementia. Bertrand had withdrawn the services of ACJ when he caught his client, the sick man's son, in some tawdry lies. His remembrance of the facility saddened him, increments of horror. He wondered once again about the futility involved in end of life approaches with humans as compared to animals who, when it was clear that the pet was dealing poorly with its life, was euthanized. It took strength of will to do it but it was ultimately seen as humane. He had made such a decision about his cherished white German shepherd Scorpio. If he had to make a list of five losses from death who could be brought back to life that dog would be on the list. All three of the great Western religions would have metaphysical and theological trauma if he voiced that opinion. Then again, the way theology was moving, he could very well have some support.

The place had two floors, one for the loss of mind, the other for the loss of physical function. He was not quite sure how the loss of both was handled but as long as Medicaid kept pumping in reimbursements he was positive that it was handled. According to Barry Fisk, Sam Liebow was dealing with both mental and physical issues. Liebow was 85 years old. McAbee went to a desk just behind the front doors and was greeted by a friendly-looking woman, aged about 40 with long copper colored hair and large glasses which took up half her face. She had a great smile, toothy and genuine. He asked about Liebow. She directed him to the second floor, east wing. He thanked her and went toward the elevator, stairs not visible. The open area around the elevator was occupied by six people in wheelchairs, old to older. They just sat there looking at the elevator door and each other, and now McAbee. Not sure what to do, he looked at them with a flowing glance and said, "Hi," with forced cheer. Three of the four women muttered a response like a hello, the other and one of the men just kept staring at him. The man to the far left, with a tray of sorts extending across the arms of his wheelchair, started to pound the tray lightly with his two hands and in moderate volume began a chant of two words repeated over and over until McAbee could no longer hear as he went upwards in the elevator, "Hot damn, hot damn," echoing in his head. He assumed the elevator to be a source of entertainment for the six of them who probably sat there hours a day.

Entry onto the second floor was less pleasant. The nurse's station stood centered between two long corridors, east and west if McAbee's unreliable inner compass was working today, which was east, which west? This woman did not have a cheerful smile. She looked beset with issues. He knew not to push at her porcupine-like exterior. "I'm looking for Sam Liebow. Would you put me in his direction?" Whatever living things porcupines feasted on, McAbee could identify with them whether they be plant or animal. Her look came down to a, 'oh you do, huh'? She looked at him with glasses a bit atilt, bloodshot eyes, and lips as tight as Ziploc bags. She never said a word yet she spoke in paragraphs with her expressions. She wrote something on a pad and then pointed abruptly to her right. A small sticky note was handed to him. On it was written 230. He went about ten steps and looked back. She was hunched over and looking at something on her desk.

The corridor had fifteen rooms on either side of it. The first room to his left was 201, across from it 202. At the end of the corridor he saw a large window. Room 230, sure enough, was at the very end across from 229. McAbee waded through the hallway filled with six medical carts, seven, at least, occupied wheelchairs and about ten aides. He had come at a busy time, just before lunch. He concluded that second floor east had to be the toughest of the units. But who knew?

Each room was about 25 feet in length, it was halved by a

white mobile screen that separated the room into two halves, and the bathroom was closest to the door thus making the front half of the room cramped as the bathroom ate about four feet of space from that sector. From his trip down the corridor he saw that all of the rooms seemed to be fashioned in the same way. It was a bleak affair, a warehouse.

The door to 230 was fully open. As he stepped in he saw a burly aide helping a one-legged man out of his bed. The aide appeared to be Hispanic. The aide looked at him inquiringly. McAbee said, "Sam Liebow?" Having settled the patient into a wheelchair the aide turned and pointed to the area behind the screen.

The window in the room was something out of Soviet architecture. It could not have been more than two feet by two feet and it was high enough to be beyond the sight line of a wheel-chaired resident. There was a man seated on a leatherette chair to the right of a standard issue hospital bed. It was Sam Liebow for certain. Sometimes it was hard to pick up 50 years of change, this was not the case with Liebow, bushy eyebrows, slightly cross-eyed, plush lips and sunken jaw. His facial characteristics had almost taken on the quality of caricature. He was in a bathrobe, around his neck a large crucifix. There was a small picture of Martin Luther on his bureau along with a copy of the bible. These two objects flew against McAbee's assumptions. There was nothing from Barry about his apparent religiosity. Liebow's use of Demosthenes' name suggesting a different mindset.

He wondered how much of Sam was left. Gently he said to the man who eyed him indifferently, "Sam Liebow of Memorial High School fame, I have come to seek your advice and opinion. My name is Bertrand McAbee." Liebow took in the verbiage but he hesitated in answering.

"You're right there. I taught there a long time." He nodded his head up and down so sharply that McAbee was alarmed.

At that moment the aide came in behind Bertrand and said to Liebow, "Mr. Liebow, lunch today?"

Again, but now a severe shake and a quick response, "No. No lunch today." The aide simply turned and walked back toward the door.

McAbee said, "I hope I'm not causing you to miss lunch. I can come back later."

Liebow eyed him more closely. "You are again?" Bertrand reintroduced himself to which he said, "I haven't had anyone seek my advice in years. Ask away."

"You were the inspiration there at Memorial for a pretty famous club whose members went on to lead extraordinary lives. The Demosthenes Club." McAbee stopped hoping that Sam Liebow would grab on.

He did. "Ah! One of my great ideas," his head snapped violently. "My advice to you is this. Take a great idea like that and bury it six feet under. Lot of trouble for me. Principal gets hollered at and then I do. That club happened only once and for one group. Bad idea in the end."

Liebow had a scratchy voice, unpleasant in its way. McAbee thought of a tea kettle and its pitch. "I've had my share of those kind of things."

"What kind of things?" he shot back.

"Good ideas like the Demosthenes Club turning into a bad idea." McAbee noting the memory loss.

"Yes. Let me tell you. Those kids, those damn kids.

Ungrateful. Never saw one of them after graduation. Not a damn one of them." He thumped the sides of his chair a few times as his head whipped to and fro.

"Those kids. That's where I need your advice. There were eight of them, nine if you included Archie Sanders..."

"Archie Sanders! A fake. Pure trouble. Had me hating black people. Me? Never. He quit. No advice on him except stay away from him," he said angrily.

McAbee slid away from Sanders. He was now sure that he had to keep Liebow in mental motion, to avoid pauses and the consequences of losing him. He said, "Anne Podreski."

Without hesitation he said, "Everyone knows that we only got half of that story. They all must have sworn an oath of loyalty because no one would talk with me. Or barely so." Head shake.

"Cynthia Power must have?" McAbee now taking a chance on a ticket of unknown value. He was apprehensive that Sam Liebow would retreat away from him.

"Better, but not much. She was just like the rest of them, no gratitude."

"So, she never came back to see you either?"

"Nope, nope. What time is it?"

"About noon."

"Always liked noon at Memorial. Teacher's lounge."

"I'll bet. About Anne?"

"Don't know. She turned on me too. They all did."

"How so?" McAbee inquired.

"Really a pack of animals. Great idea on paper. But I never understood their dislike for me, even for each other."

"I'm trying to find out about the 50% that no one knows about Anne Podreski's death. Any guesses?"

"We had a good time in the teacher's lounge. We hung together through some tough times. Did you ever know Hal Benson?"

"No, I don't think so." McAbee heard him slipping away again. "I taught. I know what you mean about teacher's lounges. Anne Podreski, that 50%?"

Liebow looked up as if coming out of a dream. "Podreski. Poor Anne. Got into knots with those other dogs. Went over to Sheriff's Department for investigation. Like having a dentist do heart surgery. A little advice. If those students grew into what I was seeing they are now monsters. Back then they were making their way." His head again shook violently but as it did the same aide came forward and began to place a seemingly heavy brace around Sam's neck.

The aide said to him, "Would you like some soup Mr. Liebow?"

"No. I'll eat in the teacher's lounge." The aide left, shrugging his shoulders.

"Sam? I need you to concentrate now. Are you saying that there was foul play around Anne's death?"

"I never said that," he yelled, trying to shake his braced head.

"I know. But if I said it would I be wrong?"

He studied McAbee for a bit and then said, "No."

From that point on McAbee's visit become one of prolonged disquiet from Sam Liebow. He spoke about his father, a Lutheran minister. Some teachers from Memorial High School, the St. Louis Cardinals, the movie *Casablanca* for which he had great admiration with a seemingly fathomless knowledge of the cast. Whenever McAbee would try to steer him back to the Demosthenes Club, Liebow would become agitated as he tried unsuccessfully to shake off the shoulder/neck device that looked as though it was forged for inquisitors to use when trying to hunt out heresy. McAbee stayed on for about 30 minutes until he heard an aide bringing back the man in the next section of the room. He noticed that Liebow was beginning to tire as even his vast knowledge of *Casablanca* was becoming confused.

Bertrand breathed deeply as he walked toward his Camry. What he learned was that Liebow had suspicions about Anne Podreski's death as well as deep resentment toward the club members. Interestingly, he was finding himself in the same place as Liebow.

CHAPTER 29

Their next meeting concluded with the handing over of $10,000 in, of course, cash. This was their standard charge for a breaking and entering by two seasoned professionals. This time there was a different demand than the arranged murder of Cynthia, that at $75,000 cash. A meticulous search for any records or documents that could be compromising – was now demanded.

The Thomas Group warned that there could very well be nothing. After all, the demanded hard disk to her computer had been removed when she was dying in her car. So no promises about anything else.

The Memorial High School library job was done by a solitary figure for $3000.

Nothing was being accomplished at the end of it all except for the main coup – the removal of Cynthia Power. But it was felt that there was some counterforce out there. There were no intentions of letting matters stand still.

CHAPTER 30

Augusta Satin's meeting with Phil Pesky was, as usual, loaded with recriminations and denouncements of ACJ, McAbee, especially Barry Fisk and Jack Scholz and now he added the gay psychiatrist Linda Rhine for good measure. When Augusta rose to the defense of Bertrand and Dr. Rhine she was silenced by his right hand's pointed finger. She now kept still. Pesky had all the cards. After a bit more of sustained abuse he went to his computer and stayed alert to it for a few minutes. He looked back at her at last and intoned authoritatively, "Anne Podreski materials are within the sheriff's purview. I'm not asking him for anything, the fucking idiot. Getting them is on you. Remember two things about it, it is ancient history and the investigation was done by inept slugs. Do you know Isaac?" She said she did but only slightly. "Well, show him a bit of leg, some cleavage, and a smile and you'll probably get it," now growling.

Augusta had no desire to find out why there was a problem between the two departments. She figured it involved jurisdiction and cooperation, a no-man's land in the relationship between the city and county. She sat there looking her most expectant self, "And Cynthia Power?"

"That's a different story. Rhine came in here horns out, making accusations against one of my detectives. Admittedly he doesn't show well, has the personality of a rock, but nonetheless he's pretty damn good. I looked over his report and saw no reason to change the assessment. So my assumption is that she hired McAbee and that's why you're here. The last time you came around here it was about the McNulty stuff. I think McAbee pulled a fast one there. When I give I expect a return."

"Chief, there are all sorts of details around that whole case. I know as much as you do but McAbee feels that he lived up to his side of the deal with you."

"Jesus!" in full exasperation.

"Come on Phil. I won't abuse your trust."

He sat back and gazed at her. They had both been detectives in the Rock Island Police Department way back when. Finally, he relented. "Okay, for old time's sake. But if I get burnt on this our relationship is over. Understood?"

"Of course."

Fifteen minutes later Augusta was walking west to the Sheriff's Office by the Scott County Courthouse. By good chance, Sheriff Tommy Isaac was in his office. She instantly remembered why Phil Pesky, a workout fanatic, would have his troubles with Isaac. He had to be 300 pounds, maybe 350, on a frame more fit for 170 pounds. His snub nose and crunched up cheeks made his eyes look odd, she thought pig-like but instantly suppressed the thought. He was an extrovert who came up to her as he patted her back and stared at her in appreciation. "Augusta Satin, I remember you from the St. Jude charity dinner. You're hard to forget.

I also know that you're a P.I. and you work for that well-known scoundrel McAbee," he snorted in, maybe, good humor.

She was sure that he had a mean streak; she wasn't about to elicit it from him. As she sat across from him while looking at the perpetual smile on Sheriff Tommy's face she told of her request. The more she talked the more he nodded. At the end of her recital, for reasons she wasn't sure, she thought it was expected that she would have to stand on his desk and do a tap dance. There was something louche about him.

He said, "Well, after I see that your P.I. license is valid I will be most happy to go to the catacombs, dig out the file, and make a copy just for you." Smiling all the way he looked away from her face and visually bore into her breasts.

He spent the next 20 minutes with her, alone and deep in the bowels of the building. She was unnecessarily touched at least ten times by him, close to but never in forbidden territory. He smiled, laughed and in a deniable way ogled her but at the end of it all she had a copy of the Anne Podreski file, with the last humiliation having to go up the stairway with him a foot behind her. She regretting wearing tight slacks.

When she entered Bertrand's office he got up and came towards her, probably to hug as was customary for them. She wanted nothing to do with it. She put her hand out in a stop motion, he did. "Let's sit at this table as I have quite a story for you about the files in my hands. If ever a woman needed a raise, it is I!"

First she told McAbee about Phil Pesky and his dire take on ACJ, that it was important for Bertrand to understand that it was necessary to give the Davenport P.D. any credit it could scrounge up and to keep it informed about happenings around Cynthia Power. He agreed and consented easily enough as he offered to get her a Coke, water, or coffee. She took a Diet Coke.

He looked at her in anticipation as if saying that wasn't all that hard. She brought up Tommy Isaac. He looked at her, was it, carefully? She asked him if he knew him.

"In fact I do a bit. Elected about three and a half years ago. ACJ actually had cooperated with the Sheriff's Department on an ID theft of one of my clients. I spent about ten minutes with him. Likes to laugh a lot. Hard to figure him. I think he's in hiding."

"What?" Augusta asked.

"I think all the laughing that Isaac does is camouflage. There is something about him that I think only his wife knows. Is there a story here?" he asked disingenuously.

"In fact Bertrand, there is a story!" She went on in full detail about the file of Anne Podreski, basement catacombs, the touching, the leers, the stairs and even her feeling that she was half expected to do a dance on the lecherous fool's desk. At that point she plopped down the two files on Bertrand's desk, took a long gulp of Coke, sat back and crossed her arms. She knew Bertrand's sense of humor and could see that he was angry on one hand at what she had to endure but, a big but, he was enjoying her exasperation and her offended manner. He once told her it was like watching a maniac walking up to a polar bear and making a fist at it. The incongruity of it all. She said after a few seconds, "Go ahead. I know. Laugh your head off!"

It took him a good five minutes of head-shaking and laughter to get back on track and to start to look at the files.

She enjoyed watching him laugh. He didn't do it enough. Through it all he was her very best friend and she knew that he loved her through his odd sense of humor.

CHAPTER 31

"I'm about to go to press on an article," Norm Schiffel intoned into McAbee's office phone. "I'd like to hear a response from you."

"What's this about Norm?" McAbee knew Schiffel. He was honest as reporters go. That meant, however, that he was frequently used as a lightning rod by people to advance agendas and bring to light matters best kept secret.

"I have information that you are opening an investigation into two deaths," he paused as if to look at his screen or notebook, "Cynthia Power and Anne Podreski. First of all, will you confirm this?"

"I have no comment on investigations done by ACJ." McAbee was taken off guard and disturbed.

"The name," he again went to his source, "Demosthenes Club has turned up in our database. Comment?"

"No. Nothing. No confirmation, no denial Norm."

"Come on McAbee, give me something."

"I'll tell you what. I will if you give me something in return."

"I'm listening," Schiffel said speculatively.

"Who would have given you this information?"

"Come on. You know I can't do that. Confidential sources."

"Bye Norm." McAbee disconnected.

He hit Augusta's number immediately. She answered, "Good morning Bertrand."

"Hi Augusta. Some bad news. *The Quad City Times* is aware of our interest in Power and Podreski. I don't know if Schiffel knows that we have the files but he was tipped about our involvement."

"Dammit Bertrand. It had to come from Isaac or Pesky. I'm thinking Pesky. Isaac was never told about Cynthia Power. Pesky knew I was headed over to Isaac. He wouldn't have to know whether or not I got the files, just that we were engaged with the two names. 95% sure it was Phil Pesky. He has never done that to me. A new low on his part. He's still steamed about Francis McNulty is my assumption and this is payback."

"Well, Schiffel is going with the article I can tell you that. So our involvement is out in the open. That's not necessarily a disaster. Maybe a rat will come out of the sewer."

The next morning Francine Korbel was about to leave her house for her three mile run. She still kept her subscription to *The Quad City Times*, the hard copy, which sat on her doorstep. She removed the protective wrapper and glanced at the first page, a story about President Trump, she flipped to the bottom half and then did a double-take. One of three stories read 'ACJ Probes Demosthenes Club.' She retreated to her study, alarmed and confused.

The byline was that of Norm Schiffel, an old-timer at the paper. Prize-winning. She knew him, having dealt with him on several stories related to Deere's international issues. He was quite good. Somehow he got the story.

She went back to her kitchen and sat at the bar area and read the story.

> In April of 1968, an honor student by the name of Anne Podreski drowned accidentally at Scott County Park. It was a heartbreaking event. Anne was a member in a very select group of students at Davenport Memorial High School. The group was called The Demosthenes Club and had only eight members. Demosthenes was a famed senator and orator in fourth century B.C. Athens.
>
> Her drowning was classified as an accident by the Sheriff's Department. It was an alcohol-related event.
>
> The Demosthenes Club is a celebrated happening because its members went on to fame and prestige. John Douthit has reached international fame in Silicon Valley. Corey Bladel is an important congressman from Illinois. Peter Waters had been an ambassador representing America in a number of posts. Megan White is a celebrated scholar at the University of Iowa and a television pundit. Francine Korbel, just recently retired, was a Vice President for International Marketing and Sales for Deere & Company.

> But death has chased the Club members. Stan Adair, a widely known litigator, died suddenly of a heart attack in 2001. Besides Podreski's tragic drowning, the recent suicide of Cynthia Power, a respected artist and social activist, has brought three deaths to the eight member club.
>
> Of great interest, however, in an exclusive to this paper, the ACJ Investigation Agency has opened inquiry into the deaths of Podreski and Power, thus leading to the speculation that the drowning and suicide are problematical events.
>
> ACJ President, Bertrand McAbee, would neither confirm nor deny the exclusive given to the paper. This secretive firm has been involved with a number of high profile cases during its almost two decade's existence.

Francine read the article twice as she muttered to herself, 'Jesus Christ, I can't believe this.' She had heard of McAbee. She recalled a piece on him somewhere. She had the strong impression from the article that he was not to be trifled with and yet she seemed to be the only one of the five club members to see this issue for what it was, a dangerous fucking dagger.

Bertrand took a call from Cynthia's attorney, Matthew Fox. Pat had indicated that he sounded furious.

"Matthew, hello."

"McAbee! I went along with your request to have your

people get into Cynthia Power's house. So you send four, three of whom were goons. They were led by some character out of the comic books. I was okay with the black woman. Enough said. I owed you, I paid. But when they left I installed a camera, it's a pen that I have. You'd never think it was a camera. So why do you send two of your creeps back there last night? They stole the pen but not before I saw them."

"Okay Matthew. What's your point?"

"My point is this. Why did you send your people back last night goddammit! What's so hard about this?"

McAbee sat back in surprise. This wasn't his operation. "Fox," he said with purposeful edge, "this wasn't my agency. We had nothing to do with this."

"Yeah right," was the sarcastic response.

"Listen to me Fox. This is serious business. I'm going to send over Augusta Satin to view what you have. Don't delete it and wait for a bit if you're going to report it to the police."

"Police! Forget it. I went to this house this morning. You'd never know they were there. But they had to be pros because they found that pen camera. They had some kind of equipment I think that could detect the camera."

"You're probably right," McAbee softened his tone, "I have another question, and by the way you have not paid your debt in full."

"Goddammit, I have to."

"No. You'll be paid when I say so. This is an important question. There might be more. I can tell you with almost certitude that they didn't find anything of value. Here's my question. Did she have a storage unit or a safety deposit box, or any other kind of location for materials? Including, by the way, your office?"

"McAbee! I saw the paper this morning. This whole thing could blow up. I've got every goddamn defense firm in Iowa and Illinois out to get my license."

"I'm sure of that," Bertrand said caustically, then catching himself for being a fool. He went on, "Strictest confidentiality. Just answer my question."

"No storage. Nothing in my office. Who am I to say that she doesn't have some aunt in Tacoma who has secret papers? Come on McAbee, give me a break."

"Mr. Fox, you are living up to the eponym. You didn't answer my question fully," McAbee left it there. They both knew the omission.

With obvious reluctance in his voice Fox said, "Safety deposit box. First Trust."

"Small, big?"

"Don't know. But yes, I have possession of the key and I am her surrogate, all rights included, and you're not getting near it."

"Can you open it?"

"Only with a notary present. I'm one but it doesn't count, obviously."

"Okay Matthew. Here's the deal to make the debt forever past and paid. I'll send my assistant Pat Trump, she's a notary, to the bank. Augusta Satin to your office to view your video of the break in – both happening today. Accommodate me please Matthew before this does, indeed, begin to spiral. If there's something in that box that bears on her supposed suicide I need it. How about it?"

"Jesus, okay!" he said in exasperation. "I've had two

cancellations today. Have them call me and I'll arrange a time. But let me say this. I hope I never see you again. Nothing is owed by either of us. Got it?"

"Yup. Something I fully concur with Matthew! We would start from scratch."

Four hours later Bertrand was sitting across from Augusta and Pat.

Augusta reported, "He only had about three minutes of video. Two people. Black clad including face cover. Gloves. They used some kind of small box that I saw just as they grabbed the pen-camera and shut it off. Pros. No doubt. Nothing else I can say. Fox went with me to the house. Flawless entry and exit. Jack Scholz would give them an A+."

"That's what I thought. Pat?"

"Let me tell you Bertrand, you hang around some freaky people. This Fox guy. Oh my God! We got into the deposit box, I had to use my notary stamp to attest to it. There wasn't much in there. Small box. A deed, car papers, envelope with some money. He counted it, $2000 in hundreds. One envelope. A three page report. He let me take it. It's not in English. Her mother's and father's birth certificates and that was it. Fox told me to say this to you, quote 'Have a nice life.' He wasn't the friendliest character I've ever met. He'd fit in with Barry Fisk and Jack Scholz if you ask me."

McAbee looked at the three pages. It was a Slavic language. "Pat, please call Zlata and ask her to come to the office. We need a translation; $300 if she can do it today."

CHAPTER 32

After the three page piece had been translated from its Cyrillic alphabet McAbee was perplexed. It was a Serbian translation of a purported Bosnian police investigation. In what way the Serbian report came into Cynthia Power's hands could only be guess work. The Bosnian report was made by an Adna Sidron, a detective in Sarajevo. It pertained to the murder of Toma Korpanja. Toma had been the name of Cynthia's lover in Bosnia; almost certainly it was the one and the same Toma in both instances. How the Bosnian report ended up in Belgrade, Serbia, a country that had battled Bosnian independence and was essentially at war in Bosnian Sarajevo at the time of Toma's murder could only be guessed at. How often had warnings been issued about the incendiary Balkans, McAbee wondered? The report read:

> Toma Korpanja, 53 years old, native of Sarajevo, was shot three times, each fatal, at the foot of the Latin Bridge. It occurred between 1:00 – 2:00 a.m. At that time the area was largely deserted. His body was

not reported until 5:40 a.m. Due to the extraordinary number of sniper-murders currently happening in Sarajevo a shade of neglect and indifference has suffused the city.

However, this particular murder is extraordinary and not explicable as are most being committed by Serbian snipers from the surrounding hills and apartment buildings. The deceased was on the payroll of the British Broadcasting Company (BBC) and he was a 'spot' reporter for Reuters and *The New York Times*, besides working for the Bosnian government.

He was known to be intrepid but also scrupulously careful in and around the streets of our endangered city. It is suspected by me that he was perhaps on an assignment for one of these news organizations. A betrayal by some supposed source is very possible.

Toma Korpanja was in a relationship with an American woman, Cynthia Power. She is involved with a Roman Catholic charity. She was questioned closely. She indicated that the subject was ensconced in an investigation about Serbian atrocities that might have a possible American association. Ms. Power was deeply distressed by the death of the subject.

A search of Mr. Korpanja's apartment found it to be ransacked. He lived three streets away from Ms. Power with his mother who at the time of the murder was visiting relatives in Mostar. The search of his apartment was thorough. Apparently all of subject's investigatory materials were removed. Neighbors in his apartment building were either ignorant of the break-in and search or were plainly uncooperative about any knowledge of the crime.

Inquiries to his colleagues and employers (BBC, etc.) were inconclusive.

It is the conclusion of this investigator that, under normal circumstances, a thorough scrutiny of the entire matter should be made. Current exigencies are unfortunately undoing this possibility. Notes will be maintained by me for some future inquiry.

Detective Adna Sidron
Sarajevo

On the bottom of the third page was a written note, 'I can get nothing further on this Miss Power. Sorry. From your friend Alexsandar Markovic'. Belgrade.'

McAbee read the police report three times, each time slowly. Cynthia Power had letters from Toma Korpanja, none was kept in her safety deposit box. But a police report was. The report was undated but he knew that it was referring to an event of about 23 years ago and that in fact, it had been prepared by a Detective Sidron. When exactly it had been secured by Markovic′ and sent to Power was not apparent but he knew that it was recent.

When Bertrand's brother Bill had been alive there were ways to answer these questions through his channels. Bill had run a massive investigatory agency with tentacles all over the world. He had been assassinated in Kabul four years back and his agency had splintered out.

He called Jack Scholz, "Need to meet privately with you. Have some time?"

"Sure. How about the City Cemetery on Rockingham Road?"

"Fine. Time?"

"Two."

"See you then."

Jack Scholz was paranoid. Sometimes he would come to McAbee's office but only on the condition that any conversations were reasonably neutral. It was understood by both of them that when McAbee said "privately" it meant out of the office, location chosen by Jack. Jack probably had good cause for his fears. He waded in dangerous waters among a cast of lethal men and women. A slight man of about five feet nine inches, he had been in the military; McAbee was never quite sure which branch. McAbee had heard, off-handedly, from one of Jack's confederates, an Irishman named Dineen, that Jack had led multiple operations into tough places deemed hostile to American interests. He was a ruthless man who had been extraordinarily helpful to Bertrand in a number of cases, Bertrand's ambivalence about his ethics notwithstanding.

City Cemetery was an isolated place in between an Oscar Mayer plant and a little to its west Ralston Purina. Almost all of the tombstones dated back into the 19th century. In that same century Rockingham had once been a city that vied with Davenport to its east for the Scott County seat of government. The election was won by Davenport. The illegalities that occurred in that election are legendary. At the end of it all Rockingham was incorporated into Davenport with only the name Rockingham being used for a street that weaved into the deep west end of Davenport. To add hurt to hurt the street traversed some of the shabbier elements of Davenport. McAbee always saw the cemetery as symbolic of a bad history, like Little Bighorn in Montana.

Scholz saw McAbee approaching him as he stood more or less in the center of this four acre graveyard. He thought that McAbee should have retired a few years ago, actually he should never have left academia. He was pressing his luck, some near skirmishes with death. His uneven tread across the pebbled narrow path was noted by Jack. He had mixed feelings about McAbee. At first he did a few odd jobs for him on the hopes that he would be noticed by his brother Bill and be brought into that international investigatory machine. But it never worked out that way. However, he stayed attached to ACJ and as the firm became more and more successful his services were called upon with frequency.

What he didn't appreciate was McAbee's hypocrisy as he would pretend to be on some moral high ground and yet when push came to shove, fully supported some of the violent tactics that Jack used. McAbee was conflicted, a bad angel on one shoulder and a good angel on the other. In his judgment he felt that McAbee was drifting to the dark side even as his two female employees, Augusta Satin and Pat Trump, were trying to pull him back.

McAbee knew, but it was always inferred, never explicit, that Jack had contacts in the dark arts all over the world and had access to a number of military advancements in weaponry and soft assets. So it was of interest that a 'private' meeting was going to happen.

"Bertrand, what's up?" McAbee's gray, blue eyes looked through glasses at him. His eyes had become more calculating and more focused than in the past when they would occasionally float around like a buoy. He was balding, stood about five feet, ten inches, light skinned and with a wide but thin mouth, high cheekbones. His weight was under control and he was clearly in shape and doing well for someone who had crossed the border into his 70s.

McAbee said, "Let's walk." He summarized the developments around the case of Cynthia Power in his well-spoken voice. He was to the point with little in the way of unnecessary embellishment.

Jack instantly realized that McAbee was putting his hand into a beehive. He asked, "You're pretty sure it was a murder?"

"Yes. There's no bulls-eye target that's been hit but there are too many arrows around the bull's-eye. Too many indirects not to be direct in sum."

"And you're linking this to the Demosthenes Club?"

"Again, indirects. I studied both investigations. The Sheriff's back in 1968 was and is a piece of crap. All eight of the students had been drinking. Cynthia Power was not swimming, she was at the campsite puking her guts out. The seven, Podreski included, were pretty wasted. The coroner determined that Podreski blacked out and drowned. By the time that was realized by the others, she was under water and dead, probably by five or ten minutes. Accidental drowning. Cynthia Power a different story. Davenport P.D. is fully convinced it was a suicide. Their report is absolute and shows no doubt. But we know differently. The missing hard drive, this new break-in, the missing school newspapers, it again comes down to around the bull's-eye. Too many arrows Jack."

"May I ask Bertrand? Why are you doing this? It's a dangerous case."

"For Augusta. Pure and simple. I'd do the same for you."

Scholz liked that quality in McAbee. It was a solid answer that he himself would have given to any of his colleagues who were asking for help. "Got it. So what do you want me to do?"

Bertrand told him about the police report from Sarajevo by way of Belgrade. He needed information on the two detectives, Sidron and Markovic´. Were they alive? Did Jack have contacts in Bosnia and Serbia who could find out?

In the meantime Bertrand was going to try to make contact with the five remaining members of the Demosthenes Club.

Jack said, "You're into this all the way, aren't you?"

"Yup," he said, as they separated.

CHAPTER 33

Augusta Satin was sure that she was allowed into Dr. Megan White's office in Iowa City for one primary reason – she was African American. Barry Fisk's background on White portrayed a woman who rode the great white horse of justice and caring. Other information that he dug up, as only he could, pointed to a mean-spirited academic jackal. So, she concluded, stay neutral until other data presented themselves.

White would not know the purpose of Augusta's visit, one that was mandated by Bertrand who was himself trying to nail down Congressman Corey Bladel and retired Deere Vice President Korbel at parallel times.

White's office gave her a fine view of the now tame Cedar River, known for its vile flooding temper every decade or two. White asked, "So you are interested in student killings? A noteworthy topic as even in Iowa City, this has occasionally occurred. How can I help you? It is not a topic to which I give scientific study, let me say at the outset. Nor have I ever personally been touched by this violence."

Augusta was still trying to figure out the best time to

drop the name Anne Podreski. "Thanks for seeing me on this short notice, I know how busy you must be."

"Oh my! You have no idea. Once you get on the national stage everything changes."

"I'm sure. You are so prominent on so many important social issues," Augusta said as she was beginning to take a dislike to this arrogant woman whose studied ways of asserting self-importance became overbearing in her speech and manner.

Megan White looked back at Augusta, waiting for her to go on. When she didn't, she said a bit exasperatedly, "Go on Ms. Satin."

"I'm looking into killings in Iowa generally, and in the past specifically."

"Twentieth century?"

"Yes," Augusta said trying to relax her a bit before springing on her.

"I imagine if your range is 1900-1999 you have quite a number. Male and female?" The social scientist was trying to get the scope and angle of Augusta's inquiry.

"Actually, it's much more precise, although it is in the 20th century and involves a female," Augusta said as she noticed Megan White's eyes narrow just so slightly.

"Go ahead," White said just short of a command.

"I'm looking into the death, and there is some conjecture, killing of someone whom you knew, Anne Podreski," Augusta said awaiting the consequences of her treachery.

"And you are who again?" Now with a full stare and a pink flash across her face.

"As I told your teaching assistant, I'm Augusta Satin.

I'm with ACJ Investigations and I'm a licensed private investigator in Iowa."

White immediately got up, walked briskly to her office door, opened it and asked her teaching assistance, Derrick, "How did this woman," she pointed back dismissively toward Augusta, "represent herself?"

He looked down at his pad and said meekly, "Augusta Satin wanting help with an investigation into student killings," Derrick responded with a tremulous voice.

She came back into the office having slammed her office door shut and quickly swished her way back to her seat. "Listen to me! I'm aware that your disreputable agency has thrust its way into the drowning of Podreski. If you had identified yourself fully you never would have gotten within a mile of this office." She concluded with full stare and stridency.

Augusta found it interesting that she wasn't commanded to leave and wondered what was behind that tactic. With all the placidness that she could summon, she looked back at unsmiling White. "Nothing that I said was untrue. You are doing me a wrong." Augusta was playing a card that she detested using but given the object she felt justified – white guilt that Megan had cultivated to her advantage for decades. She proclaimed to be an expert on it.

"Please. You were engaged in misleading behavior," Megan remarked getting a hold on herself.

"We blacks have learned to be crafty in this white dominated society," she responded in full self-disgust. She noticed that self-righteous Megan White was wavering, reluctant to get on the wrong side of an affronted black woman. The guilt card was working.

"Let me see your P.I. identification," White said probably trying to gain time. That done, she replied, "Anne Podreski drowned. She wasn't killed. Cynthia Power," she shot a pointed index finger at Augusta, "committed suicide. I know nothing else except that your agency is trying to dig up dirt to hurt the living members of the Demosthenes Club. Why any self-respecting woman would involve herself in this character assassination is beyond me. And yes I am aware that this cretin McAbee opened this case. And you're not here just about Anne. Cynthia too."

Augusta raised an outstretched hand toward White so as to slow her down and as a sign of peace. White sat back from the gesture. "No one is accusing anyone, least of all you. But some strange things have happened. There has been interference with ACJ, interference with Cynthia's belongings and house. What I am saying is this. If nothing is amiss why all the pushback?"

"I'm not aware of any of this. I don't even know where Cynthia lived. We were not friends. Never were. Same goes for Anne Podreski."

"Can you tell me about the night Anne died?"

"Not much to say. Get the report."

"I read it. Pretty thin."

"We were all drinking. We were 17, 18. Celebrating. There's a small man-made lake in that park. We decided to swim. We went down there. Yes, we took our clothes off. All of us pretty high. Suddenly someone, one of the guys, don't remember who, yells out Anne's name. Nothing. We go on frolicking. Finally, it was Douthit, screams for us to focus. We do. She's found. She's dead. We freak out."

"Any attempt at resuscitation?"

"Yes. Douthit. I remember him trying. Someone runs back, there's an office at the park entrance. Forget who. Emergency vehicles and all the rest. A disaster. It was a goddamn accident. We got into trouble, underage drinking and all that. Gets buried, forgotten. And now you are trying to get us. Who the hell is funding this?"

"Cynthia Power? Was she swimming?"

"No. She was puking her guts out, sickly girl that she was. Don't think twice about her, she was a psychological mess then and always would be. Suicide was a smart way out for her. That's enough. Now please leave."

When Augusta was driving east across I-80, she reflected that she had just met a very nasty woman. Barry Fisk had her figured out. Takes one to know one.

CHAPTER 34

Jack Scholz drove southward on U.S. 67 to Keokuk, Iowa, the southern-most city in eastern Iowa before the state touched Missouri. It had a population of about 10,000. On the way there, he had passed through Muscatine, Burlington, and Fort Madison, all Iowa Mississippi River cities, smaller Illinois cities just east across the river. He had been given the name of Jim Edgington by his source, Mason French, in the Defense Department. Edgington had been an operative for the CIA before and during the Sarajevo siege. Edgington's cooperation with Jack had been arranged already, Jack's *sub rosa* network working like a well-oiled machine. He had been forewarned by French that Edgington had a bad heart, to be very careful around him and under no circumstances cause him stress. Edgington was a good man and an ally in the underground system in which Jack played so heartily.

He lived in a trailer home on a three acre piece of land. The dirt road that led to him was about four miles west of town. Jack pulled up near the trailer and just sat in his pickup. Edgington knew he was coming. Besides the bad heart he was said to be a bit paranoid, not dangerous, but definitely suspicious and spooked. Jack just waited. About five minutes later the trailer's door opened and Edgington walk-limped to the pickup.

Edgington was 60 years old according to Mason's profile. He walked as if he was 80. He was bald and almost obese. He leaned on a cane. He came to the truck door, threw his cane into the back of the pickup, opened the door and after about 20 seconds of hard breathing and ass moving he settled in. He said, "I'm Jim. You're Jack. What do you want to know?"

"I'm going to drive. You okay with that?"

"Yeah. Probably good to get away from this area. Utility truck out here a few days ago. Alarms raised when I see that shit."

Jack wasn't unsympathetic when he heard that comment, himself being suspicious to the extreme. As they drove around the rural roads of southeastern Iowa, Jack, very carefully, started to debrief the man. Edgington spoke in a low bass voice. "I was 37 when I was sent over there. I was young and in good shape. Not the mess you see now. We, the CIA – let's be clear, had a mission over there in Sarajevo. Also had one in Belgrade but that was another affair. It would be accurate to call the Belgrade one espionage."

"CIA pretty active? Field offices?"

"Yeah. The works. The whole mess there is about religion. Moslems and Orthodox Christians. The Roman Catholics pretty much stay out of things unless you touch western Bosnia. Then the Catholic Croats act up. But I understand you're interested in Sarajevo and one of the killings there. Right?"

"Yeah, basically. Did you know any government officials in Sarajevo?"

"Sure. They knew who I was. I'm good at languages and I got pretty close to a few of them. I had a nice budget that I could dip into. The whole Balkan area is fueled by bribes. Pay for play. We were paying and playing on both sides for a while. Pro Serb, pro Bosnian until President Clinton played hardball with the Serbs who lost their sense of proportion. The breaking point was Holbrooke and the slaughter in Srebrenica."

"How dirty did the Serbs play?"

"Well, I just missed being killed in Sarajevo. They sat up on the hills around the city, some apartment buildings too, and just indiscriminately shot people. Old men, women, kids, whatever. Everyone was target practice. They used scopes to perfect their shots. Terror. As I say, they missed me by six inches. Everyone was a Bosnian to them and every Bosnian needed to be murdered unless, of course, they were Orthodox clergy. Doesn't mean that they didn't kill the Orthodox Christians, they couldn't tell that, but it wasn't intended. Terror trumped identity. It's noteworthy, however, that no Orthodox priests were ever killed by the snipers as far as I know. Their costume was easily discernible," Edgington said bitingly.

"They had a police department in Sarajevo?" Jack asked.

"Sure. Pretty thin, pretty ineffective. Law and order was a victim just like the people. You're going somewhere but you sure are indirect. Not your style from what I was told about you Mr. Scholz."

Jack laughed, realizing that Edgington had been briefed about him just as he had about Edgington. "You're right, it's not my style. I have some names that I'd like to run by you."

"More than 20 years ago. But go ahead. I used to have a great memory."

Jack said, "Toma Korpanja."

Involuntarily it seemed to Jack, Jim Edgington moved his left arm and sent a long glance at Jack. "Korpanja was murdered. I knew him pretty well. He was honest by the standards of the day, a beneficiary of American largesse. But in his case I always thought he passed the money to those who needed it. A good man. Could never figure out how he got lured out to the Latin Bridge at one in the morning. He was no one's fool."

"He had a girlfriend. American. Ever met her?"

"Yeah. Catholic stuff. She worked out of the Cathedral. Met her once or twice. But they were an item. Could tell that a mile away. But I didn't really know her."

"Any idea about Toma Korpanja's murder?" Jack asked.

"Nah. Too many possibles. The goddamn city was like the Wild West. But I'll tell you he was no lover of us Americans. He liked *me* I think, but you know how treachery parallels suspicion and distrust."

"You said that Uncle Sam played both sides of the street. You had counterparts working in Belgrade?"

"Yep."

"And they knew what the Serbs were doing?"

"Yep. The Serbs were using Kalashnikovs, dangerous as hell with good scopes. They weren't just in the hills around the city. They occupied some apartments and some sections of the city. Bigger city than you might think, about 250,000. The Serbs were getting American funding. Above my pay grade as to where it was coming from." Edgington was moving his large torso. Uncomfortable.

"Korpanja. Can you tell me more about him?"

"Nice way about him. Urbane is a good word. Slick, another. When he drank that poison rat gut alcohol they served there during the siege days he'd open up a bit. Hated the Serbs and the Russians whom he felt were their primary supporters. But he knew there was more to it. He'd smile at me and say 'I like you Jim but you represent American duplicity. American people are essentially good but your government is prone to evil. I don't think your president has a half idea of how involved you all are in dirty work and that means here in Bosnia. Someday you will be found out.' On a scale of 1 – 10 with 10 as sheer hate, the Serbs would hit a 10, Russians too. Americans? 5."

"What exactly did he do?"

"Oh. He worked in their equivalent to our spook agencies. Minor department. No resources to speak of. He used a cover, reporting for the BBC and some other organizations. I'd give him a few thousand once in a while. He didn't or couldn't give me much back. But once in a while he'd throw something out there."

"For example?"

"Orthodox clergy in the city. Always suspected them. Gave me names."

"And?"

"I was an officer. I sent the names forward. Made me look good and justified continuing to give him some bucks. I didn't sleep with the guy you know. Just occasional meetings."

"Another name. Adna Sidron?"

Edgington looked over at Jack in surprise when Jack looked over at him. He said, "You're looking into the murder of Toma Korpanja. Good luck with that," he said with a finality.

"You're right about Korpanja. But I'm asking you about Adna Sidron?"

"Well, she was a detective in their police department, homicide, for whatever that was worth, no resources. She's about five feet, weighs about 20 pounds and is intense, a ball of fire. Moslem. When Korpanja was murdered she came to my apartment. My name was in a small book that he kept. She didn't believe a word that I said. I could tell. Tough little spider."

Jack said, "Should she have believed a word that you said?"

"Hah!" Edgington laughed. "Of course not. But, actually, in reference to Toma she should've. I was very upset about his murder. He was one of the better ones over there. Look! If you think I had anything to do with his murder, I didn't."

"Tell me more about Adna Sidron. Do you think she's still alive?"

"Who knows? I can say one thing about her, one clear, indelible impression – honest. Scary honest. She smelled my job. She knew that I traded in dishonesty and misdirection."

"We have papers on her investigation of Korpanja's murder. It went nowhere. She was frustrated."

"As I said, it was the Wild West over there. Life was cheap. Murders ubiquitous."

"So let me give you some more. Korpanja's American lover, Cynthia Power. She pretty much crashed after Korpanja's murder from what we can make out. Somehow, we have no idea exactly how, she received a copy of Adna

Sidron's investigation report of the murder from of all places Belgrade. A Serb translation of Bosnian sent to Power by a Belgrade detective named Alexsandar Markovic′. We're trying to figure out how that was possible. Also, how did Markovic′ know Power as he wrote a short note to her in the translated report?"

Edgington reacted, "Well, the short answer is it's the fucking Balkans! There are no rules. I know the name Alexsandar Markovic′ but I honestly can't tell you why. I just don't remember. But the name is familiar. As to your exact question there were spies all over the goddamn place. For a bribe you could get anything. My assumption is that Belgrade might have been interested in Korpanja. Maybe they wanted to make sure that the case deep-sixed. But the Power woman? How she got a hold of this investigation report? God knows. Was she the type who would go out on her own and try to dig?"

"She had a reputation for being obsessive."

"Well, that may be the answer. Bribes could get you pretty far over there. If she got that report she didn't get it from the likes of Adna Sidron. But Markovic′ maybe. I just can't connect his name to something I know. I'll let my mind wrap around it."

"One more thing. Korpanja's murder. Is there any way we were involved?"

He glared at Jack. "No way from our operation in Sarajevo!"

"How about out of Belgrade? Our operation there."

"Anything is possible. But if we were involved it never came back to me. But our Belgrade operation was nasty, bad people. But I just don't know."

Jack found his way back to the trailer. He gave Edgington an envelope with twenty $100 bills. He said to Edgington, "If you remember, call this number."

As Jack drove through Burlington a call came through. "Yeah?"

"Got it on that name Markovic'. He was a crook. Highest bidder. But if you wanted something done he'd be it. Not a Bosnian Serb. A Serbian Serb. Similar but not identical. He was right out of Belgrade. Funny. Eating some Rice Chex and bang it came to me. Worked any side of any fence. I never had need of him. But this Power woman – she could get it from him with the right offer."

CHAPTER 35

Maria Sanchez lived in Davenport's west end. She seemed happy to talk with McAbee who sensed a lonely woman, whose expressive brown eyes had a droop to them as if she was closing off half the world.

Her house was simple, every object and wall hanging placed perfectly. He thought of Scandinavian simplicity done in Mexican style. She invited him into her small living room. Maria had a quiet elegance about herself and her surroundings. He declined a beverage.

"So you mention the name of a woman whose memory brings me to melancholy. Cynthia sought grace but it was never given to her. But I do not accept her suicide."

"Neither do I," McAbee said, "that's part of the reason why I'm here."

"How did you connect me to Cynthia?"

"Her brother Eric. He told me that a close friend had helped with her mother's funeral in 1989. I called Brook's funeral home. They keep good records and you made it easy for me since you haven't moved since then." He smiled.

"Yes. Funeral homes are quite good at that and no I haven't moved."

"When was the last time you saw her?"

Maria tapped the sidearm on her chair. She answered hesitantly. "I've known Cynthia off and on since grammar school. She travelled for much of her life. But we kept pretty close when she was in town. I am happy that you are in doubt about the suicide. Perhaps I can help."

"Your comment about grace. That's saddening to me. I never knew her but your insight strikes a chord with my observation. Did she have a shortage of luck? What you call grace?"

"Luck? No. It's about grace, the supernatural. She was a tested Catholic. I think that God was testing her. I don't think I could have held up, personally. Every time she found a ray of happiness it was snatched from her. The story of Job."

"How'd you connect specifically?"

"We were in a Catholic youth group, our parish, Holy Family. She'd always go to the extreme, though. I think that she was drawn to fire by God."

"God or her personality?"

"I have never seen much of a difference. God is in every atom, every pore of us. We are in constant dialogue with the divine."

It had been some time since McAbee had encountered this extreme version of Catholicism. Maria Sanchez was a true believer. "In my investigation Maria, I'm turning up some things that are bothersome. But it's hard to connect the dots. May I ask you some questions?"

"Of course."

"Did you attend Memorial High School?"

"Yes, I was a classmate of hers."

"Did she ever talk about the Demosthenes Club?"

"Oh yes. She was sorry she had ever consented to joining it. But she wouldn't quit. Wasn't the type."

"Did she ever mention Anne Podreski?"

"She was so ashamed of herself. She wasn't in the lake area when Anne died. She was sick. And then her conscience kicked in. She felt that she could have been nicer to Anne. Cynthia had a highly developed conscience."

McAbee inquired, "Did she ever suspect foul play around that death?"

"No," Maria looked at McAbee quizzically.

"When was the last time you saw her?"

"It was a while. We'd be like that. We'd drop in and drop out," she smiled. Then she added, "A few months. She was going to write a book about that outlandish Demosthenes Club."

"Outlandish?"

"Cynthia thought that they all pretty much hated each other. They were so competitive, so ambitious. She was trying to figure out how they all became so successful and maybe if they had changed. I thought that to be unlikely."

"Did she dislike them?"

"No. Cynthia was not a hater. I think she was perplexed."

"So when she got into the book research you weren't in touch."

"No. I was in Las Cruces for two months. She knew I was going."

"So, going back years, she's gone for a long time. She comes back for her mother's funeral in 1989. Anything of note there?"

"Her brother? Eric. A real louse. I helped her get it

together. The funeral. Cynthia just kept getting whacked, it seems to me."

"During that period, anything about the Demosthenes Club? Anne Podreski?"

"No. I can't remember anything like that coming up."

"Did she ever bring up Corey Bladel?"

Her eyes widened a bit before she answered. "Yes. She had kept in touch with him. No big deal but I recall her having a meal with him. She didn't really like him but for some reason she stayed in touch. I think it was a bad experience for her. That was an exception. She wanted to keep herself aside from them. And then, kind of on a whim, she sets out to find the key to their success. I think the article in the paper a few years ago struck her."

"She had a romance in Bosnia. Heavy. Then the man was murdered over there in 1995. From what I can make out she went off the rails."

"I see that you are digging into this. She did speak with me when she came back here. She went from heaven to hell with that relationship. It was always like that with her. She never could find peace or stability."

"The man's name was Toma. There's a mystery around his death. It appears that she made some inquiries. This Toma was a government official and a reporter of sorts."

"She said that his killing had made no sense. Once, we went out and we both got a little tipsy. We took a cab home, actually." She smiled. "But she said something that I found upsetting. Later on, a few weeks, I brought it up to her. She became defensive. I never mentioned it again."

"What was it?"

"Americans. She suspected American involvement."

"Allow me on this. American involvement around Toma's death?"

"Yes. Very clearly. It was a glancing comment but it was said in anger. Then she had moved on."

"When did this occur?" McAbee asked.

"2006, 2007?"

"He would have been dead over ten years."

She gazed at McAbee before saying, "Not in her heart, sir, not in her heart."

CHAPTER 36

The days subsequent to Douthit's dire phone call found Cory Bladel in a state of panic. He had tried unsuccessfully to speak with Megan White in Iowa City. She disconnected with a, 'Don't call me again, goddamn you.' Peter Waters, as usual, was unreachable, his wife in a dangerous New England snarl. He wondered whether New England had wolverines. And Francine Korbel launched the following at him, 'Corey, I'm glad you understand the damage that you did. Poor Cynthia. Shame on you. But from here on it I will say nothing more about the matter. I was Paul Revere and now my mission is over.' She disconnected. She sounded as though she had read a prepared message, almost as though she suspected the call was being taped. It was alarming when someone like Francine decided to back away. He was not sure how to play the Douthit threat. But it sounded as though everyone was going to lie low even though there was an awareness that some Davenport investigation firm was playing around with Cynthia's death and in turn Anne Podreski. Knowing nothing meant knowing nothing, he concluded.

Francine Korbel told herself to back off as she kept a

sideways glance at the ACJ Agency. She knew of McAbee by hearsay and had then Googled the firm. They were not lightweights. Some cases that ACJ had been involved with were extraordinary. She found out that McAbee had gotten into the investigation business through his prominent brother who was assassinated in Kabul, that he had been a classics professor at St. Anselm College in Davenport. She called a woman friend who worked for the largest local firm in investigations and asked about McAbee. Francine had taped the telephone conversation. It went like this. 'McAbee? ACJ. Don't use them.' That potential employment of McAbee was Francine's cover for the inquiry. 'He's a dilettante,' she continued. 'Doesn't belong. No one respects him in this line of work. Doesn't belong to any of the local agencies. Lone wolf. Police departments up and down the river have him on their hit list. He was a professor. Ancient Greece. Doesn't know a thing about the real world. He has some operatives who are universally seen as crooked and dishonest. Dates some black bitch who used to be a detective in Rock Island. I'm not saying you should use my firm but I *am* saying don't use him.' Francine thanked her for her candor.

When she was called by McAbee's secretary, Pat, she assented to a meeting, curious about McAbee and just what he might or might not know. He would be happy to come to her house or meet her, Pat said, wherever she designated. She chose to go to his office, intrigue again kicking in.

His secretary had a fox-like face, she was pleasant but a bit frigid in manner. She offered Francine a refreshment which she declined as she eyed the office. Nothing unusual except for a child's chair that sat incongruously among normal chairs. Pat said that McAbee was finishing off a phone call and would be with her momentarily. So much for conversation. She looked at Pat more closely and thought for a split second that she had seen her before, somewhere. Meanly, she thought of a nature show that was on PBS a bit ago. It was about foxes.

The inner door opened and out came McAbee whose picture she had seen on the Google feed. He was pretty old. He should think about retiring to Arizona rather than tangling with the formidable Demosthenes Club. But she was surprised by his vigorous handshake as he drew her into his office. There was a certain graciousness about him as she noted his quick and very mobile eyes X-raying her. By the time they sat across from each other she had the distinct impression that she had been disrobed and dressed again in that 20 second span. His eye color shifted between gray and blue depending on the shafts of sun that played hide and seek with the outside clouds. She now wondered about the wisdom of coming down to his office. They negotiated each other's names, Bertrand and Francine.

"Francine, my agency has been employed to look into Cynthia Power's death. It's a real puzzle to me to tell the truth."

Korbel thought that it was unlikely that this bastard ever told the truth. She decided to hold back and play his game for a bit. "I understand. I was shocked. She was working on a book about the Demosthenes Club. Are you familiar with that group?"

"Oh yeah. Inescapable once we started to look into her life. Quite a group. There are only five of you left?"

Undeniable fact. She said, "That's right. Am I the first to be contacted?"

"Yes, by me personally. I had one of my associates visit," he looked at his indecipherable pad, "Dr. Megan White in Iowa City yesterday."

It was time to poke the bastard a bit. "I'm sure she was very cooperative," she said blandly while thinking that Megan probably threw a hissy fit. She wondered if the 'associate' was the black bitch – probably given Megan's ultra-liberal views about identity politics. This shrewd sonofabitch sitting across from her would have figured out that tactic in a millisecond.

"Actually, most of that conversation had moved away from Cynthia Power and onto another member of the club, Anne Podreski."

"Is that right? How odd. Anne has been dead for decades," she mused disingenuously but thinking that this clever character had moved his queen in the chess game.

"You know? I didn't know anything about the Demosthenes Club until I scanned an article in *The Quad City Times*. Incredible talent. You seemed to be so together, so supportive of each other," he said neutrally.

McAbee was playing a game and he had some moves that she couldn't predict. She wasn't sure what he knew. She responded, "Well, we were high school kids. Teens. You know how that is. Everything is in fast motion. The fact is that we pretty much spread out across the globe. Contacts with each other were spare as you can imagine. It wasn't the world of Facebook."

"Got a hint of that from a perusal of Cynthia's papers and diaries."

Shit, she thought. So Cynthia left things around and this cunning bastard was leaning in on her. She cautioned herself to keep her cool. "Yes, well Cynthia was quite a travelling vagabond herself. Each, in our own way, was. So, Bertrand, how can I help you?" She was going to finesse him away from his strategy, she hoped.

"I'm just trying to figure out whether or not my limited and small agency should pursue this or not?"

"Pursue what?" she said abruptly and with a purposeful hint of her well-known acerbity.

He looked closely at her, again the stripping look but now point blank at her eyes. "Well, the possible murder of Cynthia and from things noted in her materials the questions around the drowning of Anne Podreski."

"What?" Francine said in false horror.

"It seems that one of your cohorts in the Demosthenes Club had indicated to Cynthia that Podreski's death was not what it seemed. Cynthia Power became distraught," he stopped and let his statement sit.

As she reflected on this later she made a mistake right at this point. "This is news to me."

"Oh." Silence slipped in between them. "It seems that she thought she talked to you about this very drowning on three occasions. That's what I have in my possession. Her notes you know. Was Cynthia on any psychotropic drugs by any chance?" He asked in full cuteness.

"She must have. I have no memory of such. What else can I help you with?" She looked at her watch. She desired to jump across the small table and slug the smug bastard.

"So there's nothing to her concern about Anne Podreski's death?"

"Of course not. I thought you wanted to talk about Cynthia? This street that you're going down in damn absurd," she said winding herself into attack mode.

"I assume also that you feel similarly about Cynthia. A suicide?"

"Of course. Cynthia was always a bit unbalanced. She was doing a book about the club and I think that she became discouraged."

"How so?"

"She compared her life to the rest of us who were in the club. She was a failure! A mediocre artist and a useless charity worker. Let it go McAbee. You're wasting your time and at your age you don't have much left," she said with a snarl. She arose and left McAbee's office saying over her shoulder to Pat, "Don't call me again Miss."

In the elevator down she remembered where she had seen Pat. She had been a fill-in at Deere. She was once part of an agency that provided temp help to Deere executives. The bitch had changed, of course, but once a fox always a fox.

McAbee awaited a visit from Augusta. He had a lounger in his office and there he sat thinking about this case. Last night he and Jack Scholz had driven around the streets of Moline in Jack's pickup. Scholz had reported his meeting with Jim Edgington of Keokuk. Barry Fisk had within 45 minutes determined that the Sarajevo detective Adna Sidron was still alive but she now headed a small investigatory agency there, having retired from the police department in 2005. Markovic', on the other hand, had become the assistant police chief in Belgrade. If there was a worthwhile path to them it would manifest itself eventually. In the meantime, Jack would see if more could be determined about Toma Korpanja's death.

Bertrand continued to think about the presenting case, did Cynthia Power commit suicide? It was clear that Corey Bladel was the cause of her inquiry into Podreski's death. Furthermore, that had precipitated Cynthia's re-entry into the Demosthenes Club only now with an entirely different agenda. Was it possible that one of the members of that club would be frightened enough to believe that her murder was warranted? A huge risk to erase an ostensibly small risk. There really was little information about Podreski's drowning. He decided to request a visit with Corey Bladel who according to Cynthia was an unpleasant letch. He would need leverage to get a meeting with the congressman.

At that moment Augusta Satin came into the office. She gave him a fuller account of her disastrous meeting with Megan White in Iowa City. She concluded by saying, "I don't know if they are all colluding or we are out on a limb that's being sawed off as we crawl out farther and farther."

"The tipping point for me was when someone went after the student papers at Memorial High School. It just made no sense to do that. I guess that they assumed that if I went there and the librarian, who now distrusts me, found them missing she would merely let it go as some kind of unfortunate event. I don't think I was followed. I just was a step ahead. For all I know they don't know that I have all of the relevant copies for those two years. That said, I didn't get that much from the papers. That theft backfired. Instead of just walking away from this as being inconclusive I'm getting more involved. I'm going to try to see Corey Bladel. Francine Korbel felt it necessary to lie about her meetings with Cynthia about the drowning of Podreski. She's one interesting customer."

"Who isn't in this?"

McAbee smiled and then asked Augusta to pursue Archie Sanders while he would try to track down Bladel.

He concluded the meeting with, "Augusta, I feel that there is a malevolent instrument in this. That it is parallel to us but instead of assisting us it is aiming at us."

CHAPTER 37

It took a day, some help from Barry Fisk and her shaking down of contacts in the African American community, to finally locate Archie Sanders. He was alive and living in Ames, Iowa, home city of Iowa State University located 30 miles north of Des Moines pretty much in the center of the state.

Augusta left Rock Island at 12:45 p.m. and arrived in Ames at 4:10 p.m. Sanders was retired from the university. He had been a janitor in the fieldhouse. Augusta was chagrined as by all appearances the young Archie was quite talented. Like so many events in America dealing with race she figured that much of Archie's lack of success was in the quagmire of racism. He lived in a small housing development for people 55 and over. It was located just off of Highway 69 (Grand Avenue) and 11th Street. The neighborhood wasn't hell but surely not heaven. McAbee would say it smacked of purgatory. She shook her head and smiled as she hunted for a parking place. She backed into one a block away and headed toward the three story building that looked as though it had five apartments per floor. She was incorrect. It had four apartments per floor. The end unit was apparently double-sized. Archie's apartment was on the third floor just to the right of the small elevator. The building had a smell to it of fried fish. She wondered whether Archie was home and what he'd be like. Barry could find no phone number for him or any email locator.

She knocked at his door and heard a sluggish "Yeah?" She immediately responded in her gentlest of voices, "Hi, Archie Sanders? I've come over from the Quad Cities. I'd like to speak with you about a few things. Be mighty grateful." There was a long hesitation from behind the door. Finally she heard a chain being slid across, a double lock being thrown and the door opening. Archie Sanders stood there in front of her, in baggy brown pants and a stained yellow tee shirt. He was in bare feet.

He grumbled, "Lady, if you're here to cause trouble, tell me now and we'll call it a draw."

"No. No trouble." Archie was a dark-skinned African American. He stood about six feet, matching Augusta's height. His hair was thinning and what was there was snow white. His brown eyes were full of suspicion. He hadn't shaved for a few days. He smelled badly and there was alcohol on his breath. His small apartment was in disorganization. She observed a recliner and could hear, just slightly, a Wheel of Fortune rerun. "This won't take long and if you help me there's a hundred bucks in it for you." Bertrand had always told her to be free with money if she thought that would work. One good look at Archie Sanders fit the conditions.

"Okay. Come in. But let's see the dough, sister," as he carried over a chair from a small kitchen table and put it in front of his recliner. He turned off the television.

During that time she removed from the inner pocket of

her purse a $100 dollar bill. She showed it to him as he sat letting out a low sigh. He nodded. "I'm going to need you to go back deep into your memories."

"That's all I ever do. What?" he said morosely.

"My name is Augusta. Is it okay if I call you Archie?" He nodded warily. "How long did you live in the Quad Cities?"

"Shiiit. Horseshit area. I grew up in Davenport, over near the Chiropractic College, Palmer. My father worked at Oscar Meyer. I was an honor student by the way," he said defensively. He stared at Augusta, wanting some recognition from her for that disclosure. "I left that city when I was 18 and have never gone back."

She understood the need. "I know of your ability. You were in a very select group of students. The Demosthenes Club."

He stared harshly at her for several seconds. "You know, I think about that a lot. It was a forked road in my life. I let that goddamn club get the better of me. Is that what this is about?"

"For the most part, yes."

"You can tell I could use a hundred bucks. So I'll talk. But I want to know what this is all about."

Augusta wanted to tread carefully here and not predispose him to answer falsely. "One of the members of that club died recently, Cynthia Power. Trying to connect some dots," she answered obliquely.

"Sister! That's a fucking phony answer. I need the C-note but I'm not going to whore myself for it. So once again, what's this about?"

"Okay, okay Archie. There were eight original members in the club. You were the ninth but you quit it. Read the articles in the student newspaper. Of the eight only five are alive. My firm has been asked to do a thorough analysis of them. We suspect one of them to be involved in some bad stuff. I'm not going to tell you anymore. I don't want to prejudice your response."

"Prejudice? Shit. What a word to use with me of all people. What do you want to know?"

"I don't know what you told the school board in January of 1968. I do know that the cops came and tossed you out of the meeting. What did you say?"

"Hah! Listen. I don't have to tell you about racism. It's bad now with that turkey in the White House and everything that it tells you about this country. Back then it was more obvious, more vicious. I was a stellar student, great GPA. I interviewed with that freak...Ludlow."

Augusta asked, "Liebow, do you mean?"

"Yeah, that's it. Liebow. He claimed to be unbiased. During the interview he wanted me to tell him that I should be proud to be chosen. Think about it, he says, you're a black. That's unbelievable. Like he was giving me a break. I didn't play the game and he saw that. He didn't pick me. I sat the summer and got madder and madder. I spoke with some of the brothers and they saw it the same way I did. He was a racist bastard."

"So you kicked back?" Augusta said with an understanding smile.

"Damn right. Fucking Liebow blew his righteous horn. Listen to him because he's the fairest guy in Davenport. I cornered them, they let me into the club. You know what? By that time I didn't want anything to do with them. But I joined to rankle them."

"How'd it go?"

"For a while they all played the nicey-nicey game."

"There was an article in the November student paper. You seemed to be pretty gung ho about everything."

"I was. For about a month. Liebow was scared of me. Left me alone. The eight white kids pretended to be okay. Some more than others. I don't even remember their names anymore. The boys, four of them, were all bastards. Looking down their noses at me and not just me. It was like two sides – the girls versus the boys. The girls pushed back but not as strongly as the guys. Two of the girls could mix it up; the other two were pretty damn weak. But the guys ran the show and they scared off Liebow. He was a weak dude."

"But you exploded at a school board meeting?"

"I'll admit that I was getting into the Black Panther stuff. Just needed an igniter. That happened and from there on my life was never the same. I suppose that those pricks are all living in mansions. What bullshit!"

"Igniter? What do you mean?" Augusta noticed some perspiration around his upper lip and his forehead.

"There was a Christmas show of sorts. Put on by the senior class. I think that it was a custom. Skits, you know. I wouldn't piss on it. Probably early, mid-December before the holiday. Excuse me for a minute." He went to his bathroom, half-closed the door and urinated loudly. He left there and went to his kitchen. He yelled back at her, "I'm going to have some whiskey. Want some?"

Augusta was a light drinker, mostly wine. She figured that it might be construed as an insult for her to refuse. She said, "Just a tiny bit, with some water and ice. Thanks Archie."

He brought back two glasses. Hers was watery pale, his deeply hued. The glasses were dirty. With a sigh he sat. "So here is where everything went south. Late afternoon practices for the skits going on. I was in the library doing some research for a paper. Place pretty empty. I had left my coat in the gym and I went to get it. The only light there came from the skylight and from a few red exit lights. My coat wasn't where I left it but I hear some noises from under the bleachers. It was a good coat. I'm looking around and I hear 'Shh' noises. I'm at the end of the bleachers near the exit door I look under and I see two of them. Half naked. My coat is under them. Fuckers. Demosthenes Club fuckers, neither had been nice to me. But the girl starts yelling at me. The guy puts his pants on. He's quiet. She's yelling. I'm a voyeur! Fuck the two of them. I kneel down and grab my coat from under her skinny little white ass and I leave."

Augusta saw the pain in his eyes as he relived the scene. She said gently, "Wow, that's heavy stuff for a 17 year old who was going through all that you were."

"Yeah, it was. But that wasn't the worst of it. They turned on me. Shunned me. The only one who at least spoke to me was the light redhead but she was into herself. Forget her name. The others were all fuckers. It was like being in a boiler room. I saw them for what they were, white fuckers."

"Did you speak with Liebow?"

"Nah. Why? He was already sucking up to them trying to get them to talk with him. They used to dis him. Listen to me sister; that was a bad fucking group. By the time I got back from Christmas break I was ready to break loose on them and the whole system that supported them."

Augusta understood the man's grief and how it could

have broken him. Was he beyond reproach? No. But by large proportions she favored him over the club members.

"Archie, I'm really sorry about this. The interesting thing about your observations is that I think that these scoundrels are still operating but now at dangerous levels. This is why I'm here. Try to help me."

"Go ahead, I'm listening," he said as he gulped down a goodly part of the whiskey.

"Three of the members are dead." She withdrew from her bag a copy of the picture from the student paper. She pointed at Stan Adair. "He had a heart attack. Lawyer. Sixteen years ago." She noticed that Archie put down his glass and reached for his reading glasses, now fully attentive. She continued, "This was Anne Podreski. She drowned in April of '68. You probably remember?" He nodded, lips tight. "This is Cynthia Power. She died a few weeks ago. Maybe something fishy there."

He looked closely at the picture. He remarked that Cynthia Power was the only one who didn't shun him. "She didn't go out of her way but at least she spoke to me."

Augusta continued as she pointed to the faces and stated the names of the five living club members.

"Let me have the picture for a minute." He studied it, shaking his head back and forth. Finally he looked at Augusta and said, "You didn't mention Liebow. The pig."

"No. If something bad happened a few weeks ago, he wasn't part of it for sure. Nursing home. Can you tell me anything about these five?"

"Okay. It's coming back to me more than I want it to. Top row left? Name again?"

"Megan White," Augusta responded.

"She was the nasty little pig under the bleachers. Phony liberal crap. She was furious with me when I yanked my coat out from under her ass. From then on she was more than just an enemy. As if it was her coat. These are bad memories sister." He looked away from the picture for a moment and then sipped at his drink. "Next over, the other part of the fucking duo. Name?"

"Peter Waters."

"An actor. He could get up and give a rousing speech in favor of syphilis or cancer. His heart was stone. One of the most self-centered bastards I ever met. He and that Megan turned everyone flat against me after I discovered them. Went from dislike to sheer hatred from there."

"Next one on the top is Corey Bladel. Remember him?"

"Yep. Class President. Bull shitter. Politician. Went along with the others. I see his rotten face on the TV sometimes. Doesn't seem to have changed much. Still a bull shitter," he laughed sarcastically. He went on. "This last one," he pointed to the standing Francine Korbel. "She was one scary bitch. Alpha plus female. Amazon. She wouldn't take shit from anybody. I remember once, she caused Liebow to leave the room. I think he was about to cry. That bitch would take no prisoners."

Augusta reflected as she listened to Archie that this Demosthenes Club didn't work with knives and guns. They used *civilized* tools – language and arrogance that reigned with no counterforce such as Liebow should have provided. Archie Sanders was DOA.

His finger shook slightly as he pointed to Anne Podreski. "She drowned. Some of them had at her all the time. A lamb in a wolves den. They ate her soul. The bastards," he shook his head. "Now this one," he pointed to John Douthit, "was pretty removed from things. Very quiet. Always observing. They said that he had perfect scores on the ACT and the other one too. His family ran a funeral parlor. Probably sacked out in one of their coffins. We had little communication but underneath him I sensed nothing being there, it was hard to sense anything actually. What's his name again?"

"John Douthit."

Archie glanced up sharply from the picture. "He's not the one from San Francisco that I see on TV sometimes? Is he?"

"Yes. Billionaire."

"Geez, that's amazing." He sat quietly for a moment. "This one was a lawyer's son. Rough character. Cursed all the time. Fuck this, fuck that. He gambled a lot. I remember. Ran football pools, sold cigarettes – a sharpie. Always had the feeling that he would make a good slave trader. Another sonofabitch. What was his name again?"

"Stan Adair. Dead. Heart attack," she said softly not wanting to break his rhythm.

"Next over Cynthia Power. Nice enough but she was a bit scatterbrained. I don't mean stupid. Maybe self-engrossed. She was never unkind to me as were the others but you could walk by her in the halls and say hello and it didn't register with her. It took me awhile to realize that she didn't say hi back because she never heard me. She was so into herself. I don't see suicide in her but then its 50 years later. Lot of water under the bridge."

Augusta was saddened by the whole interview. She asked him, "So Archie, what became of you?"

"I graduated and left Davenport. I was drafted for that fucking Vietnam War. Court martialed. Bummed around Chicago, LA, New York. Odd jobs. Arrested a few times. Marijuana selling, vagrancy. Ended up in Vegas for about fifteen years. Running bets and so on. Eventually I came back to Iowa. I was a janitor at the university. Yeah, I fucked up sister. I had a full bag of talent and I pissed it away. Is there anything else?"

"No. Here's the $100. And here's another too. My firm will keep you on retainer as it were." He gave her a knowing smile.

On the drive home Augusta felt great anger. Another bad racial story in a saga of bad racial stories, Archie Sanders.

CHAPTER 38

Barry Fisk noticed the first sign of trouble when he woke up his primary PC at 11:30 p.m. It was slow even though he had signed up for business speed with the local service carrier Mediacom. By a conservative measure, Barry had well over $200,000 invested in software, hardware, components and assorted highly illegal hacking tools. Years ago he had been busted by the FBI for some illegal sleuthing on behalf of ACJ. Only the intervention of McAbee's well-connected brother Bill, got him off. But the G-Men warnings had been dire. Accordingly, he had double-downed on precautions and accepted extraordinary monetary infusions into his computer capacities. Bertrand McAbee had been his benefactor. Although McAbee didn't have to throw a small fortune at him he did, primarily Barry reasoned, because he had to. McAbee owed him every cent he coughed up because Barry was so essential to his ACJ operation. Who was fooling who?

He went into his encrypted files and noticed the fades and paneling. He immediately went to his IBM file protector and ran a scan. This protection program had cost $4000. It was state of the art and was customarily used by some major

American corporations as a defender against hacking, file disruption, and malware. It ran for about 30 seconds before an ominous message appeared. 'Active attempts are currently being made to compromise your computer. Protections are holding. Contact us by phone immediately.' He did so and was told to turn off all equipment and wait until personally contacted by an IBM team. A series of confirmations were given to authenticate the message. Barry did as directed, informed McAbee, and prepared for his anger management counseling session a little later in the day. As he reflected he saw only two good candidates for such an intrusion, the FBI or something to do with McAbee's Demosthenes case. He saw this latter as the more probable.

Jack Scholz lived on the fringe of Davenport's northern border. A solitary lane was used for entry to his ranch house. The surroundings were wired to lights and sirens by numerous trip wires and observational cameras. One of his friends from the old days had remarked that if someone could get through to Jack's house uninvited they should be brought into Jack's large fold of contacts with special commendations.

Jack had just dozed at 3:00 a.m. when a peripheral trip wire had been breached. This caused an alarm to sound in his bedroom. Within two minutes Jack was black clad, night scoped, and out of his basement and through a tunnel ending 30 feet from his house. He had a semi-automatic with him as he crawled to a small bluff upon which sat a huge boulder. Within two minutes he saw the armed individuals running, crouching, hand-signaling and making toward his house. He kept looking behind them to see if it was just those two on his property. Satisfied they were alone, he moved down behind them and when he was about 30 feet away barked, "Guns down or you're fucked." One of them froze and dropped his weapon immediately. The other turned with his gun, Jack blasted his knee area as the man fell backward, gun dropped. The other had his hands-up. Jack told him to tend to the wounded man as he called a buddy, a former medic, who now ran an ambulance service in Davenport to come out to his place and be prepared to tend to a wounded man. Jack said, "Prefer to keep the cops out of this."

Augusta Satin was called at 3:45 a.m. The male voiced comment was short, "Augusta Satin, we know about your two daughters in Champaign-Urbana. Back away from the Power matter or else." Augusta had been in a deep sleep and by the time she processed the message, the caller disconnected.

McAbee had not experienced any threats during that night. By 7:00 a.m. all three of his cohorts had reported into him. Augusta would go to the University of Illinois and refresh her girls on gun care and practice, Barry was awaiting an all-clear from IBM, and Jack simply said that there had been an encroachment but all was okay. Pat Trump had not been bothered. McAbee looked idly out at the Mississippi River and south of it to Rock Island. He reasoned that whoever was coordinating the threats and attacks on his people had made a mistake. The call to Augusta was quite explicit, the 'Power matter.' Why he wasn't personally attacked was anyone's guess. But he was now fully alert. Barry called through to inform him that the effort to compromise his system was blunted but he was currently on a select list that would entail constant monitoring, his entire system now backed up through three different highly advanced IBM programs. He was told that his adversary in the matter was extraordinarily sophisticated and able. Efforts were being made to determine the source of the hack.

Augusta called later in the day to report that her two daughters were prepared and ready. McAbee remarked to her, "I promise I won't go within 50 miles of the University of Illinois now that your daughters are looking for trouble." She laughed and seemed to be relaxed. She gave McAbee a brief synopsis of her meeting with Archie Sanders.

McAbee had not heard from Jack Scholz. He wondered what was happening in that world.

He was in his Camry heading east across northern Illinois for Naperville at 4:30 p.m. He was set to meet with Representative Corey Bladel at Maggiano's Italian Restaurant at 8:00 p.m. He desired to be there by 7:30 to get the lay of the land as it were. He anticipated that this meeting might be highly charged and unpleasant.

Traffic had picked up as he drove I-88 across northern Illinois toward Chicago, although he saw that going west was worse as people were fleeing to the suburbs out of the city of Chicago. After one bad turn (not unusual for him) he found the restaurant. It was 7:35 p.m. when he pulled into a plum spot close to the busy restaurant. Augusta would put his parking luck to a pact he had with Satan, his luck in parking spaces extraordinary even by his own estimation. He thanked St. Christopher instead of Satan.

He went to the bar and ordered a Perrier with lime. He gave the empty bottle to the bartender who disposed of it. Although he assumed that he might be watched he saw no reason to give away his sobriety. Let Bladel guess. He knew from Fisk's research that unmarried Bladel was known to be a carouser. At 7:50 p.m. a young woman, quite beautiful, came up beside him and said very quietly, "Bertrand McAbee?" He looked more closely at her and saw a face yet to be etched by cynicism or disappointment.

"That's correct," he responded.

"My name is Rachel. I've been asked by Representative Bladel to escort you to a private room at the back of this restaurant. I understand that you are having a meeting with him." She smiled warmly.

He followed her around the perimeter of the fully occupied restaurant and into a corridor at the back end of the place. She stopped at a closed door, opened it and moved her arm forward. "He will be here shortly," she said as she withdrew from the doorway. When he entered the dimly lit room he saw a square table in its center with two chairs. On the table was a checkered tablecloth on top of which stood a salt and pepper dispenser, a bottle of olive oil, and a small canister of parmesan cheese. The table was not set for a meal. He assumed that there was some sort of listening device either set already or one that would be attached to Bladel. He was, after all, a member of the Demosthenes Club.

He sipped from his glass as he awaited the man who could command the restaurant to supply such a courtesy to him.

Bladel burst into the room at 8:20 p.m. He had a glass of what looked like whiskey in his hand. McAbee was startled. The stillness of the room had been roiled by the energy that seeped from Bladel. He came at the table like a warrior in battle. He sat with emphasis and looked over at McAbee in a hostile manner. He said, "So you are the ass who has set the world afire. I don't care for your tactics. I don't know how you got to the Chair of the Republican National Committee. But I'm here as a favor to him. But don't for a second doubt that I know what you're doing over in Iowa. I have been forewarned about you and your irresponsible behavior toward the Demosthenes Club and its members. So get to your point and get the hell out of my way. I have much more important matters on my plate than meeting with some bullshit gumshoe from Iowa," he was almost in a yell as he finished.

McAbee immediately sensed that the politician was in distress and already well above the legal limit in alcohol consumption. He was tempted to go directly at the man's anger, to provoke him, and hopefully cause him to shout some telling comment. But he did otherwise. "Representative Bladel, thanks so much for coming to see me. I realize that your schedule is complex and demanding. I knew of no other way to be heard by you in person, thus the Chair of your party and this meeting. Thanks for the privacy by the way, also." McAbee said this almost in a whisper. As he spoke, he witnessed confusion in Bladel's face.

Confusion or not, Bladel was riding the horse of anger and he was in a racing mood. Loudly, he intoned, "I know nothing of Cynthia Power's suicide. Hadn't seen her in ages except to interview for her stupid little book. A one-time meeting. She was crazy by the way. Charity on my part to meet her. And now I hear that you're dredging up, a proper word in this context, Anne Podreski. I'm warning you. Stop this insanity. You are taking on some very strong people and they will have no hesitation in breaking your back in two."

McAbee, for reasons that were murky, saw the congressman as an overgrown child. He felt a certain sadness for the man. Subtlety was well beyond Bladel's skill set now as he was in his late sixties. Perhaps Congress had strengthened his innate tendency to bluster. "*You already have tried as you know*," he said severely trying to catch Bladel out.

"What?"

"Right now three of my associates are under siege. You think that's going to break my back?"

Bladel leaned back in his chair, calculating Bertrand's comment. He had been stopped. "What are you saying to me?"

"If there was no fire in the forest why all of the fire trucks Congressman? We've been hampered from the outset by some entity or other. A number of unexplainable occurrences *unless* something bad is being covered up. You say that you haven't spoken to her except for Power's stupid little book. But her own words and subsequent meetings with Francine Korbel say that something was said by you. I'm not arguing that you are the one causing havoc in this inquiry. But I'm thinking that it has gotten beyond you. As you say, the Demosthenes Club has some very strong people."

He took a gulp from his glass and looked confusedly at McAbee. In a more conciliatory tone he said, "From what I hear, you're challenging the police investigation about her suicide. All the rest – Anne Podreski, associate bashing, whatever – you are connecting back to that. Unless you can break that police report you don't have anything except for Cynthia's fears and imaginary conversation with me. I'm sorry about busting out on you but you'd be better served working on a different case."

"It's too late. Too many games have been played Congressman. What exactly did you say to her about Anee Podreski's death?"

"To be honest with you I was plastered. All I remember is telling her how sad it was about Anne's drowning."

"That's it?"

"We've met, I've cooperated and I'd like you to report back to our Chair as such." He got up and as he opened the door he looked back at McAbee, "I recommend the lasagna here." He left.

McAbee concluded that Corey Bladel said a lot more than he was saying to Cynthia Power about Anne Podreski's death. That it had menace to it. A passing comment made by a drunk. But he was also pretty sure that Corey Bladel had nothing to do with all of the roadblocks that had been encountered since the investigation opened. He couldn't be that drunk and that subtle at the same time. His surprise was obvious when told of the harassing behavior. He wondered, too, how the other four club members perceived Corey Bladel. Yes, he was an important congressman, but he had some outsized personal issues. As a group they probably didn't like him. But then again, no one in the group seemed to like anyone else in the group.

CHAPTER 39

On the next morning Bertrand found Dr. Linda Rhine sitting across from Pat. Before Pat could say anything Rhine got up and said loudly to him, "I have to speak with you immediately." Bertrand looked over at Pat who gave him a quick wince and a shrug of her shoulders. Rhine looked at her watch and emitted a light 'tsk.'

McAbee didn't appreciate the intrusion thinking crossly how doctors hid themselves behind their staffs and would not as a rule violate their own protocols for an unplanned visit. He turned toward her and said, "You seem upset," as he peered at his watch. He was irked by her.

"I am. I was here at 8:00 a.m. I have many responsibilities. Your hours would be referred to as banker's hours." She looked at her watch, unsmilingly.

"No. These are my hours. I work very differently than you."

"Apparently," she said in a dismissive and hostile voice.

McAbee collected himself and led her into his office, realizing that something was wrong with her and it wasn't just about his hours of operation. They sat, he said nothing.

Linda withdrew a wallet from her large purse. "I've come

to settle up with you. I am no longer interested in pursuing the case of Cynthia Power. How much do I owe you?"

Now that they sat across from each other, four feet at best, he saw her at a breaking point. She was haggard, her eyes rimmed by a distasteful gray/black. This was not the same woman who had initiated the case. "May I ask why you've changed your mind?"

"Don't buck me Dr. McAbee. I'm out. It was a momentary slip on my part to involve myself in the woes of one of my patients. I should not have gotten involved. Give me an amount and forget you ever met me. Augusta? Keep her out of this."

Bertrand was absorbed in all that he heard. This was a proud and strong woman who seemingly was shut down. His first thought went to the threats that had clustered around Augusta, Barry, and Jack.

"What was done to you Linda? This makes no sense. You've been threatened? Compromised?"

She looked back at him harshly. "I've been good enough to come down here and square my bill with you. I never signed a contract with you so technically I have no obligation to you. Now give me an amount. I have to get back to the hospital."

"Cynthia Power was murdered in my judgment because she was concerned about a terrible death 50 years ago. This is the way I'm reading this case right now. Three of my people have been, a loose word but accurate, molested. Now you I assume. Sure. I can give you a number and it would cover my expenses so far. But here's the deal, I'm not about to let this go – your money be damned. It looks to me that you have been whipped into some kind of submission, servility, and I'm very distressed about it." He awaited the coming storm as the silence in his office gathered its seconds amid the unflinching looks of the two.

Finally Linda Rhine broke and broke hard. She burst into tears, hung her head among her throbbing shoulders and soon lowered her head into her arms on the table. McAbee said nothing but within himself felt a depression of spirit. He reached over for a box of tissues and quietly placed the box between them.

"Bertrand McAbee, let me talk," she said haltingly. "I'm 61 years old. I'm a psychiatrist. I've worked in this community for just short of 30 years. I have treated thousands of patients. I have been fervent in the proper care of my patients. In the case of Cynthia Power even to her grave." She stopped.

McAbee knew that more was coming. But he remarked, "All that you have just said makes sense to me. I know that you are speaking the truth." He let his comment stand.

"I'm an atheist. I see most of religion as dangerous and demeaning. But as in any mythology, there is a quest for insight. I won't say truth. One dilemma that all religions circle around is our inherent imperfection. None of us, in that tired lingo, is without sin, imperfection, the stain of evil. Whatever you wish to call it. Patients come to me because of their imperfections. In every way, it's the imperfect coming to me the imperfect. I am always aware that I walk with feet of clay although I have been trained to conceal this. Doctor perfection is seen to be efficacious for patient treatment and it probably is. I need a drink."

"Coke, water?"

"No goddammit. Alcohol," she said pleadingly.

"Of course." Many years ago, McAbee had been given a bottle of scotch by his students at St. Anselm College. They thought he needed it. He never could determine from them why they thought that. But he had kept the bottle of Chivas Regal in his office while at the college and had dutifully brought it to his offices when he opened ACJ. It sat next to a shelf full of Loeb Classics, the Greeks. McAbee had personally sworn off of alcohol ages ago because of an incident that caused him much self-anguish and regret. He removed the bottle from the shelf and opened it. "Ice?"

"No. Straight up," her voice now in recovery.

He poured her about four fingers, realizing as he did that that was a lot of whiskey at 9:15 a.m. As he started to sit she was already taking a huge draw from the glass.

"That's better. Let me tell you this so that you understand why I came here this morning and also why I will not be able to support this inquiry by you and my wish for you to cease." She looked at him pleadingly. "Last night I was closing my office. About 7:00 p.m. No one was there. I was about to set the latch and was turning to leave when two men pushed me inside, closed the door and dragged me back to my office. One of them whispered into my ear that he'd break my jaw and knock out every tooth in my head if I said a word. Just in case you are wondering, I did not report this to the police." McAbee saying nothing, she went on. "Six years ago I assisted in euthanizing a couple that had been married for over 70 years. They were both in advanced dementia and absolutely terrorized by their fantasies. They believed people were trying to kill them, they were going to jail, and a host of other imaginings. Their only son begged me to help. I did and did it actively by injections. They died together in the same bed, the poor things. There was a story in the paper about their remarkable love for each other, their deaths happening within seconds of each other serving as proof. I don't know how this son, who was my patient, was compromised, but he was. He made tapes of our conversations. The son was bad and I was a fool – the bottom line. The two thugs played a few of the tapes and told me to stop my interest in this case or else. That I was to pay you off and call you off. That's what I'm doing." She drank off some more of the Scotch. "I have a number to call. I am to tell them about my acquiescence to their demands." Tears flowed down her cheeks. Linda Rhine was broken.

Bertrand was quick off the mark. "Linda, pull out and tell them you did. Write me a check for $5000. I will post it to my account. I suspect that the group behind this has some kind of access and will see that you have paid me off. It will do them no good to hurt you further. But, and please hear me out on this, I will not halt the investigation. Whoever is behind all of the attacks will not succeed. By the way, what you did for those old people, I admire."

She wrote the check with a trembling hand and gave it to McAbee who asked to see the phone number. He would not call it, he promised, but he was interested in researching it. She did so and left his office without another word said.

By the end of the day, Barry had reported that his PC was in an unbreakable zone of encryption that IBM claimed was safe even from the NSA. Barry would not swear to the validity of that claim but he was impressed by their optimism. Augusta's girls had been at a gun club again in Urbana and had practiced together for two full hours. After Pat had rung Jack Scholz three times an hour for six straight hours, he finally picked up, "I'm good. Don't bother me again." Both she and Bertrand understood that as non-negotiable. Jack would appear in his own way and time.

Every effort to reach John Douthit out in San Francisco had failed, the layers of his protection most extraordinary. Pat had gotten as far as the wife of Peter Waters only to be rebuffed and sharply reprimanded. If she continued to call, she would be reported to the FBI and several other agencies that Pat had never heard of and whose existence she doubted. She did remark to Bertrand that Waters' wife had perfected the art of snobbery. Bertrand suggested that if *Downton Abbey* ever returned to television the wife could probably try out for a role.

But within himself Bertrand seethed over the out of bounds arrogance of this gang of five. He went back to the materials left behind by Cynthia Power. She must have crossed some red line. In all probability it was an act that went unrecorded in the materials but it had been understood by someone who felt that she was now a dangerous woman.

CHAPTER 40

Scholz called McAbee the next morning. A meeting was needed. "Up at the birds," he said. 10:00 a.m.? Agreed.

Up at the birds meant Lock and Dam 14 in LeClaire, Iowa, northeast of Davenport by about ten miles. In the winter it was a haven for bald eagles who had migrated south. Because of the constant water flow and churning around the lock and dam, fish were readily available for the eagles whose talons would snare them from the water, the captured fish brought to nests in nearby trees. There, the fish would be calmly eaten by the eagles. The lock and dam was a tourist site that drew people out of their homes and into the frequently bitter winter weather for this display of nature. In May, however, the birds were long gone and the parking area around the lock and dam almost empty.

A meeting here suggested that Jack Scholz was very concerned about security. It wouldn't surprise McAbee that there was a backup crew for Jack in case someone was there who didn't belong.

His pickup was already parked when Bertrand entered the lot. There was only one other vehicle there, a Honda Accord, Illinois plates. He assumed that the car had been there for a bit as no one was near it. Some visitors would walk up close to the lock and dam in order to study the workings of the complex apparatus. He hoped for the safety of the car's owner that the auto hadn't followed Jack into the lot.

When McAbee entered Jack's pickup he said, "Bertrand, how about a little drive?"

Jack gave him an extended explanation of the events that led to the wounding and capture of one man and another on his property. This was said with a calmness of manner that had McAbee mildly anxious. Perhaps it was the word 'capture.'

"When I called this is what I was alluding to. An encroachment. That's how that went down. I have two guys protecting my property in case others try again. The one who took two bullets won't ever walk right again. Tough. So, what you need to know was given to me by them. Neither one of them was particularly cooperative but they became so. You don't need the details, right?" he asked with a slight mock in his voice.

"Will they leave alive?" Bertrand asked sarcastically.

Jack looked across at him silently as he drove on Iowa 67, the Great River Road.

"No. I don't need to know how they *cooperated* with you," he said in exasperation.

"Here's what I know. It related to your Demosthenes case. These guys are well-trained at what they do. They were told about my visit to Fort Madison, Edgington. Essentially these guys are on a chain. Not at the top either. Their knowledge is limited. They were to question me about Edgington."

"Question? What does that mean?"

"Beat me up until I talked, maybe kill me."

"It sounds like they didn't know you very well."

"They were minor leaguers. Couldn't get anything about how it was known that I was in Keokuk. But it says that someone is playing hard at stopping you."

"What else?" Bertrand asked.

"Chicago agency. Thomas Group, Thomas Brothers, one and the same. They do things that I do but if you think, as I know you do, that I'm unethical, this outfit makes me look angelic. There are plenty of people I won't work for; Thomas Group will work for anyone. It's just a matter of money. One of my guys has proof that they've done work for the Chinese government against Microsoft and General Electric. That's just surface stuff. This friend I'm talking about was interviewed by them for a job. He got close enough to them to run for the hills. The Russian stuff with Trump and Clinton? They're there. You might want the midget to shake their tree a bit."

"Why go to you and not Edgington?"

"Nobody in their right mind would believe a word that Edgington would say. Ex-CIA. Too clever."

"But you believed Edgington?"

"Yeah. Within reason. He's on our side. When I saw him I was already bespoke," he grinned slightly. "Thomas outfit guys never."

At that moment Jack's cell chimed. He looked at his phone suspiciously as though it shouldn't have gone off. He held his finger up to Bertrand, pulled over to the shoulder and left his pickup. He came back in less than a minute. He sat quiet, and then gently, at first, then with some fury started to pound his steering wheel. Bertrand felt that his own presence was forgotten, as he waited for Jack to come back from his distress.

At last, through clenched teeth Jack said, "While I was wasting my time with those two scuds some others got to Edgington last night. Another crew. They figured out that my captives had met a bad end and then they decided to go after Edgington. I sent a guy over there this morning to check on him. He was dead, by about eight hours. The man I sent was a field medic. He examined the body carefully. He's 95% sure it was a heart attack. No bruises, no nothing on the body except for an injection. Blood sample showed a heavy shot of something into his armpit. Probably fright killed him. I feel responsible. After I broke those two I should have gotten Edgington out of Keokuk."

McAbee knew how deeply Scholz took the death of one of his contacts. There was an implied contract between all of the operatives in that hidden world. In Jack's estimation, Edgington was within the bounds of this contract, Jack had an obligation to protect.

He interjected into Bertrand's thoughts, "I was too busy breaking those two creeps. Too gentle with them. I should have accelerated my techniques. They didn't give me Edgington's name for quite a while."

"Do you still have them?" Bertand asked out of curiosity.

"There are some things McAbee that you need not know. Let's leave it at that."

Bertrand hoped for the sake of the two captives they had been released. He saw no need to break it down any further. Jack's world was Jack's world, an alternate universe. "This outfit? Thomas Group? Do you think they were behind the threat to Augusta's girls and Barry being hacked?"

"Augusta probably. Fisk? I don't know about that. From what you said that level of expertise? They might have that. Don't know. Did you ever think that there might be two, or even three, of these Demosthenes characters working in tandem?"

"Yes. I understand what you're saying. There's five of them. I think Corey Bladel is not part of this but he set off the cannon by mistake. Francine Korbel was the only Quad Cities local and Cynthia Power pursued her hard about what Bladel said. She knows something but I don't see her as an agency interfering with us. Augusta's take on Megan White is simple enough – she wouldn't trust her mother, that there's no way that she'd expose herself by interfering. She's seen as crafty and risk aversive."

"So that leaves two," Jack said.

"Douthit in San Francisco is unreachable. Layers of protection. Billions of dollars buys that. I don't know how to break through that and for all I know he doesn't give a care in the world about this whole matter. I do know that Cynthia Power called him out there according to phone records that Barry got to. There was a two minute exchange into his number three weeks ago. I assume that she spoke with him about Podreski. She had a much longer session with him a few months ago. When she began her book project."

Jack shot back, "What about this ambassador?"

"Peter Waters. Chicago. Another hider like Douthit. Of course, even though they're inaccessible it doesn't mean they're interfering. But someone is using this Thomas Group Agency."

"Maybe Fisk can find out?"

"I'll see. But if they're like you they won't put much on computers."

"Yeah. There's that."

"I have a long shot that I'd like your opinion on. Maybe help."

"I'm listening," Jack said.

CHAPTER 41

William Dineen considered himself a practicing nihilist. He lived alone near the cliffs of Waterford, Ireland. Born in Ireland he had found his way to the United States and then into a Special Forces unit headed by Jack Scholz. They had participated in a number of dangerous missions and were as close to being brothers as one could get. They left the military together; it was then that Dineen went back to his homeland. In short order he felt himself slide into depression, occasionally flirting with suicidal urgings. The deadly missions that he and Jack entered upon had brought him to a level of excitement that he found fully intoxicating, his life frequently at stake during them. He compared his current life to walking with crutches in a field of mud to those dangerous missions which were similar to jumping from a plane before the opening of the parachute, the thrill of danger and the unknown.

Since his retirement he had been called upon to assist in a variety of extra-legal missions, some at the request of Jack Scholz. Although as rare as these were they had the power to bring him back to some kind of life again. And so it was that at 9:00 p.m. a text appeared on his iPhone. [Shannon,

Aer Lingus #19, tomorrow 9:30 a.m. Same]. He instantly returned a message to Jack. [Got it].

He would be back in Waterford tomorrow by noon with an encrypted CD which came by way of a flight into Shannon Airport. Neither Jack nor Dineen trusted any level of communication as safe except for their unusual relationship with the Vice President of Operations at Aer Lingus and the security that such guaranteed.

When he opened the CD he read a tightly written summary of ACJ's case around the Demosthenes Club and in particular the suspected murder of Cynthia Power. He smiled as he remembered several of his missions that involved ACJ and the odd ex-professor McAbee. A host of supporting documents were also included by way of appendices. It took Dineen about two hours to grasp the essence of the case. He shook his head and wondered how it was that McAbee continued to wander into complex and dangerous cases.

He went back into the materials and reread the personal note that was written by McAbee.

> Dineen,
>
> I never thought we'd meet again and perhaps we won't if you can't get any cooperation. However, knowing you and knowing fate, I feel that there is a certain inevitability about us. By now you have read all of the attending materials. Most of my focus is on the Balkans (of all places) and in particular the murder of Toma Korpanja. I

am most interested in the Sarajevo detective (former) Adna Sidron. I sense a connection to this case 'through a glass darkly.' Too many missing data points to bring this beyond speculation.

Best,
McAbee

Dineen booked a flight out of Aerfort Bhaile Atha Cliath (Dublin Airport) at 9:00 a.m. the next day, landing in Amsterdam's Schiphol Airport and then a flight into Butmir Airport in Sarajevo. He arrived around 4:45 p.m. in downtown Sarajevo, already having booked a room at the Hotel Metro. He was to meet Danny Finnerty in the hotel bar at 5:30 p.m.

Dineen sat facing the small but well-stocked bar at the hotel at 5:15. The huge mirror that was placed behind an array of carefully tended bottles gave him a heads-up as to when Finnerty would enter the hotel. He hadn't seen him in five years or so but they both knew that Danny Finnerty owed his life twice over to Dineen.

Finnerty grew up with Dineen. They had been close friends during their troubled childhood and adolescence. Then Dineen crossed the Atlantic to the United States and Finnerty crossed the Irish Sea into England and from then to now became an accomplished crook, blackmailer, pimp, arms dealer, refugee smuggler, confidence man, etc. To the best of Dineen's knowledge he had never personally crossed into violence. But violence found him and that's where Dineen was owed by him. He shook his head slightly as he remembered the extraordinary skills that Danny possessed, among them, a kid who could draw, with extraordinary accuracy, anything that he saw. Additionally, his handwriting was artistic as the nuns would praise him while in the next breath tell Dineen that he was an oaf with no skills. His other skill was his ear for languages. He was speaking Gaelic and French fluently by the age of nine.

When Dineen called him in Vienna, Danny promised to be in Sarajevo, driving from Austria. And sure enough at 5:30 p.m. exactly Finnerty entered the hotel and headed toward the bar.

He was as dapper as ever, about five feet, eight inches, thin as a rail, energy surging from him. His eyes were a peppery black that took in the entire scene rapidly. About 20 feet from the seated Dineen he yelled, "Ah Dineen, I'm on to you. You had me made the minute I came through that front door." They shook hands, laughed, and hugged briefly.

He was happy to see him again even though he knew Danny was as crooked as an S-curved mountain road. It took them an hour of chat before the two Irishmen were prepared for business. In that hour old friends, past events, and assorted other of life's underpinnings were reviewed by each. Beneath all of the talk, though, there was a hard rock of trust between the two. In that hour, Danny had offered a job to Dineen as the overseer of a group of operations in Slovenia, Croatia, and Montenegro, "Outrageously good money William. And safe. Bribery and corruption are the currency there." Dineen told him he'd think about it, already knowing that he wanted nothing to do with any of Danny's operations.

"So Danny, as you know this isn't why I asked for this

meeting, although it's wonderful seeing you again and hearing of your successes."

"You know William, I was thinking that too."

"So you've been hanging out in these environs for a good 25 years or so. Do you know any of the languages just out of curiosity?"

"Ah William. I've had three great gifts from the gods. I can draw anything, write elegantly, and I've a terrific ear. So yes, I can hold my own in the old Austro-Hungarian Empire." He smiled, his nervous energy sparking like a wet log on a fire.

"What were you up to when Sarajevo was under siege?"

"Well, I wasn't walking the goddamn streets, I can tell you that." He signaled the bartender for a refill for both of them as he pointed to each empty glass of Connemara, neat. He looked around. Only one other patron sat at the bar. He whispered to Dineen, "How about over there in the corner?"

Dineen figured that Danny had some tasty secrets for him. They took their drinks and went across to the other side of the bar area, far away from anyone's ears.

Danny, in a low voice said, "William, buckets of money were being tossed around at that time. The Russians, the Serbs, the Croats, and especially the Americans. What's new about the Americans who piss away fortunes on faithless allies? And I should know since as you understand, I'm the number one faithless fucker of them all." He laughed, in his skittering manner.

"What was your angle?"

"Guns, ammo, cigarettes and booze. I had great routes across the mountains. Not easy but doable. The fucking Croats had lapped off a huge section of Bosnia in the southwest and so had the Serbs in the east. Yugoslavia was shattered glass. But the Balkans are all about bribes. Everyone had hands out. I always knew the way to people's hearts, money, and of course everything that it could buy. The fastest way to prove this theory is to live around here."

"Did you operate in Serbia?"

"Yeah. But very carefully. That's a gangster regime. But safer there down south in Nis. Tough in Belgrade. They have a queer way of looking at things do the Serbs. They grow gangsters, killers, lots of them, but they think they're doing God's work. Orthodox Christian horseshit. Ergo, the Russian involvement. When the Russians are involved they're shooting adrenalin into Serb veins. And believe me the Orthodox don't forget 1349 and fucking Moslems coming out of Turkey à la the Ottomans. The crazy bastards make the Irish look like Quakers," again the skittering laugh. "I know you're going somewhere William." He now smiled in a coy way.

"I am Danny. I need your help, but I don't want to get you in trouble. As I listen to you I see you as a cynical diplomat in a war zone. The American Kissinger comes to mind. I'm not judging you, mind, just trying to see things through your lenses."

"I think that's fair but one big difference between myself and Kissinger is that I don't sit in hotels 40 stories above the street and spend people's lives. I'm a ground man, always will be until I check out and retire to my place on Lake Como or I make a mistake and I'm done in. Always a risk when you're on the ground."

"And it's the ground that I need here Danny."

Danny nodded.

"Sarajevo, during the siege, Serbs sitting on their asses up in the woods, some in apartment buildings, indiscriminately murdering people on the streets is where I'm heading. Sarajevo has a police department, uniforms, detectives, just like everywhere else. Ever deal with them?" Danny nodded. "Corrupt?" Dineen asked.

"The sniper killings gave the Sarajevo's a firm sphincter. They were alert as hell. Some of their cop colleagues were picked off by the Serbs. It was one thing for me to help the Sarajevo Bosnians with guns and ammo. They'd look the other way. The Sarajevo police easily distinguished the helpful from the unhelpful. Most of their cops were like that with a little give and go on graft. Not anywhere like in Serbia where the bribing was massive. I'm listening for a drift here William?"

Dineen took out of his pocket some sheets of paper. "I'm going to tell you a story and give you some names." He went on from that comment to give Finnerty an outline of the killing of Toma Korpanja, the love affair with Cynthia Power and the police analysis done by Sarajevo Detective Adna Sidron plus the involvement of Alexsandar Markovic′. Danny listened intently. Dineen concluded by saying, "So I'm talking here about 1995. I think about as low as low gets in this bad history."

Danny Finnerty sat still for about two minutes after the recital. Dineen just waited on him knowing that Danny's quick mind was processing a huge trove of data. He was pretty sure that he'd tell him most of what he knew. All? Maybe, maybe not.

Finnerty eye-checked the environment closely before speaking quietly, "You have it right. Terrible times. I never would have thought I'd be talking with you about that mess. I don't remember anything about the murder at the Latin Bridge. I don't know of a Toma Korpanja or a Cynthia Power. But I'll ask around. Markovic′ I knew well and still do. Exhibit number one for demonstrating corruption in the Balkans. He's a slitherer. Now he's the Assistant Police Chief in Belgrade. In reality, he's the Chief because his boss is a drunken fool who couldn't tell his left hand from his right. Markovic′ is very important. He has to be fed euros like a pig, slop. And like a pig his appetite never lets up. But he has one great redeeming quality – he will oink for euros. Expensive dance partner but he dances. But you would need an introduction before he'd even look at you. In other words, he's not reckless."

Dineen noticed that Danny had picked up the habit of sucking in air through his bottom teeth. This became more obvious as he shared information. It was as though he was sifting the shared information through his bottom row of teeth. He waited for an analysis of Adna Sidron, the person McAbee was most interested in and the one that Danny had so far avoided.

Finnerty wiped his mouth with his sleeve and then motioned the bartender for another round. After it was brought and the bartender back to his station, Danny leaned forward and spoke softly. "Adna Sidron is a Moslem, Sarajevo type – moderate, no extremist shit about her. She's the exception that proves the rule about graft. Straight arrow. Not to be fooled with. When she retired, what was it, about ten years ago, I was a happy man. Not that I had to deal with her often. She was homicide and I don't involve myself with that *but* once in a while it touches one of my operators or contacts. She's into private investigations now."

"Have you ever met her personally?"

"Oh yes. Three times she had me in for questioning. She's a tiny thing. Smart, street-wise. Tricky. Astute interrogator. Your question was how Markovic′ could get her report? Easy. Money. I assume that Cynthia Power got nowhere with Sidron. But Sidron's report could easily have been taken from her file by some operative in the Sarajevo police headquarters. Is there reason to think that Sidron knows that her report was taken?"

"Don't know," Dineen responded, "probably not. This McAbee I mentioned, he wants to speak with Adna Sidron by phone."

Danny shook his head back and forth. "I'd give that a one percent chance of success. Let me explain this again. She's a tough little bitch. She'd be all over him as to how he even knows about her."

Dineen responded, "Knowing McAbee he'd tell her. He can be disarming as hell."

"Well, you should forget the telephone. Just to make sure, you're not trying to get me to speak with her on this? The woman has no love for me."

"No. You are my Google for this operation. Should I talk with her?"

Danny thought hard and long on this proposition. "Keep me out of it. Worth a try. I'll do some feeling around. You up for some bar hopping?"

"Of course. Let's."

CHAPTER 42

Barry Fisk was exhausted, triumphant, and depressed all simultaneously and in a continuous arc over the past three days. Whimsically he thought of Dante's hell, purgatory, and heaven, experiencing the three at once rather than in the stepped approach of Dante. It all needed sorting and he came to McAbee's office for that to happen. Difficult as it was for him to admit, McAbee was the person he felt closest to, not that he would even admit it to him. Happily, Pat Trump was conveniently missing from her station in the reception area of the ACJ offices.

After the customary courtesies they sat. "So Barry, you seemed to be a bit… ah… scattered when you called. I cancelled a few meetings in light of how you sounded. And by the way, you don't look well Barry. Are you okay?"

"This is hard for me McAbee. A lot of things going on, hardly any sleep in three days. My mind is unusually clouded. Hear me out."

Bertrand made a hand wave and said, "Sure Barry."

"If beaches could think and feel I would compare myself to Normandy during D-Day. I have been beset. I need someone to look at what I'm dealing with through a distant lens. Thanks for seeing me. I met with my court-ordered therapist two days ago. I didn't want to go but I had to. I already had cancelled twice with him. I was dealing with the computer hack as you know. I was furious about it and once I got back on my PC I was in attack mode. I took that attitude into the football player's office."

"Football player?"

"Court appointed stiff. Former jock at the University of Iowa, now allegedly doing therapy on behalf of the people of Iowa. Guarding them from the likes of me. At any rate, he starts pressing me about my feelings about hate and anger. So I tell him. He doesn't like my tone of voice as I start telling him what I think. We argued, of course, I turn my hatred and anger on him. We're dealing with all of this as I am recovering from the hack. I shouldn't have been there. I know that but he doesn't get it. So I send out a full blast of anger and hatred directed specifically at him. At the end of the session, only 25 minutes, I am warned that if I ever use that language again at him he will turn me into the judge. God knows what that means. I could be sent to jail," he said in exasperation.

McAbee saw first-hand that this proud man was scared. Jail would be a disaster for him. "As I listen to you I hear that you have no respect for the therapist?"

"Of course I don't, he's a dumb jock. It's disgusting that he sits there judging *me*. Humiliating." He slammed his hand on the table.

"He's licensed, right?"

"Yeah, so what!" Barry said harshly.

"The two previous cancellations. Were they based on this sense of humiliation?"

"…Yeah. Mostly anyway."

"If you had not been hacked and you weren't physically and mentally exhausted would your comments to him have been so personal and nasty?"

Barry reflected before saying, "No. I'm not that unfiltered. I know that these sessions are five in number. Finite. I just want them to end. My being sent to him should never have happened," he said angrily.

"So Barry. How can we stop the bleeding?"

"That's it. He's going to lord this over me and probably set me off again. Then he might call the judge, then I'm in jail."

"You're giving a person for whom you have no respect a tremendous amount of power over you," McAbee observed.

"Noted,"

"So, how do you turn the tables on this?"

"I'm so angry it's hard for me to find a way out."

"Do you ever try to win over people?"

"Not a strength of mine."

"I see the following. You have a disdain for all athletes. They're stupid. That's outrageously fallacious. Think it through Barry. You chose him. Yes, he was a football player and thus he's had to deal with anger. Football is a hard game. Lots of feelings, anger among them. If he's so dumb and incompetent, how is it that he can control it? You have to be prepared to give him some credit, Barry. Send him a note of apology and explain your situation relative to the hack and your exhaustion. Ask for his ideas on how he handles anger. You'll probably win him over. You know why?"

"No. Tell me."

"You're attending to him, complimenting him and

asking for his help and insights. And you know what? You might learn some useful things. The issue after all is about anger."

Barry thought for a bit. Then he said, "Yeah. You're probably right."

"The exhaustion?"

"That's a result of the hack. Otherwise, I could handle the therapist, unpleasant as it is. I've gotten to the bottom of the hack by the way." Barry's legs started to move back and forth.

"Before we get to that, tell me about the exhaustion."

"Three days no sleep. Maybe two or three hours, just naps. I feel that I can't see right mentally."

"Have you ever gone that long without sleep?"

"Once or twice at Yale."

"And you were a lot younger then. Will you be able to sleep tonight?"

"For sure. I have some sleeping pills. I'll take them just to ensure that I sleep."

"So that should take care of itself Barry. Sleep, therapist-handling. So tell me about the hacking."

With legs shaking, Barry began his recitation. "Remember that money you gave me? You called it a grant, $15,000. Hate to admit it but your generosity has been marvelous. You know from past cases that I have purchased state of the art software. Some of it enables me to get into places where I'm not welcome."

"It's called hacking? Or does it have a new name? Justifiable snooping? In depth research?" McAbee asked with a sarcastic smile. He noticed that Fisk's face did not show an appreciation for his humor. McAbee couldn't remember Fisk smiling in ages but he'd persist in trying to get him to lighten up.

Ignoring McAbee, he went on, "There are great hackers all over the world. Governments fund them, special agencies created only for that purpose. Corporations too. Criminal networks, loners. So the big game now is in defense against the aggressors. It's like a wild chess game operating across thousands and thousands of boards. As you know Bertrand, I'm in this game and on some of these boards. And I'm a sore loser as you have probably figured out." McAbee tipped his head slightly and closed his eyes for a second so as to show his understanding. "When the FBI cornered me all those years back I said 'never again.' Up to three days ago no one ever treed me. So we are in the middle of this Demosthenes stuff with its heavy hitters and suddenly after all these years I'm hacked. And it's major league. I pay handsomely to IBM to forestall any hacking. IBM freaks out. Like they hadn't seen this approach before. Bottom line, the hacking was stopped. But I'm put on a high alert status by them. But I'm not about to accept the encroachment as you can imagine. There is a group of what I call good people, Estonians. They have worked vigorously in the defense aspect of hacking. After all they are on the border with the fucking Russians who work assiduously at messing them up. By necessity some groups in Tallinn have become great defenders. To make a long story short I purchased, bitcoin, $14,000 of defensive software. Defensive in the sense that it can turn up aggressors. For $50,000 I could get a reverse stab and create havoc on the aggressor's end."

"How come the U.S. government doesn't do that?"

"It's a no-man's land. It would be like starting a nuclear

war. An observation – has Estonia been assaulted lately by way of hacking? For a long time the country was regularly hacked. It stopped. Why? Pretty obvious. Cyberwar is cyberwar."

McAbee leaned in, "I take it you didn't spend $50,000."

"No. I think it could ultimately be a losing proposition, especially for a loner like me."

"So the $14,000?"

Barry's legs had been shaking and stopping depending on where he had been in his recitation. The shaking renewed itself. "The attacking group is associated in a network run by the Thomas Group out of Chicago. Once I got that I did some research. They're pretty much all ex-CIA, NSA types. So they did it but I can't tell who they were working for. So the $14,000 gives me the source of the hack, Thomas Group. But it's a high risk to try to get into their files. Which is not to say I won't try some time but not now. But I am happy to have solved this puzzle. The $14,000 software package was worth every penny."

"I'm thrilled by this Barry. It ties together a few more strands. For now I think you should go home, relax, and get some sleep. I think momentum is starting to turn in our favor."

After he left McAbee now had a second confirmation about the Thomas Group or by its other name Thomas Brothers. He saw them as a hired gun. The question now is who were they serving? Their client? He thought of Douthit and Waters.

CHAPTER 43

Dineen walked toward the Miljacka River. Adna Sidron's office was located on the Obala Kulina Bana about 300 meters from the Latin Bridge. Her office was on the second floor of a shortened three story office building. He had not called ahead. He was placing his success in the hands of luck. If Scholz heard that, Dineen would never hear the end of it.

The offices stood in a white painted hallway with black wooden doors. There were four offices on the second floor. Sidron's was in 103. There was a bell and intercom that had an attached camera. The other three offices did not have these. Dineen hit the soundless buzzer. The screen lit up and a shrill feminine voice said, "Da?"

In his gentlest of voices he said, "I'd like to speak with Investigator Sidron about an issue from the past. It's confidential."

"Your name?"

"William Dineen."

"Please put your passport up to the camera."

Dineen did so while noting that it took about five

minutes before he heard a buzzer and her saying, "You may enter."

The secretary was an older women, maybe 60 or so. She wore a white hajib. Her glasses were thick but circular like her features. The office was spare but professional. There were three pictures on the walls, all relative to Bosnia and each pointed to some scene of horror from two decades plus ago. One was of the bombing destruction of the Sarajevo city hall. Dineen knew that an extraordinary amount of historical documents were lost in that incident. Another was the famous scene of a person shot by a sniper – lying dead on a bridge in Sarajevo. The last was a gruesome picture of the about to be slaughtered men in Srebrenica. The pictures told Dineen that Adna Sidron probably would not serve him milk and cookies. "She will see you soon. Please sit."

She came out of her office door and was standing in front of him in what had to be in less than two seconds. What a face he thought to himself. She had, at first glance, two extraordinary features, a long nose and intense brown/black eyes. She wore a hijab and only a fraction of her black hair was evident. There was a stern look on her face. As he took her in after the surprise he saw that she was no taller than five feet and if she weighed more than 100 pounds he'd be surprised. She had a small thin mouth that topped a narrowing chin. He saw a lot of Ottoman Turk in her. No hand was offered. She said, "Come into my office Mr. Dineen."

There was one picture in her Spartan office. It was of the mosque in old town Sarajevo along with the clock tower adjoining it. He sat in front of her desk absorbing her hard and suspicious look. "You can call me William," he said mildly.

She responded, "My name is Adna Sidron, as you know. So William, what is it that you want with me?"

"This is a long story. You may not want anything to do with it. I'm here on behalf of a private detective in the United States. A murder has occurred there that it is thought could relate back to Sarajevo in 1995. You were an investigator. A copy of *your* police report is in this detective's possession."

"As you can see I'm not with the police anymore. I need details about what you're talking about."

Dineen recounted most of what he knew. As he did so not one feature on Sidron's serious face changed. In fact, only once did he see her blink. Tough little babe, he thought to himself as he concluded his presentation by handing her a copy of her police report from 1995, the Serbian version.

She looked out at the 50ish Irishman. He could easily fit in with the Serb killers, thick-necked, large-faced, and with a pair of violent eyes. Through a friend in the Sarajevo Police Department a profile of William Dineen was run through Interpol for her. While he sat in the waiting room she was informed about him. He was no innocent lamb. His name was involved in several open cases, the most prominent around a number of unsolved murders on the island of Lesbos and some foul play in London. Added to that was his past service in the U.S. military, most of which was considered classified.

"You gave me a report in Serb. I don't write things in that language. So how do you know it's mine?"

He removed from his pocket some notes. "It came from a detective in Belgrade who presumably accessed your report somehow and translated it into Serbian. The name is Markovic′."

Sidron startled at this name. A nemesis. Someone in Sarajevo headquarters had leaked it to this crook. She didn't like Dineen. She felt that he had dropped Markovic′'s name as a way of upsetting her. Dineen was crafty as well as violent.

She said, "Many murders occurred in Sarajevo in 1995. What do you want from me? If this Serb copy of my report is accurate then you know what I thought about the matter. Sorry you came all the way over here for nothing, Mr. Dineen," she started to rise.

He looked intensely at her while saying, "Look, I'm not part of this. I'm here on behalf of a private investigator, like yourself, McAbee by name. He feels that there's a connection back to this murder. He'd like to come over here and spend some time with you. He's a bulldog of sorts, probably like you."

"What makes you think that I have anything on this case other than what I formally reported?"

He sat looking at her for about a half minute. Then he said, "Lady, I'm going to be honest. Because I can smell it on you."

"You can go now. You're at the Metro? I might be in touch, leave your room number with Salma."

At 11:00 p.m. sharp she rang Dineen's phone. He said, "Yes?"

"Adna Sidron here. Send this McAbee over."

CHAPTER 44

Francine Korbel decided to take a ten day cruise out of Seattle. She was in need of Alaska and fresh air.

Corey Bladel alerted his staff to keep a close eye on the local Republican network. He was worried about a possible contender in a primary. It was all about any new money. He was drinking pretty heavily, Douthit on his mind.

Megan White, after some initial refusals, decided to take the offer of a visiting professorship for two weeks at Uppsala University in Sweden.

Peter Waters was informed that he was indeed on the short list for the ambassadorship to Iceland. The vetting process, a mere formality he was told, was about to start. He encouraged his wife, Courtney, to take a few weeks in Nantucket. She consented; he was thrilled on his way back from O'Hare Airport, happy to have an unkissed face during her departure from the car.

John Douthit remained in a somber mood. His aides were aware, surely, that he was distracted, his mood dour.

It was too crowded in McAbee's office, in Augusta's estimation. Pat Trump sat to Bertrand's left, pad resting on her crossed right knee. She looked stressed but this was nothing new when Barry Fisk was around. Speaking of that devil, he was on Bertrand's right conveniently out of Pat's view. Across from these three sat Jack Scholz and herself. Scholz was in a diagonal to Barry Fisk, Augusta to Pat Trump.

Bertrand had called Augusta last night. William Dineen had cleared the way for Bertrand to meet with Adna Sidron. He was going to Sarajevo, what did she think? From the tone of his voice she knew his inquiry was only a formality. He was already committed. But she told him that there might be danger and for him to be careful. What else could she say? He informed her that there were contacts on the ground there controlled by a man named Danny Finnerty, a good friend of Dineen. He'd have them if needed. Dineen was back in Ireland. Augusta wanted to say that a friend of Dineen was no friend of hers. But she didn't.

Marching orders were given by a decisive and intense McAbee. She was glad to see this. He would be at his best over there, she was sure.

During the office meeting, Jack Scholz was commissioned to try to get some foothold into the doings of John Douthit. Scholz said that Douthit was in a fortress but he'd feel things out.

Barry Fisk was to zero in on Peter Waters, in particular. If he had some spare time his attention to Douthit would be appreciated.

Findings from either of them were to go through Augusta who would be running the office with Pat Trump.

Bertrand explained about his mission to Sarajevo. He had no idea of what to expect. He mentioned that his phone call to Adna Sidron's secretary was met with a terse message,

"Investigator Sidron does not do business electronically. But she is aware of your inquiry and will meet you in her office."

Two days later Augusta was driving Bertrand to Chicago's O'Hare Airport. He was scheduled to take a flight on Austrian Air to Vienna and from there a flight to Sarajevo. If all the connections synced, Bertrand would be in Sarajevo in 13 hours and 45 minutes. There was no scheduled time for his meeting with Adna Sidron; however, he would be met at Budmir Airport by either Finnerty or one of his employees and then driven to the Metro Hotel which was only a five minute walk to Sidron's office.

"So Bertrand, other than what you have by way of Marković's translation of her report, what do you think she can give you?" Augusta asked.

"I'm not sure. But the very fact that she accepts a meeting may open up something that will never see the light of day without that meeting."

"And Marković in Belgrade?"

"I'm not planning a session with him. Serbia is another story. But who knows what will happen? I do know one thing for sure."

"What's that?"

"I'll miss you my friend."

"Well, same here Mistah, same here."

When she dropped him at Terminal Five, O'Hare's International Terminal, they kissed, they hugged, and she watched him disappear into the maze of that terminal. For reasons that she would never be able to explain, because it was now becoming a constant, she cried as she headed back to the Quad Cities.

CHAPTER 45

Adna Sidron stared quizzically at McAbee when he was led into her office. She stood as he came close to her desk and she extended her hand, "Adna Sidron. And you are Doctor Bertrand McAbee?"

He nodded and said, "Please call me Bertrand. Thanks for seeing me." He was already on alert about her usage of the title Doctor. He'd been checked out by her.

They sat. She said, "Call me Adna. You have come a long way about a cold case. Yes?"

"It surely was cold. But events have occurred that have given it warmth."

"So this friend of yours, William Dineen? What is your connection to him?"

"I have an agency in the States. I have used a contractor who served in the U.S. military with Dineen. Dineen was asked by this contractor to come to Sarajevo to see if you'd be open to talking about the murder of Toma Korpanga. I didn't need the trip if you wouldn't talk about it."

"This Dineen? Are you aware of his background?"

"He was in the U.S. military. He's retired, living in Ireland. Close friend of my contractor."

She looked at McAbee with a bemused expression. "There's a lot of information out there on him. An odd ambassador for a former classics professor. He is said to be dangerous by Interpol. Is your agency in that farming state in the U.S. into heavy-handedness?"

Adna Sidron was telling McAbee that he, Dineen, and ACJ had been vetted. Also that she probably still had use of her contacts in Interpol. He wondered just how much she knew as she doled out small slices of information. "Adna, take one look at me. I'm not heavy handed." He smiled. "I just do cases that come into my agency and try to bring resolution. I hope that William didn't say something that distressed you."

"No. He was a perfect gentleman *given* what he represents," she responded.

McAbee was dealing with a woman who dwelled in a river of undercurrents. She wasn't going to open up about anything related to Toma Kopanja's murder until she could find some common ground and level of trust with McAbee. It was evident that there wasn't trust of Dineen by her. "So, I'm aware of the information that was given to William but I'm not sure how much of it he shared with you," trying to shift the meeting away from Dineen's character.

"You know Bertrand that you have entered into a zone where many murders took place. A terrible era. In my own apartment, I had to keep my shades down and curtains closed for several years. Those Serbian killers could mean death. They had many marksmen who were quite able to perform random acts of killing and then there was the shelling."

"I've read a bit. A nightmare. And it can't be a good event to have me resurrecting that era."

"Oh," she smiled sadly, "This is not resurrection – the events and tragedies have never been buried. Isn't that a precondition for resurrection, burial? Burial never happened for me and never will. The brutality and what my eyes have seen will never die away until I die away."

"I see," he said feebly.

"So allow me to enumerate the areas that Dineen brought up and to make sure I understand. Cynthia Power is murdered but it is made to look like suicide. You found letters, reminders of Toma's murder in 1995. Cynthia and Toma were lovers. His murder broke her heart as she sought reasons for the unusual killing. As to the strongbox, you call it a safety deposit box, I am very curious about your possession of the Serbian translation of my report about the killing. The name Marković is used. Am I incorrect in anything so far?"

"You have it right."

"You have brought the original Marković piece that was actually sent to Cynthia Power? Not just the copy given to me by Dineen?"

"Yes," he took it out of his valise and handed it across to her.

She removed her glasses and bent over the paper. She pored over it for at least two minutes. By his estimation she could have read it 20 times. "Thank you for sharing it with me. Is it permitted for me to make a copy?"

"Of course." She got up and went to a small table that had a printer/copier on it. She made two copies, came back and handed the original back to McAbee.

"Marković had no business with the report that I issued. He was given a copy by a traitor, probably in my old detective bureau. To conceal that betrayal he translated it into Serbian or had one of his agents do it. Cynthia Power would be none the wiser."

"Had she asked you for a copy?" McAbee inquired.

"No. His note to her is of interest. I do recall her wanting information from me while I was investigating the case and questioning her. I had told her that there was nothing that I could do. She didn't believe me. Someone put her onto Marković who then got my report. You have no notes to that effect?" Adna gazed at McAbee pensively. He shook his head. "She must have paid him a fortune for his effort. He is a dishonest man. Highest bidder gets his service. What else do you have on this?" she inquired.

"There's near certainty that someone was frightened by Cynthia Power's concerns. Also, she received it recently. If you have the time I will tell you the story, the long version not William's short one. But I'd like to buy you a cup of coffee and tell you while there."

She looked at him skeptically for a bit and then said, "Yes. I will do that. You have come far on a quixotic mission. I respect that."

He had his ways, this McAbee. She did believe him when he said he wasn't heavy-handed. Maybe he not personally but if he knew and used people like William Dineen his distinctions about himself, his agency, and his contacts were inadequate and seriously in need of refinement.

His blue-gray eyes seemed to be in a frequent change of hue, also in constant motion as he eyed her office with something beyond curiosity. When his eyes fell on her she felt as though he was trying to get into her brain. But there was some quality in him that she liked and it was not just that he was an older man trying to run down an old case. Investigators always appreciated other investigators who took that extra step of diligence. She observed that quality in McAbee. They each ordered Turkish coffee. As she looked at him sip from his cup she thought that he did not enjoy the experience. She smiled to herself. She indicated to him that she was prepared to listen to his story, after reassuring herself that they were in an isolated corner of this shop.

McAbee spoke for about 20 minutes. She only interrupted him twice for some clarification. She was impressed with his delivery – concise and to the point. He had some interesting data especially about the exchange of letters between Korpanja and Power. Cynthia, unsuccessfully, had tried to conceal the depth of her relationship with Toma during her investigation of Korpanja's murder. The Marković intrusion into her report angered her. She was glad that the only official report she had made was a skimpy and uninformative one. Only if one read closely between the lines might it be inferred that she would come back to the Korpanja case. This was a datum that no one other than herself had knowledge of.

He sat back and took another sip of his coffee, wincing slightly. She said, "You should have a slice of lemon cake. It's quite good here, helps the coffee go down," she said half-teasingly. She was surprised at herself, it was unlike her to loosen up, especially with strangers. To her mild surprise, he did order the lemon cake but not to her surprise he liked it even as he remained intensely serious. He sipped his coffee as if it was laced with arsenic.

"Bertrand? Do you have a guess about the exact age of Marković's correspondence to Cynthia?"

"No. No envelope, no dating. But I had a chemist friend from the college that I taught at do an analysis. He's quite good. He is a consultant to several companies that use dyes. He said that there was one ingredient in the ink that was not introduced into the market until 2015."

"Your conclusion?"

"There's only one conclusion – that Cynthia resurrected this issue recently. That maybe it had something to do with her interviewing members of the Demosthenes Club. The book that she intended to write as a type of therapy became a chain around her neck. I believe that it brought back bad memories but also insight. But how she could get in touch with the likes of Marković is beyond me. That she would even know about his existence is difficult for me."

Adna listened to McAbee closely all the while wondering if it was safe and wise for her to open up with him. Certainly, he gave her new data about her investigation but so what? She was now in private practice and the reality was that Sarajevo had half-buried its vile past. This confusion of purpose did not mean that she was only meeting with him to drain him of what he knew. She understood that she would feel terrible remorse if she played that game of non-reciprocity with McAbee. "All of this, however, can be explained Bertrand. The key is to understand the Balkans, and all Balkan people get this. I know that it may sound paranoid to you, a leap of logic, but we have it right more often than wrong. The Ottomans when they came and conquered here in the 14th century imposed a system upon the area that you Americans would call corrupt. It was a system of favors, bribes, family connections, and generally under the table dealings meshed with violence for those who offended this system. The system became part of the Balkan DNA. About five centuries later, the 1800s, pushback against the Ottomans became intense. But the pushback did not take on the system. So that as Serbs, Croats, Greeks, Montenegrins, Slovenes, Albanians, the whole gang that revolted against the Turks did not revolt against the system that was so thoroughly etched into our souls. I think that the Austro-Hungarians who succeeded the Ottomans never mastered the system here and they lost the area, naïve fools. So here we are in 2018, all ethnics fully defined but all subject to the same system, an Eastern system in a Western world. The Balkans area is a European anomaly. Add to all of this the hatreds that fill each volcano of each ethnic group and you begin to see why we are trouble plus for outsiders. Am I boring you?"

"No. I could listen to you for hours Adna. You belong in a university."

She smiled. "The last place I would wish to be. So let me travel the road that I am on. Cynthia Power was here for about eight years. She was involved with Toma who would understand the ways of the Balkans and in all probability share his analysis with Cynthia Power. When she left here she could not have been a novice to our ways. We understand from the letters and her just actually being here that she knew about the slaughter of 8,000 Moslems in Srebrenica. She was not, what do you Americans say, a snowflake. She knew people and had contacts here that we will never know about. Toma Korpanja was not her only contact is what I'm saying. Back to the DNA. Someone, somewhere, could know about Marković. Remember the system. Money talks in the Balkans, money can move mountains. Cynthia had money. Cynthia had contacts. A thread is easily observed. If she connected to Marković it would only be a matter of money. An old police report, mine, could easily have been unearthed in the files, translated into Serbian, and passed on through him to her."

"Marković? Tell me more about him."

"Marković is a man who is the archetype of Balkan corruption. To work against him is to attack the very DNA of the Balkans. I dealt with him, never one-on-one, but through his people. He is high on a chain, the top I sometimes think. I was left to deal with rungs lower down. Killers, thieves. I feel that he did extraordinary damage to Bosnia. That he most likely," she pointed up to a large hill to her right, "was up there on the hillside gunning down and shelling our people. My hatred for him has no boundaries, Bertrand." She saw that McAbee sat there, quiet, absorbed. Probably trying to connect the dots that she illuminated. But she knew that what she just disclosed was a shadow of what she knew.

"So it doesn't surprise you that he'd cajole his way to your report? Since this is recent we can only assume that she used a very knowing intermediary."

"Certainly. That is a viable scenario. If she had a contact into Marković and produced enough of a bribe it would happen. But as you say, a reliable intermediary."

"That would mean that your police department is corrupt."

She didn't know him well enough to know whether irony was a quality of his. She smiled and said to him, "Bertrand, it's the Balkans!"

Adna had another appointment. McAbee asked her out to dinner. She said 'no' as gently as she could. He seemed disappointed. She asked him to meet with her tomorrow at 10:00 a.m. It was agreed to. They parted ways at the coffee shop. After a few seconds, each walking in opposite directions she turned and watched him. There was more to him than he let on. She wondered what else he knew. Tonight she would devise a plan for tomorrow's meeting. As she watched him disappear into a crowd she noticed that he couldn't for the life of him walk a straight line, she shook her head and smiled. She liked him, he wasn't a typical American. He had that going for him, also.

CHAPTER 46

That night Adna removed her casebook from beneath her mattress. It was a ten by fourteen inch tome of almost 400 unlined pages. She had filled 371 pages in a small and neat hand. The materials in this book never made it into the formal police files of the Sarajevo P.D. After all, she knew the system – everything could be compromised.

The death of Toma Korpanja in 1995 was just one of 32 investigations that she undertook well beyond what was put into file and typically considered closed by Bosnian standards. Of the 32, 23 involved the period of Serbian slaughters undertaken by snipers and shelling units placed around the city. It was one thing to wrap a body in plastic and attribute it correctly to a sniper but behind the apparent sometimes another dimension loomed. That dimension was part of what this book explored.

The casebook was a reminder of her limitations and of the hiddenness that would stay hidden in dead-ends, the disappearance of principals, and the sheer protection provided to murderers in the conduct of this war of slaughter.

But of the 23 cases that went well beyond what was expected of a police investigation of killings, only four shone light into the hiddenness. Toma Korpanja's murder was one of these cases. Off and on she had pursued an inquiry into his killing, one which made no sense in her judgment. It was not the typical random act of violence that comprised the vast majority of the slaughters in that ugly period of time. Occasionally, she had actually made headway only to hit another layer of hiddenness that she ultimately knew she could never penetrate. And so it was that she perused pages 305-316 of her unofficial case book. There was so much that McAbee did not know. She wondered about the wisdom of sharing this information. What good could come from it? She would see him tomorrow morning at 10:00 a.m. Perhaps sleep would display an answer for her as to how much to share with him.

Bertrand left his hotel early for his walk to Sidron's office. He went to the Latin Bridge, the scene of the assassination of Archduke Franz Ferdinand in 1914 by a Serb radical bent on freeing the Balkans from the Austro-Hungarian Empire. The murder of the Archduke and his wife precipitated World War I. As an act of Serbian defiance, the bridge would be named in memory of this assassin – Gavrilo Princip. However, the nameplate for this bridge with Princip's name highlighted would eventually be delivered to Adolph Hitler as a piece of war booty by his military, a not so subtle putdown of Serbian dignity. Decades gone by, the bridge would be renamed the Latin Bridge. Soon his thoughts drifted back to Toma Korpanja and Cynthia.

He didn't know what to expect from Adna Sidron. Instinctively he liked her, but he sensed a wounded woman who had to attend to a very dark side in her soul. She had probably seen too much and eventually that could become a spreading stain of indelible poison on a good spirit which he perceived in her.

When he entered her office, he observed an outsized book on her desk. She was all business, her face had a worn quality to it. He said, "You appear strained to me Adna, if I may take that liberty with you."

"I can see why you're a private investigator," she said sarcastically but with a slight smile.

"I have other observations too," he said so as to lighten up the atmosphere.

"I'm sure you do but maybe you'll keep them to yourself until you visit me the next time you come to Sarajevo."

So, he realized that this was the final visit. Whatever she had to share would occur right now. "The book tells me that you might have some notes?"

"Yes Bertrand. I will share with you what I know. But do understand that what I will say cannot be attributed back to me," she paused, "as a homicide investigator I would file a formal report. You actually have that via Marković. The Serbian translation was adequate, by the way. But there were some cases that I dug into beyond my official duties. This book represents those efforts. Your case, Toma Korpanja, is one of those. I will tell you what I have and share my speculation with you. After this what you do is your business. But I will tell you that nothing good or uplifting is in this book." Bertrand nodded. She went on, "First off, in 1995, Korpanja would never show up at 1:00 a.m. at the Latin Bridge unless he was convinced that a worthwhile story or information was coming his way. So, it was a very planned and targeted assassination. Someone convinced him that something important was coming. I found a witness to the murder, a prostitute about 100 meters from the killing. The murderer was tall, dressed in black, came up behind Korpanja who was looking the other way. Shot him three times point blank and just walked away. The prostitute ran. It took me three days to track her down. The area was her place of business. She had nothing else to say. Clear, an assassination. When the investigation turned up Cynthia Power's name, I informed her, and she fell apart. She had no knowledge why Toma would be at the bridge. She said that Korpanja was going to Srebrenica. Something was bothering him but he didn't share precisely what with her. She said that he had been on edge for a few days. But then she says," she read from her book, "who isn't on edge in this city?" So she didn't give his trip any particular notice. His apartment had been savaged, right after his killing. I got one resident to talk. She heard heavy, thudding steps on the way to his apartment the night he was killed. About 1:30 a.m. She heard furniture being tossed, glasses breaking for about 20 minutes. She hid behind a couch in her apartment, one floor down from Toma's. She estimated three people from the sounds of their steps. She saw nothing, just heard the cacophony. Conclusion – Korpanja knew something or had something. Did they find it? I don't know but I doubt it. Colleagues at City Hall saw him as a Bosnian patriot, his soul was bleeding over what was occurring during that filthy war. He wrote an occasional piece, usually in conjunction with a *New York Times* correspondent, for that paper. Also, he was a go-to person on the ground for the BBC. He received small stipends from both of those sources. The only constant that I was getting from nineteen interviews was the word Srebrenica. Couldn't get anything specific."

"How about enemies?" Bertrand asked.

"Ah. His enemies were the same ones we all had. Serbs or Serb sympathizers and there were plenty in Sarajevo but they had to be very careful about ever proclaiming their sympathies, obviously. I rattled around that area but I couldn't get anything. Bertrand, I'm very sorry about this. Given what we were up against in those days I gave this case a lot of time. I can say this, however, from talking with some of his associates. He had no great love for Americans or Russians. Reading between the lines I got the impression that missing pieces in his assassination would be possessed by the Serbs, the Russian or even the Americans."

"It had to be dreadful for this to end up this way for you."

She pounded the book and stared harshly at McAbee. "I sleep with this under my mattress Bertrand. It tugs at my back and side every time I turn. I want it that way."

There was a long silence before McAbee said, "It sounds as if this all points to Serbia."

"Yes it does. What's new?"

"What would happen if I went to Belgrade?"

She stared at him for a bit. Finally, she said, "Nothing would happen. You would need a contact and please don't send Dineen." There was a touch of a smirk.

"Can you help with that?"

"I had a counterpart in Belgrade. To a degree I trusted her. Not with my life but she never betrayed me. We would make occasional disclosures to each other if it was to our mutual advantage. For being a Serb, she was a good person."

"She? Police?" McAbee asked.

"Oh yes."

Lightly he asked, "Would it be possible for me to see this Marković?"

Adna looked at him curiously before saying, "What did I tell you about the Balkans?"

He responded, "Everything is possible with the right amount of money."

"Precisely. Let me play around with this. How about us meeting at the coffee shop at 1500? Oh, and by the way, do you have access to a lot of money?"

Adna found her contact Maja, alive and well, still a detective in Belgrade. Indirectly and subtlety, she told of McAbee and his desire to meet Alexsandar Marković about a case he was investigating. The contact's first response was "won't happen." In ways they both understood and in a manner that would fool a listener, Adna was eventually told that the price was 5,000 euros and it would come under the cover of a private consultation with Marković. Adna told her she'd be back in touch.

When they met for coffee, lemon cake included, she told McAbee the cost of a meeting. When he consented she confirmed to herself why she liked McAbee. Hiding in his soul was a bulldog.

They would meet again in her office tomorrow morning at 10:00 a.m. As he was leaving she said to him. "Bertrand, have you seen the roses on the streets and sidewalks of Sarajevo?"

"Yes, I have. A sad remembrance."

The roses were crafted into the cement streets and sidewalks and painted red to remind citizens that that was the spot where someone was murdered during the Serbian siege of the city. Adna took McAbee's arm and pressed it hard, "Seventeen of those roses around the city commemorate my relatives and closest friends. Please remember this if you actually do go to Serbia."

On the next morning Adna detailed some of the arrangements for McAbee. There was an Air Serbia plane leaving in mid-afternoon for Nikola Tesla Airport in Belgrade. It was only a 40 minute flight. He would be picked up at the exit gates by Maja who would have a sign with his name. Arrangements were made for the Hotel Belgrade in the city center. That would be the extent of Maja's involvement. Tomorrow he would be contacted around noon about a meeting with Marković who demanded ten 500 Euro bills for the *consultation*, the latter word used with unmasked scorn. McAbee was listening very closely as she detailed this information to him. The airline was holding a reservation for him if he chose to go.

He asked, "Is there any danger in this?"

"No, I don't think so. Maja has never betrayed me. She works for Marković, two levels removed but it seems to be a clean contact. By the way, it would be appropriate for you to give her 200 euros for the trouble."

"Okay," he said evenly.

"Remember Bertrand McAbee, this is all about your request. Nothing is guaranteed. Marković is extremely corrupt and dishonest. A killer. It is possible that he will take your money and just walk away with it. You have no recourse, you are in Serbia," she said flatly but with a touch of commiseration.

He asked, "You don't think this is a good idea, do you?"

"I have two answers for you. I like you a great deal. I want this to be resolved by you for your sake and the victims; that no harm come to you. So I will worry for you.

My other answer is it is a fine idea. My casebook is in terrible need of good news, a resolution of sorts for my display of failure. So as they say, nothing is easy in the Balkans, even a simple answer to a simple question." She smiled.

"Well, I will report back to you."

"Of course you will. It is written in your nature Bertrand."

Bertrand stood up, she also. He had a look of perplexity on his face. Finally, he said, "Adna, if I get something from Marković I'd like to return here immediately. I will need your counsel and wisdom. Perhaps we can share a meal."

Without her customary hesitation about personal matters, she said, "Absolutely I will. I would look forward to it."

"One other thing," he paused, "how much do I owe you for all that you've done?"

She gazed at him. There was a certain innocence to this guy that he probably didn't even realize he possessed. She wanted to be very careful and diplomatic with her answer, a trait that she did not have in large amounts. "Bertrand, let me say something to you. I have had a history of bad luck in dealings with men. I generally find them to be outrageous, insensitive, and stupid. With you I found a good soul, William Dineen notwithstanding. So, I had a very good experience with you during these past bits of time. You probably realize that it is very easy for all of these good feelings to evaporate in me given what I perceive you to know about the darkness that lies in my soul. That inquiry about money knocks at the dark part of me my good friend." She went across to him, touched him on the cheek, hugged him, and led him from the office.

CHAPTER 47

The Hotel Belgrade was in the city center. After checking in, McAbee walked up the long closed off boulevard near the hotel. It was full of life, shops, restaurants and outside displays of art. He took a cab to the refurbished corniche area aside the Sava River that advertised the promise of a bright future of malls and housing developments. The city gave the impression of a renewed spirit in the troubled country. Money was flowing into Belgrade from Israel and the United Arab Emirates. As he walked back to his hotel he passed by a construction site for three towers. Only recently had the government torn down the bombed out former Federal Interior Ministry building where the towers were being built. The Ministry building had stood for years as a reminder to the Serbs of American savagery.

Although Serbia was pursuing a path for entry into the European Union, its President, Aleksander Vucic, was perceived by some as secretly pro-Russian. His former friendly association with some tried, or in the midst of trial, war criminals, his appointment of a Defense Minister with strong Russian affinities was offset by the appointment of an open lesbian, Ana Brnabic, as Prime Minister, an open plead to the EU for acceptance of a "new" Serbia. This pro-gay movement caused an uproar in Serbia given its historical connections with the Eastern Orthodox Church and its avid condemnation of *perversity*. McAbee came into Belgrade when it was in the midst of this extraordinary array of cross signals, cultivating as it were, both the European Union and Russia. At 8:00 p.m. he witnessed a candlelight procession of about 50 people on a busy boulevard near his hotel protesting the lesbian appointment.

At noon the next day as he sat in his room reading from Cicero's correspondence, there was a sharp rap on his door. He opened it and saw a middle-aged man wearing a beret. He had a mustache, a narrow face and lips that appeared to be permanently whistling.

"Bertrand McAbee?" he said in a hollow, baritone voice.

"Yes?"

"I'm here about your request to meet Deputy Commissioner Markovic'. May I come in?" McAbee spread his hand out to his room. "May I sit?" he asked. McAbee nodded as the visitor took the seat near a desk and McAbee sat in an easy chair about ten feet across from him. "My name is Dragan. I work for an agency that facilitates consultancies for Deputy Police Commissioner Markovic'. I will bring you to him shortly when the set conditions have been met. I am to collect ten 500 Euro bills. If you please," he held out his hand.

McAbee was offended by the nakedness of it all. He said, "I have the money. But I want to know exactly when this *consultation* will occur."

Dragan looked at McAbee with eyes from some corner of hell. He finally responded, "It is now 12:15. We will walk across the great park to the walls overlooking the juncture of where the Danube River meets the Sava River. There, he will give you 20 minutes. If this is unacceptable I am commanded to leave the hotel and to notify you that there will be no further contact possible with him. It is nonnegotiable."

Bertrand hesitated, mindful of Adna Sidron's warnings about Serbia and Markovic′. He felt that he had no alternative cards to play except, of course, to leave, money intact. He removed the envelope from his pants pocket and silently handed it across to Dragan. The envelope was not sealed, Dragan glanced down at it when he raised the flap. He looked at the contents for about two seconds, but he didn't count the ten bills. Serbian trust, McAbee thought.

He said to McAbee, "We will leave now. It will take fifteen minutes to reach the area. Please stay 20 meters or so behind me. When I come upon Deputy Chief Markovic′, I will remove my hat and continue to walk. You will then approach him. Remember he has committed 20 minutes to you. Questions?"

"And after 20 minutes?"

"There's Nikola Tesla Airport for your consideration. Unless you become a police matter there will be no efforts on our part to communicate with you," he said sourly and sternly.

McAbee followed him as directed. They passed through a pedestrian mall and then into a fortress/park area. One sector looked as though it served as a moat in days gone by. It housed jeeps, tanks, howitzers and other assorted outdated military hardware, an open-air museum of sorts. They walked a cement path and came up to a rise which ended at a three foot high stone wall. He observed Dragan slow his pace and remove his beret. His right arm moved to just behind his back as if to tell the man he passed that Bertrand was coming.

When Bertrand was about five feet from him he said, "Dr. McAbee, I'm Alexsandar Markovic'." Bertrand had seen several pictures of Markovic' but none of them could do him full service. He was about six feet tall but he exuded an immense presence. It was almost as if he was six feet square. An energy, a force, flowed from him. His head was huge and almost squared. It seemed that all of him was about squares and rectangles. His eyes were blue but there was a heavy squint about them that weakened his presentation. He held out his hand which engulfed Bertrand's hand that had a strong grip but which was now imprisoned by Markovic''s. He said, "My time is limited. I don't consult regularly but once in a while I do. Let us walk. This is a beautiful view, two great rivers merging right at that spot," he pointed down and across. His English was satisfactory.

"I appreciate your giving me access," McAbee said in cloaked sarcasm.

He laughed. "You're paying handsomely for it. It was as a favor to Maja, I want you to understand that. Not that sullen hateful bitch in Sarajevo, Adna Sidron. I was and am amazed at your skills in passing her inspection. If I have any regret about the Serbian siege of that cursed city it is that she escaped a sniper's bullet," he said this as his conversation flowed from his beginning laugh to a voice of full hatred.

"I haven't come about her. I'm here about another *consultation* that you had, Cynthia Power."

He looked at McAbee with derision. "An interesting

woman. Still mourning a dead man from ages ago. Is that some American trait? Here, we get over our deaths in a day. Death is the natural condition, Eternal. Life is the anomaly, transient. Yes. I acquired a copy of Sidron's useless police report and I had it translated into Serbian and sent to Miss Power. She had a friend come to me for my *consultation*. It was not difficult to acquire a copy of Sidron's useless analysis."

"I've read what you sent her. Cynthia Power was murdered, did you know?" McAbee said with purposive casualness.

Markovic′ stopped and turned toward McAbee. "Is this a joke?"

"No."

"Are you sure about its being a murder?"

"99%. Carbon monoxide. Made to look like a suicide. Very professional."

He nodded and then started to walk again, heading downwards toward the Danube still far away. "And? Why did you need to see me so desperately?"

"When did she ask for your help?"

"Recently. That's why I thought you came here. To follow up for her. This is what Maja was told."

"Well, that's true. But the back story is different."

"Yes, quite. So what do you want from me?"

"Toma Korpanja – what can you tell me about him?"

"I had nothing to do with Korpanja's death. Understand that right away. About him? He was a pain in the ass. He was Bosnia government, he was a news correspondent and he was, what would you say? An activist. He made enemies.

He nosed around things that were best left dormant. There were facts on the ground that he could not accept."

"Like what?"

"Bosnia is a square peg in a circular hole. A new country out of the ashes of Yugoslavia. Good luck with that. This new entity was in the teeth of the Croatians to their west and south and the Serbs to their north and east. Neither the Serbs nor the Croats wanted a nation called Bosnia. The teeth closed on them. The Croats, the filthy bastards, fascists really, Nazi sucklings, did their share of killing but they got away with it on the world stage. The bridge in Mostar caused them trouble. A lousy bridge, not the slaughters, but a bridge they destroyed. The Serbs, though, became targets of the EU and the Americans. Those asses went out of their way to protect Moslems by protecting the Bosnians. They turned against Christians! Have you seen pictures of the bombed-out shell of the Federal Interior Ministry building? Goddamn Americans! It was just demolished recently. A reminder!" he said bitterly.

"I did see them. Why keep those ruins up so long?"

Markovic′ turned toward McAbee and grabbed his arm, "Sir? You know so much? Your fucking government has the nerve to bomb us, an independent country. The Serbs in Bosnia are not the Serbs in Serbia. But Serbia is bombed. And the USA, so innocent, so sincere. But beneath the surface you are playing both ends of the string. Filthy hypocrites." He released Bertrand's arm and went forward.

McAbee said, "But the Serbs were killing civilians indiscriminately."

"Ah! What the hell do you think the Moslems did when they took our lands?" He gazed at McAbee scornfully. "This so-called new country was going to ingest their Serbs! Please! So we have the Republic of Srpska. The Serbs in that area of Bosnia will never accept rule from Sarajevo. They are Serbs but they are not part of the country of Serbia. It is these Serbs – Srpska who shot up Sarajevo. Did they get help from Serbia – yes, but as an ally. So you ask about Korpanja. I did investigations about him McAbee. Did not send it to Miss Power. He was going to go to Srebrenica, to investigate. Not smart. He was crossing a line. As a correspondent he was seen to be dangerous – BBC, *The New York Times*. Here's something else you need to know. Toma Korpanja hated Americans, Miss Power the exception. The CIA was highly and secretly involved with Srebrenica. Somehow Korpanja found this out. That murder? I think it was an American hit, 99% sure to use your language. There was a man on the ground, a roving ambassador he called himself. I did not have the heart to tell Miss Power. Let her think away from the sordidness of the killing."

"The American name?"

"I will not give that to you. That would mark me as a spy. In the communication with her representative, he said that Ms. Power was exploring some club that she belonged to as a teenager. A name was given. It is a name that connected to this murder."

"Peter Waters!" McAbee said softly.

"You said that, not me. Do you think that everyone in your State Department is beyond working for the CIA?"

"But why would the CIA be involved with the slaughter in Srebrenica? That doesn't make sense."

"Don't you see McAbee? It was a chess game. Toma Korpanja was onto it, somehow. BBC, *The New York*

Times? No way. Behind the supposed tip that brought the sonofabitch to the Latin Bridge was a poisoned arrow. And that arrow was dipped into poison by the CIA needing to cover up its involvement."

"Did you inform anyone of Cynthia Power's request?"

Markovic′ paused, too long for McAbee, then he said obliquely, "There are courtesies." His tone was clear, don't ask more. Would that courtesy extend to Peter Waters?

They had been walking downward, ultimately toward the Danube and Sava, but they came upon an Orthodox Church located in a plain on the hillside. Markovic′ asked, "Do you know why I came down here?"

"You're religious?"

Markovic′ laughed at that absurdity. "No religion will save my soul McAbee. I came here because it was churches like this that kept Serbian hearts together when the goddamn Moslem Ottoman Empire tore us apart for centuries. It's a reminder to me to stay strong."

He looked at his watch and said, "Your consultation fee has been used up. Actually by 30 minutes. McAbee, you know the story of the bread crumbs. Not every diplomat is a diplomat. Have a good trip back." He left McAbee standing in front of the church as he entered it. There was a bench to the side of the church. McAbee realized it was a shrine area, much larger than just the church itself. He sat and thought.

CHAPTER 48

Bertrand barely caught a return flight from Belgrade to Sarajevo, arriving there at 4:35 p.m. A taxi brought him to the Metro Hotel. While in the cab he called Adna Sidron. They arranged to meet at the Sebilj Fountain, a landmark in Sarajevo. She would take him to a restaurant that she thought he'd enjoy. She sounded enthusiastic. The fountain was a ten minute walk from his hotel. He arrived there at 5:55 p.m. He knew from a guidebook that taking a drink from the fountain supposedly guaranteed a return visit to the city. His concern about water safety caused him to reject the temptation to drink. Still and all his sense of Sarajevo was quite positive. They, by necessity, had to be a tough and proud people.

Adna came from behind him. She said, "Hello Bertrand. Just follow but stay behind me. Ten, fifteen meters or so." She proceeded forward. Minutes later they sat in a quiet restaurant a block from the Sacred Heart Cathedral. She nodded to the manager or owner who nodded back knowingly. They walked deep into the place. She pointed to a seat for Bertrand and then she sat across from him. She held her hand outwards in a stop motion and peered back toward the restaurant door. McAbee sat there quietly. After a few minutes she smiled, "Welcome. I was just checking on surveillance. I feel that you have become a person of interest. If not now, expect it in the near future. So, you came back. I take it that Markovic′ gave you some information?"

"He did. But I need you to give it context. Believability?"

"Hah. It is a good thing to do when handling the bite of a lethal serpent. Let us order first. I am hungry. I have been fasting this day. A penitential prayer for your success and safety," she smiled.

After they ordered he said, "I'm not that hungry really." He was conceding his distrust of foods that he was unfamiliar with, thus, his request for grilled chicken strips. She ordered a fish dish.

"You don't drink alcohol Bertrand? You would not offend me."

"I don't drink Adna."

"I see," she said skeptically. "So tell me what was the most interesting disclosure from *saintly* Markovic′?"

"CIA!" He responded flatly.

She picked up a spoon and slowly stirred her cup of tea. She stroked her chin and then nodded her head just so slightly. "You use those initials and then I use them as a key that could unlock the door that would open up to a room of discovery. I will say this. The initials fit the lock but I will need to hear more in order to turn the lock."

"Of course. Markovic′ claimed that the CIA was playing both ends. Serbs and Bosnians. His major assertion was that the CIA was supportive of the Bosnian Serbs. That somehow Toma Korpanja discovered this. Given his credentials with the BBC and *The New York Times* he would be perceived as extraordinarily dangerous by the CIA. Any disclosure of CIA involvement would blow the roof off America's supposedly being a trustworthy peace seeker. That trail leads to his assassination. Or this is where Markovic′ wanted to take me."

"It is wise to be very suspicious of him. Lies are like air to him and his ilk. They are deep breathers. I am puzzled. Why would he expose the CIA?"

"Perhaps they don't pay consulting fees to him anymore."

Adna laughed. That had to be a rarity for her but she did actually laugh out loud. "Good, Bertrand. You are developing Balkan humor. Stay here for a month and I will get a slot for you in one of our comedy clubs. But you might have hit the nail on its head."

"There's more. He wouldn't give me a name. But he gave me a trail that allowed me to voice a name. When I did he showed no surprise. He merely said that name came from me, not him. This named man was a roving ambassador to the Balkans during those times. None other than a member of the Demosthenes Club, Peter Waters."

"Diplomacy and spying in one person. Not at all rare. Conceivable. It is odd, perhaps, that he did not say 'Peter Waters?' as in 'who's that?' He allowed you use of the name without denial, but not affirmation either. Continue."

"He advanced his cooperation, clearly implying that Waters was involved with the murder of Korpanja. When I told him of Cynthia Power's likely murder he was visibly shaken. While not personally done, Waters could have licensed the killing at the Latin Bridge. But what I don't see is why America would want anything to do with the slaughter of 8000 men in Srebrenica? To what end? Why would someone like Waters get anywhere near that?"

Sidron nodded understanding. She said after a bit, "Dealing with the Serbs is like sticking your hand into a beehive. Roving ambassadors frequently do just that, engage with the worst. Your trouble shooter, Richard Holbrooke, forced the Dayton Accords, the bombing of Belgrade and that finally gave Kosovo a type of peace. Holbrooke was not in any way a CIA character. He saw the problem and went after an answer – peace talks. But your CIA is a different animal and it has agendas that do not necessarily correspond to your State Department. If Toma Korpanja had any information of American involvement in Srebrenica he would be prime for an assassination. Was he compromised? The Balkans are famous for betrayals after betrayals. I believe that these revelations throw light into dark places."

"Maybe the CIA thought that an atrocity would force peace?"

"Maybe at first. But Srebrenica got out of hand. There are atrocities and there are atrocities. Even the CIA would hide given how bad it became. If they were holding the hand of Radovan Karadzic′ they would feel that hand become fire as he engineered that massacre over there near the border of Serbia. The Moslems were a minority in a bad area at a bad time. Defenseless even as the United Nations was a presence there and promoted a false sense of security. But Toma Korpanja? How did he fall for a setup on the Latin Bridge? It had to be someone he trusted. We will never access that datum."

"Maybe it was the same person who gave him the original scoop. When the atrocity got out of hand it was decided that Toma's information was too dangerous," Bertrand speculated.

"Arguably so."

"But back to Markovic′ and what he nodded to. Peter Waters opens up a trove of possibilities. Cynthia Power knew something, maybe unconsciously, and the death of Anne Podreski quickened her intuitions. Just like Toma Korpanja she became dangerous."

Bertrand understood her when she decided that she needed to think and make a phone call. She said, "Bertrand, there is a plane to Vienna tomorrow afternoon at 1400. I would like to escort you around Sarajevo in the morning and have lunch with you. Then I will take you to the airport. You need to see some things. They will inform you in a way that books cannot. May I pick you up at the hotel at 8:30?"

"It would be an honor."

She let him to pay for the meal. As they were at the doorway of the restaurant she said, "Allow me also to escort you to the hotel. I am armed if it comes to that."

CHAPTER 49

Adna Sidron arrived back at her apartment at 9:35 p.m. She called Vedad Mahmuljin. He had been the Chief of Intelligence for Bosnia during the entire siege period of the war between 1992 and 1995. He had been compromised by some enemies within the government and forced out of his position shortly after the war ended. Adna had never learned the full story and it was irrelevant to the object of her call. Vedad, however, had been a childhood friend of her father and the families had deeply rooted connections with each other. It was that undercurrent of understanding that had maintained over the years.

Vedad was dying of lung cancer. She had learned this from his daughter at a lunch two weeks previous. With tears in her eyes she had put a cause to her father's condition, "Papa was a chain smoker. He still is."

Mahmuljin picked up his land line at the second ring. He said, "Yes?"

"My dear Vedad. This is Adna. I am calling you for two reasons, my sorrow over what has befallen you and a need to speak with you urgently."

After a silence of several seconds he said through a cough

and a rasp, "Adna my dear. Yes I am heading to a bad end. We all are aren't we? But thank you for your commiseration. As to the urgency you can come now if you wish. It seems that I hardly ever see anyone anymore. Your company would be welcome."

Adna was in his apartment twenty minutes later. Vedad's appearance distressed her. In his prime he had been a muscular man about six feet tall and probably 200 pounds, his calculating and intelligent brown eyes his most prominent feature. She estimated that he had lost about a third of his former weight, his hair was gone and his eyes had been dimmed by the cancer. He shuffled back to this seat after the brief hug.

He said, "Adna, sit and remove that pitied look from your face." He smiled wanly as he took a cigarette from a case beside his chair and lit up with a long wooden match. The smell of sulfur and tobacco embracing the room. "As you can see the end is near for me. My attention span is not good, Adna, so talk to me while I am together."

She told him of the murder of Toma Korpanja, the visit by McAbee and finally the revelations of Markovic′. He sat stoically, never once interrupting her presentation.

"Adna, I was aware of the murder of Toma. He was a man of many faces. Many of those faces brought him enemies. His murder did not shock me but I regretted it. At heart he was a patriot. There was no doubt about his hatred of the Serbs. I knew that you were investigating his murder back then. I calculated that it was unsolvable. From what you say you have confirmed that. So, out of the wilds of America comes this McAbee. I can see that you like him, appreciate his efforts. I will tell you that I was dealing with so much in those war years. I knew nothing of Toma Korpanja's love affair with the American woman, Cynthia Power. Too much detail for my level. But with this McAbee comes the name of a most hated adversary, Markovic'. It is nothing, really, that he has stolen your police report of the murder. We know how porous things are. But the scoundrel only sends a translated report to Power. He takes the money and runs. Pure Markovic'!" Vedid started to cough from deep within his chest, it went on for about 30 seconds ending with his spitting up mucous into a soiled handkerchief. "So, with this McAbee Markovic' surrenders more detail. The CIA! You are asking me to weigh credibility. I can confirm one detail in what he disclosed. America *was* double dealing. There were some Americans on the ground at Srebrenica. You gave me a name, Peter Waters. I knew him personally. His cover was as a diplomat. He was a CIA agent. On at least three occasions he handed over bags of $100 bills to me. The monies were used to buy contacts and to support our efforts."

"What was he like?"

"Arrogant. Know-it-all. An American who knew all the answers and how to make things correct. He was the type who could crawl through a two centimeter opening. He'd give us reports about the Serbians, pretending to be one with us. He underrated my networks who told the other side of him, at ease and doing the same with Belgrade. He was like mercury, at once useful and dangerous at the same time."

"Would he have the power to order the killing of Toma Korpanja?"

"Of course he would. Would he use that power? Absolutely, if it suited his purposes."

"Markovic′ said that he gave McAbee the trail of crumbs. But he wouldn't verbally confirm on Peter Waters."

"No, he wouldn't. He would be committing espionage. He is far too clever. But he went further than I thought he would. So, Adna, you ask my opinion on the matter. I'd say that there was a strong likelihood that Peter Waters was somehow in on the death of Korpanja. Not as a trigger man but as a distal agent who would be more than capable of ordering the murder."

Adna was in bed near midnight. Her murder tome was particularly edgy as it jabbed at her back and side making for a fitful night of sleep.

As they sat at lunch the next day McAbee was trying to absorb the rapidity of the morning in an effort to keep so many sights and events in his mind. Only with a slight surprise did he observe that Adna was well-known in Sarajevo. Everywhere they went nods were given to her, people stepped aside, bowed, or voiced hellos in her direction. Between the walking and the driving to different places he was given a solid introduction to the city and country especially as to how it absorbed the punishment of the Serbian violence. The one place that he found to be etched in his memory was the uphill visit to the Olympic stadium built for the 1984 Winter Olympics. Across the road was a cemetery. It was an older burial ground but from that hillside where it was located he saw across the city a large swath of cemeteries with their white burial stones all standing in mute recognition of the slaughters that had taken place during the war with the Serbs.

When she drove him to the airport for his flight to Vienna she parked her car by the terminal and turned toward him. "Bertrand, it was a joy to meet you. I am pleased with your involvement with the case of Toma Korpanja. We will probably never find the shooter but I think that you might discover the identity of who ordered the murder. I am at your disposal if needed." She extended her hand. They shook and he opened the door of the car. He retrieved his bag from the back seat and then leaned in, "Adna! You are a good woman. I admire you." With that, he entered the terminal for his flight back to the States.

CHAPTER 50

There was no way around it. Cynthia Power had been dealt bad hands. The more she lived, the worse the hands became. Over a trajectory of about 50 years the course of her life appeared to be pre-set with her entry into the Demosthenes Club. The finale of it all was her murder.

Back, now by two days, McAbee called Dr. Linda Rhine. After five minutes of transfers and holds, she picked up. She said, "Sorry about that Bertrand. The threats stopped by the way. I think you were right in how things were handled. What can I do for you?"

"I'm making some progress, Linda. We'll talk sometime about it. But I have an important question for you. Why and when did Cynthia decide to do a book on the Demosthenes Club? Do you know?"

"The idea came from John Douthit."

Bertrand exclaimed, "What? Silicon Valley Douthit?"

"Yes, I'm sorry. I thought you knew."

"Tell me more. This is very important."

"Well I gave you summaries of our sessions. Isn't it in there?"

"No Linda. There's nothing of the sort in there."

"I guess I just didn't see any reason to mention it. Sorry. I still have all my raw notes. I have a patient waiting. I'll call you back."

A connection into Douthit was new to him. He knew that Cynthia interviewed him but there was no record of their conversation, presumably that disappeared with the missing hard drive.

An hour later Rhine called McAbee. "This is what I have in my notes. Cynthia and I had been working through hobbies and creating new interests for her. We had been at that and her making of adjustments on other issues for a bunch of sessions. Suddenly, one day she comes in super-charged and elated. I commented to her enthusiasms. To her shock she was called by John Douthit, out of the blue as it was. She was surprised by how much he knew about her, including that she was back in this area. He knew about her stints in Washington, Sarajevo, New York, and the rest. He ran the idea of a book about the Demosthenes Club by her. Said he'd be her first interview. She knew that was a big deal as he is often cited for being a recluse. She sought my counsel. I thought it was a great idea and told her so."

"Did she interview him?"

"Oh yes. But we didn't really talk all that much of her sessions with the club members except for one overriding theme."

"Which was?" McAbee inquired.

"She was dealing with issues of success. She thought that all five of them, each in their own way, was patronizing toward her. We had to work through that in the sense that perhaps that was coming from her rather than them."

"And?"

"I think we saw it as combinatory. Some from them, some from her. But as you know she realized that in many ways there was a moral bankruptcy in them."

"Douthit too?"

"Nothing that I remember but as a matter of deduction it would include him. May I ask Bertrand, why is this so important? Douthit?"

"Just some fill-ins. It probably doesn't mean anything Linda."

Actually, it meant a lot to McAbee. It was another trail that had to be traversed. His assumption was that it would be a formidable task to get beyond the phalanx of protectors that John Douthit used.

He called Barry Fisk.

In full crankiness Fisk said, "Yes?" His voice was particularly raspy.

"Barry, what's been going on with your research?"

"I've got some information for you."

"I need to get access to John Douthit and Peter Waters."

"Is this a result of your trip?"

"In part, yes. Especially Peter Waters. But now I've taken still more interest in Douthit too."

"These are elusive characters. All sorts of interference. As you requested before you left for Europe I have been hot and heavy on the two of them. In the parlance of investigations these are tough gets. By the way, I have a terrible cold. It's in my lungs. I am coughing up a storm. I mailed a hard copy of my research on them to you. You might get it today. But I can tell you a few things. John Douthit hid behind a steel curtain for years. He was a mysterious presence in Silicon Valley. Great eye for comers. Got into Apple big time when

Jobs was spreading his wings. Microsoft before that. Initial investor in Facebook. He's worth several billion. Famous for his secrecy. No record of giving to charities, museums, universities, etc. Not well-liked, loner. Lot of envy operating around him. Doesn't interview. About four months ago he starts to peek out of his cave. Gives five million to Stanford, nothing for him given his wealth but a significant change of behavior. Soon *Barrons* has a piece that explains it. Hans Schlimmer of muckraking fame has an advance of two and a half million to do an unauthorized bio of John Douthit. Schlimmer is a first class bastard who will print anything as fact. No such things as fake news. While you were in Serbia, Douthit throws 20 million to St. Jude's Children's Hospital."

"I wonder if Schlimmer has gotten near the Demosthenes Club yet."

"There's so much out in California for him. No doubt he'll get there but I don't see it now."

"Anything on Waters?" McAbee asked.

"He's been around the block in the State Department. Lots of posts. But his files are carefully protected. I did some stabs in the State Department. That's a tough site with all sorts of warnings. After the bust by the FBI, I'm scared. Your brother isn't around to save me. I can give you the public record on him which is full of praise, generally. He has been given credit for some of his work around the Dayton Accords. Does that help? I know that dovetails with Cynthia Power. But he's a closed book."

Bertrand sensed that Barry had more, his pause a giveaway. He asked, "That's it Barry?"

"Well, I do have more. There's a website called the *Staters* that I hit upon. It has a chat room. Password protected and all that. I got in there, unannounced, unseen, and unwelcome. It's a rumor mill and a killing field for enemies of enemies. It's loaded with inside information. Has to be brokered by ex and current State Department types. It was not easy to get into it. I left one comment in it, "Peter Waters is a great patriot." It was like throwing a body into a pond of piranhas. The basic smack-downs on him are snob, arrogant, ambitious, and duplicitous. But he's not alone in getting whacked. It's a dirty, mean-spirited place. The only other thing of note is that he's pursuing another appointment. Several commented that it was Iceland. But who knows? His wife is universally detested, his fourth. I confirmed that, as someone posted she was his seventh, a lie. As I said, nasty site."

"The Thomas Group?" McAbee asked.

"Well, that's a different story. They are very sophisticated and scary. I have been circling around them the last few days. They have utilized extraordinary protection around their computer security. My conclusion? Someone from inside would have to gain access. I'm not done, of course, but I'm sorry I have to lie down and rest. This afternoon I have another session with counselor Hawkeye Hank about my aggressive personality. I have to stay on my toes; this jock is sharper than I thought he'd be."

By just about everyone's estimation, C.C. Balthazar owned Omaha, Nebraska. He had bought out an entire Embassy Suites smack in the middle of downtown. His employees working for his mega-successful investment enterprise occupied the refitted third to eighth floors. His personal quarters and a variety of executive offices occupied the ninth floor. It was where he lived and worked.

Balthazar, way back when, had graduated from a small liberal arts college in Iowa, Baden College. His love of the school knew few boundaries as he had gifted a fortune to it but, in particular, a large part of those monies were devoted to the college's classics department. His desire was clear – 'best in the world'. And arguably it was a world-class department even though Balthazar had to admit that Oxford and Cambridge were untouchable.

As he sat in his office at 4:00 p.m. he reviewed with his secretary occurrences of the day. She had been with him for years and knew him so thoroughly that he had full trust in her to only bring forth the necessary for consideration. She had her usual handful of notes that were read from diligently. Decisions were made by him as he considered each matter with his studied but rapid analysis. "One other note of interest," she uttered with surprising hesitancy, "there was a call from Dr. Bertrand McAbee. He said you'd remember him. I do, at any rate, but perhaps you don't?"

C.C. was immediately brought back to Baden College and its infamous professor who had gone on a systematic murder spree. This professor was eventually shot and killed and the entire affair hushed up thus saving Baden College from the glare of the world. Bertrand McAbee had broken the case while being positioned as a visiting professor at Baden. Bertrand and his, presumably, lover had almost been killed. McAbee became involved because of his now deceased brother, Bill, who ran an international investigation agency. All of this came back to him in a flash. He had met Bertrand twice through the crisis. One thing was sure to

C.C., Bertrand's call was not social; their relationship was strained. He told his secretary to call him immediately.

Their politely strained openings ended with Balthazar's comment, "So Bertrand, you have called for a reason, I'm sure."

"Yes. I am in the middle of an investigation. I have suspicions about two individuals. Both are hard to reach, one in particular. He is the one with whom you could help."

"I'm listening."

"Are you familiar with a man by the name of John Douthit?"

Balthazar laughed. Then he said, "I do know him. I don't consider him to be a friend. He's not as isolated as Howard Hughes was but he is thought to be of like temperament. As you know, I have been active in trying to shake down the super-wealthy to give away significant portions of their money. Over the years I have met him a few times. Twice I was in the same hotel. I went to his room once and made my pitch. Two minutes later I was escorted from his suite. Other times were met with the same results, passing by him in seconds. I have spoken with friends about him. The take on him is universal I'm afraid. He's a miser. Now that's among his peers, people like me. But he has cultivated an image of the solitary pioneer. Many see him as a cheap bastard who would not give a nickel to his dying mother. I noticed that he has started to donate recently. I was hopeful that he had changed. But then I was told that an unauthorized biography is in the works. So his generosity is probably a means of defense. What is the problem around him?"

"Is he dangerous C.C.?"

"Most wealthy people are dangerous Bertrand. The law

is their assassin. But knowing your business you are asking a different question. Is he physically dangerous? Is that what you mean?"

"Yes, either as direct agent or through intermediaries. Do you have a sense of that?"

"My first response is no. He's quite shrewd. He would not get himself tangled with something that would potentially come back and hurt him. He wants to sit and be left alone, count his money and be perceived as a solitary genius. I think that he'd hide rather than fight. But I really am only guessing."

"Do you know of anyone who could get me access to him?"

"I'll have to think about that Bertrand. Don't count on it but I'll put out a feeler with someone who just might be able to facilitate something."

"Thanks C.C."

"Bertrand, I miss your brother Bill. Take care."

CHAPTER 51

All told his payments were now at $147,000. The Thomas Group reminded him of a dance – one step forward, one step back. The fact was that they were watching McAbee's investigation moving forward, punctuated yet inexorable. The peripherals around ACJ had been intimidated and yet they persisted. He was told by the older brother, Edgar Thomas, that a hit on McAbee, himself, would take $100,000. He had the money, of course, but one murder was enough, Cynthia Power. McAbee's death would draw the FBI. And God knows what happened to the two who had disappeared on the property of Jack Scholz. And by the way, did that bastard break them?

Seth Thomas, the meaner of the two, was very clear. They did everything they were going to do. The discounted cash payment of $147,000 had them and him dead even. Pay for play if he wanted them to do more.

And then the fucking stranger yesterday. A Chicago Serb named Zivko who spoke on behalf of none other than the crook Alexsandar Markovic′ in Belgrade. "Mister Markovic′," he said in broken English and with the face of a murderer, "has some information that he is willing to share with you. He said that it goes well beyond what Cynthia Power had tried. A 'new danger to you' Mister Markovic′ told me to quote him explicitly. He has concerns for his own reputation. I have a written communication that I am permitted to read to you but not give to you. His consultation fee is $10,000 cash."

"Listen! You and Markovic′ can go straight to hell. Fucking crooks! Get out of here."

"Of course. I will leave my number should you change your mind. Mister Markovic′ sends his regards."

Five minutes later he went to his in-built basement safe and removed 100, $100 bills. Two hours later this Serb, Zivko, crony of Markovic′ was back in Peter Waters' office. The money was handed over and counted, meticulously. The Serb gazed at him with a scornful and arrogant stare as he took out from his coat a sealed envelope. The holstered gun beneath his left armpit was also noted.

"I read now: 'My good friend! It was with some shock that I heard about the death of Cynthia Power. Her simple request about Toma Korpanja was passed on to you as a courtesy, waiving my customary consultation fees. I became aware of this death from an American by the name of Bertrand McAbee. He says that she was murdered. Perhaps you are aware of this man. He is a private detective from your region called Iowa. He paid for my consultation during which I found out that you are in his sights. He has knowledge of Srebrenica and maybe of American involvement there. Oddly, he has engaged with a formidable adversary in Sarajevo by the name of Adna Sidron. None of this can be seen positively. Please take precautions and *bon chance* on your future.' That is what I was to read," he said.

"Read it again," he ordered the Serb who looked at him reproachfully. With studied impatience he did. He then walked out of the house after a brief exchange. He watched him pull away in his Cadillac Esplanade. He wondered just how deep the Serbs were embedded in Chicago. Those bags of money for the Serbs in Bosnia in the mid-90s? Not all of them were received by their intended targets. Here and there some of the contents rested in his basement safe. Alexsandar Markovic′ was not the only rogue in this evil world.

He went to his study and gave himself a generous pour of Jack Daniels. He felt like Robert E. Lee toward the end of the Civil War, too many fronts. He needed a breakthrough event.

When word got back to Markovic′ that Zivko had successfully extorted $10,000 from the American he smiled to himself. Peter Waters was playing a high stakes game. He regretted the professional courtesy of alerting him to Cynthia Power's request for Sidron's file. The fool had told Zivko that he was seeking an ambassadorship and was grateful for the information. Zivko had reported that he was given a $500 tip. Cynthia had gone through channels known only to a few. It led to her death. He did not appreciate that she was murdered. She was a client after all. He had forgotten just how duplicitous and vicious the American bastard was. He was tempted to leak to the American State Department the information he had on Waters' involvement in Srebrenica. That would undo him. But that would be an act of espionage, a third rail for Markovic′, ever so careful where he stepped.

His thoughts then flew to Adna Sidron. Any involvement of her in this 1,000 piece puzzle bothered him. She had come dangerously close to a network that he was running back in 1994 in Sarajevo. Her efforts had forced him to erase two principals. Unfortunately, they were sons of two close family friends. It was not the first time nor the last when the Moslem bitch had gotten too close for comfort. And now her name again!

CHAPTER 52

C.C. Balthazar called Bertrand at 10:00 a.m. sharp. He owed McAbee more than he would ever admit. In his calculation, Baden College had avoided a debilitating scandal due to McAbee's efforts. Balthazar's call to John Douthit was received graciously enough, much to his surprise. He figured that this was due to Douthit's efforts at trying to lower the harsh light that was being shone on him. Whatever the reason he asked Douthit to grant an interview to McAbee. To his mild surprise, he was informed by Douthit that he was knowledgeable of McAbee and ACJ. Douthit would be in Minneapolis tomorrow and would spare time at 4:00 p.m. at the J.W. Marriott in downtown Minneapolis. Needless to say, McAbee was thankful. For unclear reasons he could not identify why he did not like McAbee on a personal level and he could sense that it was reciprocal. But a debt is debt to be paid.

The two guards, though hatless in this case, reminded McAbee of the Blues Brothers. They both escorted McAbee into the vestibule of the huge suite at the top floor of the hotel in downtown Minneapolis. He was frisked and asked to hand over every object in his possession from cellphone to

Fitbit to keys and so on. When that was done the shorter of the two went forward, beyond McAbee's field of vision. He came back in a few seconds with a tall, impeccably groomed man of about six feet four inches. He looked down at McAbee who saw a man to be pitied as he was so studied in his behaviors that he could be mistaken for a robot who was now saying with a vague English accent, "Mr. Douthit will be with you shortly." He turned and left. McAbee looked at the two Blues Brothers, their faces a study of iron ore.

Shortly he was led back to a small sitting room. Was he a butler, this stiff robotic man? He announced at the doorway, "Mister Douthit, Dr. Bertrand McAbee." He closed the door and left.

With the help of a low wattage lamp in the room, curtains closed, he could see enough of him to know he was the real item. Douthit sat stiffly in a high backed chair. "Dr. McAbee, please sit." No hand was extended as McAbee sat in a duplicate chair.

"I appreciate your seeing me Mr. Douthit."

In a low, carefully modulated voice he said, "I see you as an agent of sorts. A sword bearer with a mission. I am a man under siege and because of that I must have an understanding from you. Balthazar vouched for you. But that is not sufficient, necessary but not sufficient you understand."

"I understand the distinction. You need my consent to conditions around our conversation?"

"A conversation?" he said with a touch of scorn. "Isn't this rather an inquiry and a necessary probe by you? More of a questioning, maybe a cross-examination?"

"I do have questions, yes. As you know I'm not here to seek your investment advice," McAbee replied gently.

After a pause Douthit said, "I have researched you as well as I could. It is said that you honor promises. I need that promise from you that what is said here stays here. Your response to me must be unequivocal."

"I accept that condition."

"Very well. You should know that I have been under psychiatric treatment for much of my life. I could not handle as a youth my parents nor their profession, funerals. I am not clinically autistic but I do have a degree of Asperger's Syndrome. I know that some question the distinction. Regardless, because of that I am misunderstood. Many traits are projected on to me by others. I have learned to accept that. I am quite confident that you have been affected by some of these projections. Am I right?"

"Of course I have. Much of what is said about you is negative. But accept that I am a natural skeptic and I draw my own conclusions."

After another long pause Douthit continued, "There is fear among the members of the Demosthenes Club. I share that only because my reputation is in shatters primarily because of what I have told you about my problems. It is rare for me to reach out to people. When I do I get hurt with frequency. I feel responsible for what happened to Cynthia. I had kept track of her, I did with all of them actually, although unknown to them. One morning I woke out of a dream. A published book about our club back in high school. It was compelling. I heed my dreams. They are causative of much of my wealth. Cynthia Power came to my mind. She was the most gifted writer among us at

Memorial High School. I offered to be her first interview as an inducement to her. As you probably know, I don't do interviews. She said she needed to think about it. She did and she accepted but she was leery about the task."

"Why?"

"She was inclined to see the club as a bad place. She used the phrase 'Animal Farm'. I didn't say to her that I agreed but I actually did agree with her. As you probably know she did abandon the project. In the course of our relationship she inquired about Anne Podreski because of a comment made to her by Corey Bladel, an outrageously foolish man. I froze her out and said goodbye to her. The details of that tragedy had never found their way into the negativity that I was enduring. That's the last thing I wanted explored. Bladel's disclosure caused me to call him and threaten a primary against him. I was that upset... Tell me, who in the club have you met?"

"Francine Korbel, Corey Bladel, and my associate has met Megan White and Archie Sanders. The only one we cannot get to is Peter Waters. But I will eventually."

"Archie Sanders was a victim of racism, that of others primarily, but then of his own. The Anne Podreski matter had nothing to do with him. Your associate? This I take it to be is Augusta Satin? I have read about your firm, of course."

In a studied neutral mode McAbee responded, "Yes."

"And your joint conclusions?"

"Dysfunction," McAbee replied. No response from Douthit, he continued, "A pretty hateful crew of kids it seems led by a teacher with high insecurities. I did speak with him by the way."

"Yes. Sound analysis. Cynthia was slightly hopeful about

maturity and redemption in some of the club members. She found immaturity trebled by the age of 67, 68, and clear and studied turpitude. Myself included. She was heartbroken but Anne's drowning was a bone that stuck in her throat. But before I tell you about this understand one thing – Anne was not murdered by any type of commission. She did drown. I found her and brought her to shore. She had been under too long. I worked on her for ten minutes at least, crying as I did so. There was some vomit in her throat and sinuses. Her lungs full of water. It was the very worst experience of my life. Me? An adept swimmer knowledgeable of life saving techniques. I failed Anne!"

Bertrand could feel the tension rise in Douthit's voice. Did he hear a sob? Carefully, he asked, "Why Corey Bladel's comment then? It was an accident, yes?"

"All events have a context. It's the context that darkens the incident. Let me explain. We had all been drinking, me the least of all. I am not a drinker. I had been warned over and over again by my psychiatrist not to mix alcohol with the drugs that I was on at that time. Five of them were splashing and cavorting in one area of that small lake – Corey Bladel, Megan White, Stan Adair, Francine Korbel, and Peter Waters. I had swam away, maybe 50 yards, but close enough to be within hearing distance of them. Anne had also moved away. The lake was unevenly bedded. Three feet here, six feet there but no deeper than that, I think. I heard someone yell. I think Megan White but maybe Francine. "Where's Miss Iowa?" It was a typically mean comment directed at Anne. A few minutes later I heard, loud and clear, "Fuck her! Let her drown." Peals of laughter from the five of them. I went into overdrive looking for her.

It took me minutes to find her. I don't know how long but I did find her. I got her to shore and yelled at them to come, to get help." He stopped and stared downwards. The telling was hurting.

"I'm so sorry for you."

Douthit's hand flew out toward Bertrand, dismissive. "Long after we knew she was gone we had a few minutes alone before all of the help came, fire department, sheriff, ambulance, and so on. Everyone sobered up quickly. It was decided then and there that we knew nothing except that I tried to resuscitate her after I heard someone say 'where is Anne?' And we stuck to that story all these years through thick and thin. It was our secret. And then Corey Bladel alerted the only one not part of that contract and who would that be? Poor Cynthia Power who was put on this road to write about the Demosthenes Club by me. So you see? Anne was not murdered. No one took her down as it were."

"Who yelled 'let her drown'?"

"Ah. Only one voice among us had that timbre and resonance. Peter Waters. When you get to visit with him you will hear my meaning. His voice is quite distinct. But I want to reiterate there was no murder, teenage insouciance at best."

McAbee noted that very little eye contact was given to him, he attributed that to his Asperger's. "Why would any of you have Cynthia murdered?" he asked quickly and sharply. He observed that no portion of Douthit moved.

"I know that you have come that far in your work. We would all have a motive, of course, disclosure. All of us have built legacies. Yet in the end it is all incidental about Anne. So why do you go to murder?"

"Cynthia, as you say was reaffirming, 50 years later, the rottenness in the DNA of the club and its members. So she decides to stop the project but not her inquiry into Anne's death. She probably hears about the malignancy of Peter Waters' comment. I can't get a straightforward account of what exactly Corey Bladel said to her. I know he was drinking heavily, though, when she met with him. Maybe he revealed Peter Waters to her. But let me tell you what you don't know." He went on and recounted to the silent John Douthit the harassment of his people, the break-in at Cynthia's residence, the school library, and the reigniting of her inquiry into the death of her lover, Toma Korpanja.

At the end of his recitation Douthit sat back in stillness. Then he said, "Peter Waters," he paused, "Anne Podreski would be a stair to a much higher landing. Cynthia was so intuitive. If anyone could connect dots it would be she. But you are on thin ice, aren't you? You are relying on oblique comments from this known deceiver, Markovic'. The Thomas Group. That's a real clue but they sound quite dangerous. All three people in the same vicinity, Sarajevo, in 1995, Korpanja, Cynthia, and Peter. But creating a case? Murdering Cynthia? Why?"

"She was vigilant and unrelenting. He is in line for an ambassadorship according to a chat room of State Department cronies. He wanted back in the service and if any of this material found its way into FBI vetting he would be dead on arrival. She was a danger to him. My assistant tried to call for an appointment for me with him. She told me that Waters' wife was over the top in meanness. Sometimes it's as simple as that – maybe he was trying to escape from her. I don't know."

"If all of this is accurate, he must be paying a fortune to this Thomas Group. Can that be traced?"

"We can get nothing on that. I think that it is underhanded, perhaps all cash."

"Who is funding your investigation?"

"Myself. Her psychiatrist withdrew under threat. I will see this through no matter about the money."

There was a light knock at the door. It was the robotic butler. John Douthit was late for his meetings. He dismissed the man and then turned toward McAbee. He said, "I am impressed with you." He withdrew a business card from his inside jacket pocket and handed it to Bertrand. "This is my number. Call it if you need to, please."

Bertrand was back in the Quad Cities by 10:00 p.m. via Delta Air. He felt that John Douthit was a misunderstood man, some by his own doing, but maybe, largely on the doing of others.

CHAPTER 53

It took three distinct phone calls to Adna Sidron before she felt that they had a secure network. Her call to his number was made from a secured number to Bertrand's encrypted phone supplied by Jack Scholz. "It is good to speak with you Bertrand. Has there been any progress in your investigation?"

"Same suspect but I need an incontrovertible fact. My best chance is with you."

"Go ahead, I'm listening."

"The friend you visited. The man who is dying. Files, pictures, informants, anything on Srebrenica. I have reason to believe that my suspect was on the ground there representing himself as a roving American ambassador when, in fact, he was really CIA and a Serbian paymaster. If I can establish his footprint I think that I could begin the process of smoking him out. I believe that he is in line for an ambassadorship. Even the slightest hint of his presence there during the roundup and slaughter of the Moslems would create the necessary connections to the murders of Korpanja and Power. Possibilities?" McAbee asked.

"I need a picture of this man who you refer to. A series of pictures through his life. I know a man in Mostar who has compiled a gigantic inventory of pictures and articles about Srebrenica and what he doesn't have in his possession he would know where to find. It would help if he could access facial recognition software. Understand, I want nothing from you. But he might need financial assistance. He is poor of course as are many of us. I will inquire and hopefully this investigation can move forward."

For two days there were a variety of communications between Adna and Bertrand and then between Barry Fisk and the man from Mostar called Hamza. By the third day Hamza had in his possession costly state of the art facial recognition software developed in Israel. It did not distress McAbee that Barry had brokered a discounted deal that enabled him to also receive a download of this same software.

On day four Adna called Bertrand. She was excited. "Hamza has done it. He has five photos from the thousands he examined that clearly show your suspect in Srebrenica. One of the pictures is alarming, disturbing as you will see. He is next to Colonel Ljubisa Beara whose hands were drowning in the blood of our kin. They are standing in front of a pit. Smiling. There is no visual of what is in the pit. Perhaps enhancement might bring something up. But what is clear is that a prominent American was present on the ground. It is not a posed picture. Hamza feels that it was taken without their knowledge. Hamza is quite sure that bodies lie in that pit. In the background you can count eleven soldiers with automatic rifles. Beara was sentenced to life imprisonment by The Hague for war crimes. He died a natural death, the bastard, in February of 2017. These pictures will be transmitted to your man, Fisk. Hamza holds this Fisk in high esteem Bertrand. Stay in touch. I must go."

CHAPTER 54

McAbee and Scholz walked the perimeter of the Rockingham cemetery. He had brought Jack up-to-date on the progress of the investigation. He concluded, "So Jack, this is what I see. Peter Waters is a desperate man. He is striving for an ambassadorship. Cynthia Power links Waters to a comment about leaving Anne Podreski to drown. Corey Bladel has to be the source. She already had intense suspicion of him around her lover Toma. Somehow she got Markovic′ to pursue a copy of Adna's murder report. I'm sure that Markovic′ informed Waters of her request. A courtesy. Cynthia becomes an endangerment to Waters. He gets in touch with the Thomas Group, CIA tentacles et al., a firm of former spooks and/or murderers. From then on the shadow of that firm acting on behalf of Waters has been hovering over our operation. Now Waters' personal involvement with Srebrenica has been authenticated. Neither the Thomas Group nor Waters knows what I have. When they do, Waters will be in a spiral. His reputation is being held together by safety pins. It would be a cinch to crush his hope for a foreign posting. But the thing of it is I think he's a murderer, using this same Thomas Group as his enforcers. But I don't know how to get that established. Too many moving parts and I admit some guesses. I think that the only way to get at Waters is to somehow threaten the Thomas Group. Put a wedge between them. Get them each nervous of the other. See how they act out."

"Fisk has hit a wall with the Thomas outfit?"

"Yes. He cannot break into their systems. He admires how advanced they are. He did get a hit on Waters and he found him super cautious on his personal computer. We do know that his wife is in Nantucket. An email to a friend suggests that divorce is coming from one or the other. But even that detail has to be inferred. Equivocation is his code. It is as if he assumes that he is being monitored."

"Then you should aim for their instinctual distrust. A good idea Bertrand but you do understand that they are all complicit in the murder of Cynthia. Getting to Waters may not get to the Thomas Group. In fact there is a good chance that they would snuff Waters. They are a bad crew operating just below the surface of the water."

"The two guys you captured on your property? Are they alive?"

"Yes they are. At least they were when I released them in Dubuque. Had a change of mind about them. I didn't need a war with the Thomas organization."

"What will they say?" Bertrand inquired.

"They were had. They don't know anything – they'll say that to the Thomas Group and they'll lie about their disclosing the Thomas Group organization to me. They'll get broken once again by them and own up to what they said to me. I have no idea what will be done to the two idiots. I am hopeful that a peace will be declared between me and the Thomas Group."

"So, they know that I know about them."

"Most assuredly," Jack said emphatically.

"The way I look at it Peter Waters is in the weakest position. I don't see how he can counter the muscle of the Thomas Group. He's cornered."

"You took this case to find a murderer. You found two murderers. Your best hope is to nail one of them. I don't think that you can lay a glove on the Thomas Group. You can destroy Waters, though."

"This all saddens me but I think you're right. I hate to see this Chicago gang, the Thomas Group, get away."

"Sometimes the best you can get is 50%," Jack looked hard at Bertrand.

CHAPTER 55

Exactly thirteen days from his meeting with Scholz, McAbee went to the stoop in front of his condo and picked up *The New York Times*. In the top middle half of the first page he saw the now familiar picture of Peter Waters and Colonel Ljubisa Brea standing on top of a trench. Beneath the picture the following headline was read: [CIA Scrambles over Involvement in Srebrenica Genocide]. The picture identified Brea as a recently deceased war criminal and Peter Waters as an alleged diplomat with CIA credentials.

In the course of the story Waters claimed the picture was photo-shopped, that he wasn't near Srebrenica and was 100 miles away in Belgrade; he had never been to Srebrenica. However, the story went on, Waters' presence in Srebrenica was confirmed by three reputable sources. The article went on to report that he was on the short list for the ambassadorship to Iceland. McAbee concluded that Waters' enemies picked up by Fisk in the chat room had been given their moment for revenge.

With the *Times* as the igniter, the story broke across CNN, Fox, MSNBC, and the others in the business of instant news. Twitter became energized. Crews from various networks now staked out Waters' house.

Two days later *The Quad City Times* had a feature story on the 'bedeviled' Demosthenes Club. Megan White, Corey Bladel, and Francine Korbel all in their own way said they hadn't seen Peter since the funeral of Stan Adair in 2001. John Douthit was unreachable.

Augusta Satin sat in Phil Pesky's office. Attending the meeting was the County Attorney Mike 'Iron' O'Connor. Pesky was hostile toward her as she informed him that Cynthia Power's cause of death needed to be reopened. "I've been asked by ACJ to share information with you. Proving this will be a nasty climb." She noticed that 'Iron' O'Connor just sat, observing. Any criminal case would come under his jurisdiction. O'Connor, she knew, rarely lost in criminal court, primarily, word on the street had it, because he wouldn't prosecute any cases that had a one percent chance of being lost.

At the end of their meeting which went for two hours Pesky said, "You know something Augusta. Your chum McAbee never shares with us. Now you share and it's metaphysics. Pure hype and speculation. I can't do a damn thing with this."

"Sorry that you feel this way Phil. We wanted to recover our relationship with you."

"Yeah, right."

Iron O'Connor finally spoke. "A fantastic piece of speculation. May all be true. It's the Chief's call. But right now I wouldn't touch this with a ten foot pole. From what I hear this Peter Waters guy is ruined by his own doing. I will go this far. I will interview him. He would have to admit the crime and then implicate this Thomas Group. He's been around the block enough, by his credentials to say the least, to sidestep the hell out of us. That's the best I can do Ms. Satin."

Pesky interjected, "I'm not lifting a finger on this until County Attorney O'Connor has taken a bite out of him."

To Augusta's dismay the session ended. Cynthia Power was not going to get justice.

Peter Waters was called by O'Connor within two days of the meeting with Augusta and Phil Pesky. He was startled, his life in shreds since the pile on from *The New York Times* article. That O'Connor was sniffing around about loopy Cynthia was disastrous. He called into the Thomas Group. They could come by to strategize. He was relieved.

Seth Thomas looked over at his older brother whose face was ashen. In Seth's judgment Edgar would overthink the inherent problems that were presented by Peter Waters. Simply put, Peter Waters was now an impediment and a danger to the Thomas Group. He knew too much, especially about the murder of Cynthia Power. Yes, it was a cash payment, no records kept. All of his other payments, as well, were done in cash. Not for the first time did Seth wonder about how much thievery this fraudulent ambassador had committed to get that kind of cash reserve. The time to strike was now when Peter's life was in disarray and his vile wife was gone from his premises.

His brother had that inward look about him, the look that perpetually caused hesitation. Seth came hard at him, "Do you recall the cellar to his house. The pitch of his stairs. Sixteen as I remember. His incredible wine collection?"

"What about it?" Edgar asked distractedly.

"He needs the whiskey treatment Edgar. This is a way to sever all connections. No one wants him around. He's toxic. The State Department? The CIA? All the books get closed when he dies, drinking too much, and then flying down the steps to a cement floor. Broken neck, a sad story. There is no other way. We have to protect ourselves and the firm. Against our better judgment we did some stupid things for him. We were led by his cash."

Edgar gave back a morose look to Seth. Edgar was an old CIA hand who was adept at compromising enemies with honey traps, blackmail, drugs, but he was not given to violence. That was Seth's specialty. After all, he had been the guy behind the murder of Cynthia Power. In Seth's hand all murders were done within the boundaries of confusion and doubt, Cynthia Power as an example. Peter Waters was a prime candidate for overdrinking and falling.

Their method had twice been employed over the years. Bring a bottle of costly Scotch. Get the victim as lit as possible, all the while speaking with him in the kindest and most collaborative of ways. At the right moment have two reliables come and hold the mark, squeeze his nostrils and pour as much alcohol as possible into the victim. In one previous happening the mark had been rehabbing an old Mercedes in his garage. They wrenched it up and collapsed it on the chest of the poor bastard. The other time it took place on a boat.

Edgar Thomas reluctantly consented to Seth's plan with the nod of his head.

CHAPTER 56

McAbee was called at 1:30 a.m. by Barry Fisk. He had just fallen asleep. Groggily, he said, "Barry, yes," as he noted the time of the call.

"I have news. Just came across on CNN. Peter Waters is dead, a fall in his house. No other details. Sorry to wake you," he disconnected.

McAbee was now fully awake. He threw on a bathrobe and went to his study. He sat in his lounger and thought. He gave an accidental death about a 10% chance of truth. More about the death would be found out. Perhaps he was wrong but he doubted it. He figured a murder. He also knew that he came to a dead end in his case.

There were now only four of the eight left. He recalled that Demosthenes, the Senator from ancient Athens, had committed suicide rather than face Macedonian revenge for his insolence. The old Macedonian Empire had included what is now Bosnia. Somewhere out there in an ever expanding universe there seemed to be some indelible line of connectives. Coincidence? He just didn't know. The thought fled from his mind as he whimsically reached his hand downward to pet Scorpio only to touch empty space. To himself he whispered, "Vanity of vanities and all is vanity."

AFTERWORD

- The Thomas Group is still out there hawking its discreet services.
- Barry Fisk completed his five session counseling with Hawkeye Hank. His anger is still at the very hot level.
- Eric Power has moved into Cynthia's house. It took three days for the moving firm to relocate his stuff.
- Peter Waters' wife had his safe opened by a professional outfit. At the end of the day she found $2,300,000 in $100 dollar bills. She smirked.
- Corey Bladel, Francine Korbel, and Megan White continue on their way through life, undaunted.
- John Douthit wired $100,000 to ACJ. A private note to McAbee merely read, 'Appreciated.'
- Adna Sidron scrawled across the first page of her notations on the Korpanja murder – MCABEE. Her casebook didn't hurt that night as she slept soundly.
- McAbee went back to Plutarch's *Lives*. He opened to Demosthenes. A sentence struck him, easily worked from the Greek. He mulled over it, "If the 'Know Thyself" injunction of the Delphi Oracle was a simple thing, why is it a divine command?"

ABOUT THE AUTHOR

Dr. Joseph McCaffrey is a Professor of Philosophy. Years ago he was offered a job at a private investigation agency. He declined but the proposal renewed a long held objective of his to write a mystery novel around a character who actually took the offer he refused – thus, Bertrand McAbee. The Demosthenes Club is the eleventh in this series that began in 1997.

Printed in the United States
By Bookmasters